Covert Danger

Mata Hari Series, Book 1

Jo-Ann Carson

Copyright

Covert Danger is a work of fiction. Names, characters, places and incidents are the products of the author's imagination or are used fictitiously. Any resemblance to actual events, locales, or persons, living or dead, is entirely coincidental.

Cover design by Nina French
Photo of NYC Metropolitan Museum of Art
by Eric Baetscher

for Piet

who helped me find my voice.

Love always...

The Mata Hari Series

#1 - *Covert Danger*

#2 - *Born of Magic*

#3 - *Ancient Danger*

Smart Sexy Suspense

www.jo-anncarson.com

CHAPTER 1

Venice, Italy
March

Standing at the helm of his yacht, international art dealer Sebastian Wilde watched the mysterious woman roar through the dark waters of the Grand Canal in a high-speed motor boat, the Italian military police hot on her tail. He grabbed his binoculars for a better view. In the translucent morning light the stunning red head accelerated, steering around boats as if she'd been running from the Carabinieri all her life. She moved with desperate recklessness, as if she had nothing left to lose. If her hand slipped, she'd smash into one of the gondolas gliding along the famous waterway lined with fading pink palaces sinking slowly into the sea. One slip and someone would die.

Horns blew, telegraphing danger, and the boats in the channel cleared a path. Sebastian shook his head. She had to be crazy. Like a savvy pirate she focused on the water in front of her and made her way.

Unbridled and brazen, the woman dominated the scene.

His breath caught as he waited for her to fail.

As she roared closer he lowered his binoculars. Their eyes locked—just for a moment. A wise man would let the cops catch her, but his blood rushed south of his brain. She had the beauty of an enchantress. A smile spread across his face. And the balls of a Navy SEAL.

As she passed his vessel her wake rocked his hull. He needed to make a split-second decision: get out of the way of the police who pursued her, or...? He swung his steering wheel and slid his yacht into their path. He might have a lot of explaining to do, but part of him wanted to help the daring woman who risked everything. Irrational and stupid—he could already hear the names he'd call himself later. But it felt right. And he trusted his gut.

A hundred yards ahead, a small barge loaded with boxes of bananas, apples and oranges for the market moved towards the woman. The white-haired skipper yelled to the second mate, "Porta. Porta, stupido." Cowering at the tiller, the gangly boy yanked the stick completely to starboard, steering directly towards the woman.

Sebastian's muscles tensed. Sweat beaded on his brow. He grabbed a life ring. At the last second, the woman maneuvered her boat around the barge in a smooth arc. He exhaled slowly.

The boats neared the picturesque twelfth-century Rialto Bridge with its elaborate twenty four foot arch over the canal. People leaned over the sides taking pictures. Gondolas glided along the edges. Sebastian prayed no one would get hurt.

The police boat slowed to get around his hull. They cleared him, but had to make a sharp turn to avoid the barge. Little room remained. The woman had left an obstacle course of boats scattered in her wake.

The Carabinieri's boat with double engines roaring at high speed didn't have a chance. There was no space left for them to maneuver. Five times the police horn blew, the mariner's warning of imminent disaster. "Porca Madonna... Dio."

The cops threw their engines into reverse to slow their momentum. But a collision with the barge carrying fruit could not be avoided. All the sailors reached for a hand-hold. The two vessels collided with a loud, solid thud followed by a grinding that made Sebastian wince.

An officer standing on the bow of the police boat smacked his head with the palm of his hand. "Dio... Dio." Men ran around on both boats checking for damage. The barge listed, but no one landed in the water.

A vaporetto chugged by with a full load of people gaping at the scene. Other boats moved in to take a closer look. People shouted from the bridge. The barge captain swore and gestured with his hands. His young helmsman shook.

Sebastian turned to look at the woman at the helm of the cocky speed boat. Watching the auburn-haired beauty wrapped in a cloak of green silk disappear into the morning mist made his pulse race.

***

Sadie's shoulders relaxed. Once again fate had saved her. She halved her speed and eased into the morning traffic.

Hot guy on the yacht. Not many men would take a risk like that for a woman they didn't know. He must be crazy, or a lousy sailor.

Five minutes later, she turned into a side canal and brought her boat to the edge where her business associate Delilah waited. Tossing her the bow line, she cut the engine and pulled the drain plug.

Dirty canal water gushed into the hull with a swishing sound. As the craft slowly sank, Sadie climbed out, holding a diamond and ruby necklace in one hand and Italian stilettos in the other. The expensive motor-boat she'd borrowed from a gentleman friend had served its purpose. Glancing over her shoulder, she grimaced as the last visible part of the bow sank below the surface into the darkness below, where it would rest on the bottom of the canal amid centuries of relics and sordid tales. She took off her designer cloak and threw it in. At least she wasn't joining the artifacts yet.

Delilah, a short, buxom brunette who looked a Botox thirty-five in good light helped her onto dry land. The woman smelled of Cuban cigars. Her knowing eyes scanned Sadie as they walked, arm in arm, down the narrow back street like sisters out for a stroll.

The crowds thickened as people came out of their hotels to find breakfast. The smell of espresso and fresh pastry floated in the air.

Delilah leaned towards her. "You're one crazy bitch." As usual, the hard edge in her tone cut deeper than her words.

"Just tell me what the necklace is worth."

"A quarter million, at most. It's a well-known piece. I'll have to take it apart to get anything."

Sadie released the woman's arm and took a step back. "Two hundred and fifty thousand Euro. That's all?" She pressed her lips together.

"Dollars."

Sadie shook her head. That was even worse. They walked in a brooding silence. She kicked a pebble with her toe. "I've got to find a better way to make money."

"Are you in trouble... drugs or something?" Delilah's eyes softened.

"Not exactly." Sadie hesitated. "I'm turning thirty."

Delilah broke into a throaty bar laugh. "Honey, it happens to us all."

"But not like it happens to me. When I turn thirty, my modeling contracts will dry up. The Luscious Lips campaign already dropped me for a fifteen-year-old. The lipstick writing is on the wall. I'm running out of cat walk. No one wants a model with wrinkles.

The world wants fresh meat. No matter how much I diet, I'm going to be yesterday's cover girl and worse—I'm going to be a penniless one."

Delilah's eyes narrowed. "I don't understand why you steal. You've made heaps of money."

"And spent even more." Sadie kicked at another pebble. "Yeah, my modeling career's been great. I've been on lots of covers, traveled the world and met interesting people. Problem is, soon I won't be able to afford the life I'm used to. Modeling is a short term career. You come in hailed as a beauty queen and in a blink of a false eyelash you end up tossed aside like yesterday's salad. The money I made I spent, or invested in stocks that sank faster than that boat.

I suck at saving money." She shook her head like a dumb dame. "The bucks came so easy in the beginning, but now that I'm older, things are changing."

Her insides cringed. It took a lot to sound so whiny. But she wanted to convince the woman. Sadie gave her a doe-eyed look. Delilah needed to buy the whole image: Sadie Stewart, international model—empty-headed bimbo—willing to do anything for pretty shoes.

She could never let the fence suspect her real reason for turning to a life of crime.

A mischievous glint came into Delilah's eyes. "So, find a man to pay your bills. Beautiful women have been doing that since the dawn of time." She did her version of the Gallic shrug, which on her looked awkward and out of place. "What's the problem? You could probably snare royalty with your mane of red hair, not to mention the rest of you."

Sadie rolled her eyes. "There's no way. No way on God's green earth I'll resort to relying on a man—for anything. Been there, done that. Being married is like being caged. There's no room to be yourself. And there's the stinky-sock-washing expectations to boot. Let's not even talk about what happens to romance. Marriage is not for me." A shudder ran through her body. She didn't need to act this part.

"Sadie, sweet Sadie, do you really think you can keep evading the police by sneaking around, or leading them on spectacular boat chases? Get a grip, woman. I give you six months as a jewel thief and then you'll be in some cold European jail cell with Bessy."

"Bessy?"

"A big girlfriend you don't want to meet."

"Oh. You gotta help me, Delilah. You know people. There's got to be a better way. I figure I need twenty million Euro to retire in style. That's all—twenty mill."

Delilah smiled her gotcha-smile. "If you're not going to marry it, honey, you're going to have to steal it or..."

"Or what?"

"Smuggle it."

CHAPTER 2

Amsterdam, The Netherlands
March

With a nod of his head Bakari al-Sharif motioned for his two bodyguards to stay on the cobblestoned street lined with seventeenth century, canal houses. He scanned the horizon one more time before descending a rope ladder down the steep, brick, canal wall to the barge below. His feet hit the metal deck with a thump and he turned towards the door.

Candle light flickered through a burlap covered window on the side of the cabin. The faint smell of incense hung in the air. His scalp tingled just as it did the first time he saw the great seer twenty years ago. He'd only been a teenager then.

He clenched his jaw. She could evade him no longer.

As he opened the cabin door without knocking, the pungent smell of the ancient Egyptian incense, kyphi, swamped his senses. He swallowed. Learning about the mysteries of life could be both elevating and terrifying, but he trusted the way Djeserit took great care of him. The kyphi she prepared combined twenty-eight ingredients and had been blessed with an ancient incantation known by few. The aromas of wine, honey and raisins brought memories of his childhood in Cairo rushing back. So long ago, and yet so near when he sat with her. She was more than a woman—more like a timeless portal to the past, present and future. Once he'd been awed by her gift. Not anymore.

He was pissed. She'd held back on him. No one could defy him like that.

Her sea-gray eyes met his, but she made no pretense of smiling. In her day she'd been a beautiful woman with fine bone structure and the full figure of a Greek Siren. Once he'd fantasized about screwing her, but that was a long time ago. Now, the lines ringing her wizened eyes spoke her age. The tone and luster had drained from her skin. Her body sagged and had grown frail. She broke their stare and looked down at her hands on the table. Trembling.

Did she know how angry he was? Nothing could get in his way. Not now. Not even Djeserit, the most powerful living Egyptian sorceress.

She sat behind a small table covered with a black cloth. A tall, gold candelabrum he'd given her as a gift sat to one side. It gave the room light, but not warmth. The damp chill of the approaching night penetrated his cashmere sweater. He hated the cold Amsterdam spring. Placing her tarot cards beside the candle, she looked directly at him. "Sit," she said.

He folded his five foot ten frame into the rickety wooden chair opposite her, hearing it creak under his weight. "I need answers," he said.

She grimaced. "My answers will not change your future."

"Just tell me what you see. That's all I ask." He leaned back. "I'll take care of the future."

She tilted her head to the right. "Bakari, you are too full of pride." Her eyes narrowed crinkling the skin around them. "You must listen to me."

"Tell me." He pounded his fist on the table.

She reached for the candelabra to steady it. All softness drained from her eyes when she looked back at him. "I can tell you only what I see. The vision of the cards is not to be used to manipulate the world."

How dare she lecture him? Heat rushed to his face. He would have his way. The silence in the room was deafening.

He let it sit for a minute and then he began. "You tell me the cards are meant to show me my spiritual path. But I'm not a spiritual man, Djeserit. I am a man of action." He leaned forward until his face was within inches of hers and he could smell her morning tea on her breath. "And I know your vision extends beyond the cards."

Her eyes flickered and she looked back down

at the table. Her mouth firmed into a straight line. "The cards are sacred. They are meant to help us on our spiritual journey on this plane. They should not be misused." She looked back at him. "I fear for you. You have been a good friend to me. It is not wise to upset the natural order."

"You've never been reluctant to give me a reading. Why now? Have you seen something in the cards? Did you hear news on the street? What are you so afraid of?"

"It is all in the cards."

He'd never heard her voice so flat. "Tell me!" He hadn't meant to yell.

Picking up the deck she held it for a moment in her hands as if it held the weight of eternity. Whispering words he could not hear she brought the cards to her heart. Then her eyes locked with his once more. "Only if you are sure."

He nodded. If she didn't do as he asked soon, he'd wring her neck. His people could get him out of the country. Sweat beaded on his forehead. "Now."

She fanned the cards face down in front of him. "You want me to tell you what you want to hear. I know this, Bakari. But I cannot."

His chest tightened. "No. Listen to me, woman. I want you to tell me the truth. That is why I come to you. I know you will never break your sacred oath. You vowed to your teacher before your gods to never lie about the cards."

Her eyes narrowed. "And then you will kill me."

Ah, so that's it. He leaned back. She's frightened of me. After all these years. She must have heard I killed my third wife, Safa. He exhaled. "I didn't kill her because she told me the truth."

"Then why?"

"She..." He stopped for a moment. It was complicated. "She betrayed me."

Djeserit looked at the flame of one of the candles and then back at him. "Ask your question. I will not betray you. Know that the cards will tell you what you need to know, not what you want to know."

He'd heard these words many times over. His scalp tingled again. In his mind he asked: 'How do I gain the power I need?'

Gathering the cards in his hands he sensed their strange, ethereal warmth. He shuffled them until they felt like his and then he cut them and placed them in three neat piles. Breathing in the incense he cleared his mind of everything but his question.

She stood and raised her hands to the sky. Her shimmering red silk robe looked otherworldly in the candlelight. Long wavy tendrils of black hair framed her brown face, which looked colder than a stone statue. "I, coming forth am Amen, the hidden one."

Her words reverberated through his mind and body. His chest expanded and he felt a lightness of being.

From her pocket she drew an ivory wand inscribed with hieroglyphs. She waved it once in the air. "I am the keeper of Akashic Records. All of which is, and which shall be. Eternity and Everlastingness, open your portals." She put her left hand on the deck. "May I fly like a golden hawk. May I see the truth revealed." She stood absolutely still. Her eyes were closed and the lids trembled, as if she listened to distant voices.

Bakari forced himself to breath.

Her eyes opened, so glazed over they no longer looked human.

She waved the wand once in front of him. "Son of Isis, Searcher of Truth. Your time has come."

CHAPTER 3

Florence, Italy
May

Sebastian clenched one fist at his side as he entered the thirteenth-century Italian palace in Florence. He had to attend the fancy party because he'd lost a soccer bet with his friend Gregor. Dressed in a tux, he braced for the inevitable; being offered around like an appetizer to further his friend's reputation.

He took a deep breath and blew it out slowly as he scanned the scene. With luck, the night wouldn't be a total loss. According to rumors, a shady art deal would go down soon. He might overhear a conversation about it and pass the information along to Interpol. People talked when big money surfaced. He took a glass of champagne from a tray carried by a waiter working the crowd.

Gregor had organized this event to raise money for a local orphanage and had wisely chosen to host it in the Palazzo del Bargello, an art museum with a storied past that housed renaissance sculptures by Donatello, Michelangelo and Cellini. People dressed in elegant evening clothes wandered around the old courtyard chatting; cleavage, jewels and perfumed hair dominated his view. The men looked like bobble-headed penguins nodding their heads at one another as they spoke. He probably looked the same. He'd much rather write a check than hob-nob.

An older woman in a blue, sequined gown approached him. "Sebastian Wilde," she said in a breathless voice. "I understand you know everything there is to know about art."

What could he say to that?

"I'm looking for a painting in green for the main foyer in my Spanish villa."

"Green?" He swallowed hard. *Why do people choose art to match their décor?*

"Yes. We painted our walls a pale pistachio."

"Light green," he said, rubbing his chin. She didn't look like someone who would buy ancient Egyptian art. That's what the rumors said would be traded. "I may have just the right piece for you. Please, take my card." He pulled one out of his pocket and placed it in her hand. "Come by my gallery, Eros, next time you're in Amsterdam. I'll personally see what I can do for you." He walked past her towards another group of people.

"But, but..." the woman spluttered to his back. "I might want blue." The tone in her voice told him he'd made a sale in some color.

He saw his friend Gregor standing beside the ancient stone well in the middle of the courtyard. His eyes darted around, and his body fidgeted. A classically handsome man who could be mistaken for Clooney, he ran a diamond company. But at this moment he looked more like an annoyed gargoyle on sentry duty than a successful businessman and philanthropist.

When Gregor saw him he walked over and shook his hand. "Thank you for coming, Sebastian. So many people want to meet you."

Seb winced.

Gregor laughed. "You're a rising star, buddy. You turned your art gallery from a hole-in- the-wall establishment to a multi-million dollar international business in five years. You have the golden touch when it comes to art. Soak in the glory. Eros is famous. You're famous."

Seb shook his head. "I keep telling you, I don't collect art to impress others. The only reason I'm here is that I lost our football bet."

Gregor waved a hand in the air. "But your collection excites others."

"Art is man's greatest gift to the world. As Michelangelo said, 'a shadow of the divine.' I collect it because I love it."

Gregor's mouth tilted to the side. "Use that line on my guests while I get you a Belgian beer. That'll make you more sociable."

Seb grunted. "Two hours. That's the deal."

Gregor smiled. "I invited a few beautiful models. You might change your mind."

***

"Why am I here?" Sadie asked her friend Mitchell. He pushed firmly with his hand at the base of her spine to move her through the crowd in the courtyard of the Palazzo del Bargello.

"Business, sweetheart. It's all about business."

She wanted to kick him hard in a place he'd remember. He'd been her best friend for years, but that didn't matter at this moment. "I've been on stilettos for seven hours. Seven. I don't need this crap. I need to soak in a hot bubble bath." She grabbed a flute of champagne from a tray that floated by with a waitress.

"Honey, you're the one who's worried about money. You have to network. Your career horizon is fast approaching." He didn't need to say more. They'd been talking about this subject for over a year.

She stared him down. Mitchell had the soulful brown eyes of a Labrador puppy, but they couldn't melt her mood tonight. "Don't 'honey' me." She spat the words out like bad meat.

"Why look, darling, there's Alfred. You remember Alfred."

"He grabbed my ass the last time I saw him."

"And offered you a contract with a leading lingerie firm. If you were nice to him, he might forget you kneed him in the groin."

"Hah." She choked on her drink, spurting it in all directions. "The guy's an asshole."

"But a rich one. All you have to do is smile. I'll stay with you so he can't..."

"Rape me in public? That kind of creep would find his time and place. Just the thought of his hands touching my skin. Yuck."

"Okay, how about the hotel magnate in the corner." Mitch nodded with his head towards an older man who looked like the Kentucky Fried guy. "He knows people."

She crossed her eyes, twisted her mouth and made a gagging sound. "I'm just too tired. I feel like road kill left out in the sun."

"Well, suit yourself. I think he looks interesting." Mitchell headed towards him.

She hated the schmoozing part of her job. It made her feel empty and phony, but Mitchell was right. She needed to connect with people. Grabbing another drink, she wondered if it was her third. Not caring, she tossed it back.

Even from this distance she could hear Mitchell laughing. His charm, an integral component of his DNA, grated her nerves.

As she scanned the room for familiar faces, the secret phone strapped to the inside of her thigh vibrated. She made for the ladies room.

After checking she hadn't been followed, Sadie entered. The room appeared empty. She searched each stall. Finding no one, she entered the last cubicle and sat on the throne. She unstrapped her cell and pushed in her code.

Her CIA handler, Jeremiah Cole, answered in his southern drawl. "Havin' fun sugar?"

"Barrels."

She imagined her boss on the other end of the line, sitting in his office back in the States. His lean body, fit from running marathons, would be folded into a well-worn, office chair. He'd be wearing a Wall Street business suit. The collar of his white shirt would be open. His face would be clean shaven. While he spoke to her, his eyes would scan the screens of the three computer monitors on the wall facing him. On his desk beside his laptop, his vintage chessboard would be sitting with pieces positioned in an intriguing end game. Next to it would be at least two unfinished cups of Earl Gray. She could almost smell the spicy aroma of the tea she'd come to identify with intrigue. Cole was a legend in their shadowy business; half master-mind, half elite athlete—and complete master spy.

"You have to move faster," he said.

Wonderful.

"There's a lot of chatter on the Internet. Anubis is in Amsterdam," he said.

Anubis? The strange choice of code-name for her mark made her skin crawl. The jackal-headed Egyptian god associated with the after-life who weighed your soul when you died was an esteemed figure. Giving that name to an evil man not only lacked poetry, it tipped the scales. A sleaze-ball being likened to anybody's god was plain wrong.

Still, he was Egyptian, and maybe he had wild animal eyes or something. Someone had thought the code name fit. "I'm heading to

Amsterdam tomorrow for a magazine shoot," she said.

"I know. The timing couldn't be better. Make sure you're in tight with Delilah and push for an introduction."

Sadie took a deep breath. "About that."

"What?"

"Dee bought my cover story, but she's not easy to manipulate. I can't promise..."

"Anubis moved up his timeline. He'll hit the Met Museum of Art in New York next week. He's collecting ancient Egyptian amulets. To stop him, we need details about his attack plan. You read his file?"

"Yeah. He thinks they'll give him power." Another crazy in a crazy world. Sadie checked the time on her cell phone. "I'll be here another hour, then I'll work on Dee and report back to you."

"Be careful."

What? Her breath caught. Jeremiah had sent her on many dangerous missions over the nine years she'd worked for the CIA. He'd never wasted time warning her before. "Careful?" she said.

"The Egyptian police found his wife's head buried in the desert this morning."

"I'm not planning on marrying him." Just her head?

Jeremiah sighed. "Sadie, no joking. Anubis is violent and volatile. Don't get caught."

The line went dead.

Great, my guy is like a box of TNT ready to explode. She walked out of the stall and used the large mirror to re-apply her lipstick, seeing both the spy and the model in her reflection. One more hour.

When she re-entered the main courtyard, she came to an abrupt stop after a few steps. Ten yards away, beside the medieval stone well stood the man from Venice.

She sighed as she scanned his perfect body. *Damn, he's hot even without his yacht.*

At that moment, he turned her way and their eyes met. Her pulse quickened as a current of acknowledgment passed between them.

He walked towards her in long strides. She smiled and did her best not to show how much she liked what she saw coming her way. His blue eyes, the color of the morning sky, danced with mischief. He stood six-six at least, had the kind of broad shoulders a woman could really nuzzle into, and lots and lots of muscle. His sun-streaked blond hair fell loose and wild to his shoulders in waves. His sensuous lips held a sexy, bad-boy grin that kicked her libido into a full roar. Her mouth dried. Talk about forbidden fruit. She needed to focus on her mission.

It took all her willpower to arch an eyebrow. "Have we met?" she said.

"You know we have." His low-pitched voice raked her senses.

She'd met many men in her life, but none had made her feel so hot, bothered and flustered in such a short time. It must be a side effect of the romantic Italian palace, or the champagne, or something like that.

"The Grand Canal," she said, tossing her long hair over her shoulders and waiting for his response.

He moved closer and touched her hand. Strong fingers. Cool skin. A jolt of sexual awareness flowed through her body.

"I suppose..." she said, "I should thank you."

"Hell, yeah. The police went up one side of me and down the other for three hours. They accused me of getting in their way on purpose." His grin widened. He had the kind of face that looked comfortable with honest smiles.

She laughed. Hard to imagine such a large man being contained by anyone. On the other hand, it would be fun to try.

"Yeah, you're the thief. You can laugh," he said. "The carabinieri told me about the cat burglary."

She pulled back her hand as her stomach hit the floor. "Excuse me?"

"Sweetheart, you heard me."

"Things aren't always what they seem," she said.

"I'm not here to judge you. At least not until I have all the facts." He stepped closer. His scent hit her system like an intoxicating drug. It'd been too long since she'd been with a man she really craved. That's what was getting under her skin. Had to be. A simple biological response to a perfect specimen of a man.

She gave him a come-hither look.

It took only a second for his pupils to dilate and his nostrils to flare. She took a step back and said, "Later, sailor."

He laughed. "Sebastian. My name's Sebastian Wilde." He flicked a card out of his pocket, and handed it to her.

She took it and walked away feeling oddly flustered.

***

Sebastian watched her disappear into the crowd. She wore those spiky high heel things that made most women walk like lame horses, but they didn't stop her from flowing like an angel. The low cut in the back of her evening gown drew his eyes down to her ass. He imagined holding it in his hands, pulling her naked body against his. He laughed out loud. *What a woman.*

Five minutes later, he heard her scream.

CHAPTER 4

Sadie could feel Sebastian's eyes on her butt. Her face warmed. What should she do? He looked like a Viking though he had no accent. A giant of a man. Ruggedly handsome in a tux, he looked out of place here, a rough diamond amongst the gravel of gentry. She sighed. Being near him stirred a longing within her. A longing for connection... But she couldn't let anything or anyone get in the way of her mission, even if he did send delicious quivers through her body.

He wasn't for her. She bit her lip. After all, what kind of man was he? Without even knowing her, he'd helped her escape the police. Bent the law! That put him on the shady side of her universe, a place she had no intentions of going. Laws weren't made for bending. *Why are bad-boys so damn sexy?*

She laughed. They could have an interesting relationship. Lady jewel thief and accomplice. Wait—a relationship? Oh hell, she didn't have time for one of those. How had this man slipped through her guard so easily?

What about a one night stand? She winced. They weren't really her thing. Not that she didn't like sex, but one-nighters reminded her of gymnastic workouts that satisfied body parts, but left her feeling empty and more alone than ever the next morning. She preferred serial monogamy with men who knew her a little bit, but not too much.

Still, Sebastian's directness and charm, not to mention his body, made her want to know more about him. The way he laughed so easily… Images of straddling his naked body flooded her mind, raising her heartbeat into her throat. She'd been alone for far too long. That's what was wrong with her.

Gripping his card in her hand, she walked up the stone stairway to the loggia, the second level balcony overlooking the courtyard. Moonlight flooded the stone patio. A dozen people in small groups chatted as they walked up the wide, stone stairway. After scanning Sebastian's card, she slipped it into her purse.

Sensing a body closing in behind her, she readied herself for an encounter. Excitement coursed through her blood. This dude was way too potent.

She turned to face him. But it wasn't Sebastian. Her gut clenched. "You!"

"Sadie, darling." The sound of the man's familiar voice froze her words in her throat. Her ex-husband, Jonathon Moore, the last person she wanted to run into tonight, or any night for that matter, stood looking down on her with the same damn smirk on his face he'd flashed for the cameras when the divorce courts awarded him half her life savings. Or was it more than half ? She'd been so eager to get rid of him she didn't care. Jonathon "the Lothario" asshole. His tie undone, face unshaven, and long black hair pulled into a pony tail at the nape of his neck; he looked like the rake he'd always been, fit for a romance cover page or a torrid affair. How could she ever have loved such a man?

"What do you want?"

"Not glad to see me, darling?" His chocolate brown eyes narrowed, but his slimy, slick smile stayed in place, rooted in his deep, black hole of a heart.

Wishing her eyes could burn through that friggen hole she stared back.

"I hear you've got a new job." His hand grazed her shoulder.

She stepped back out of his reach. How the hell did he know? "I've got a few new contracts."

"I'm not talking about modeling." His voice lowered, the way it did when he wanted her to do something for him. He reached out to touch her again.

She shoved him away. "Don't you dare." She put her hands on her hips

He smirked, grabbed her arm and pulled her towards him.

Stepping hard on his foot with her six-inch designer heel, she screamed, "Don't touch me." People turned to stare.

"Bitch."

She pulled away from him, turned and ran for the stairway. But she ran right into Sebastian. It was a bit like running into a wall.

In one smooth movement he pulled her behind his massive body with a firm hand. His eyes focused on Jonathon. She could smell testosterone vibrating in the air. Her ex stood still, taking in the giant.

"Relax, man. I just want to talk to my ex-wife," Jonathon said. He put up his hands like an innocent guy. Talk about sleaze that walks.

She came out from behind Sebastian to stand by his side.

Sebastian's soft blue eyes turned to steel. He glanced at her. "Lady, I'm guessing you don't want to talk to your ex right now."

"Hell, no," Sadie replied. "Maybe you guys could talk this out..."

Both men said, "No," in such tight unison you'd think they'd rehearsed it. Their voices echoed off the ancient stone walls. Looking from one to the other, she grimaced. The flush in Jonathon's cheeks spoke of too many drinks and a bitter itch to hit someone if he couldn't get what he wanted. The blond warrior-guy didn't look as though he'd back down. Wasn't in his character. A nasty tremor of impending violence hung between the men, like a spark about to ignite into a full flame.

Sadie took a quick intake of air. How could she explain herself to either of them? Tell her husband she now smuggled looted art, but it wasn't his business? Tell the hotter-than-hades, supersized stud, that this creep was the biggest mistake of her life? And yes, she had been that stupid. She opened her mouth then closed it. When did her life get so complicated?

Bottom-line-time. Under no circumstance could she risk giving information about herself that might expose her covert mission. She had to lose them both. Now.

It hurt like hell to run in heels, but it wasn't her first escape from a rodeo. She pushed through groups of people as she fled down the stone staircase and headed for the palace entrance. Not a classy exit, but her best option.

As she slid through the crowds, she heard the men getting to know each other. First, a solid punch, then a grunt, then another smack. Hearing them scuffle quickened her step. Guilty pangs of regret shot through her mind. What had she gotten Sebastian into? No time to look. He'd have to take care of himself. And he sure looked like he could. She needed to escape.

Her left heel twisted and she hit a stone step. She went down, scraping her knee and then her face. "Shit."

A bystander helped her to her feet. Blood gushed from a cut on her cheek. Her knee looked worse. Shit, shit, shit. She had an important shoot in the morning, and the magazine owner would be furious with her when she arrived injured. This never happened to James Bond. Hell, he didn't even have to wear panty hose.

"Grazia, grazia," she said to a stranger who helped her up. She gathered herself with as much dignity as she could muster and continued her exit with her shoes in her hands. People flooded past her, taking in the spectacle of the two men in tuxedoes duking it out on the second floor.

When she reached the cobblestone street, she looked for a place to catch her breath. Spying a darkened side road she made for it. How much did Jonathon know? How the hell did he know anything? He couldn't mess up her op. Jeremiah would be furious with this turn of events. Limping along on the cold brick surface in her bare feet she hobbled in the direction of her hotel.

A blue compact car drove up beside her. Delilah, alone in the driver seat, rolled down the window. "Want a lift?"

Sadie tipped her head to the side. How did Dee happen to be in the right place at the right time? The thought of taking her weight off her feet trumped her worries. Delilah knew all the back streets of Italy, so maybe it wasn't that odd. Sadie would get her to the hotel safely, and that's all that mattered. Right? Well, maybe.

She needed to talk to Jeremiah. The sooner the better. She got in the car.

Delilah let her off at her hotel and waved goodbye. The woman smiled, but a voice from the dark recesses of Sadie's mind whispered—*be careful.*

CHAPTER 5

Once inside her hotel room, Sadie collapsed onto the double bed gritting her teeth. She ripped off her shoes and threw them at the wall enjoying the bumping sound they made when they hit the old plaster and fell to the tiled floor with a thud.

Just when she had Delilah reeled in to where she wanted her, Jonathon turned up. What a mess. This wouldn't impress her boss. Did Jonathon think he could blackmail her? Unbelievable. Her blistered feet burned, her knee bled and her head ached. On top of all that, her stomach churned with a foul acid. Oh yeah, *Jonathon* had returned.

She needed to get things straight in her mind before she called Jeremiah. How did Jonathon know she had a new moonlighting gig? She ran through every possibility she could think of. Could Jonathon be connected to Delilah? She hadn't seen any evidence of that. She went over and over the chain of events since the beginning of the op, but couldn't see a hole large enough for him to have seen through. She cleaned and dressed the cuts on her knee and cheek. The sting of the antiseptic brought tears to her eyes. Jonathon had known that she was a cat burglar, back when they were still together. Did he now know she'd upped her game, or was he guessing?

The knocking on her door jarred her. It took all her willpower to pull her body up and hobble towards it. Two new blisters swelled on her right foot from the stilettoes. One bled. Looking through the peep hole she spied Delilah. Now? She took a deep breath and opened the door.

Delilah's curvy body left a chill in its wake as she brushed past Sadie and took a commanding stance in the middle of the room. She held a bottle of red wine in the air like a crucifix in one hand, and two glasses in the other, by her side. "We need to talk."

Sadie rolled her eyes. "Let's talk in the morning. I'm done in."

Delilah gave her a knee-buckling stare. "What happened between you and Jonathon?"

"Ah. You heard about us." That took less than twenty minutes. Clearly someone had been watching. Sadie walked over and sat in one of the two chairs by the windows. She accepted a full wine glass and took a demure sip.

"Talk." Delilah's cheeks reddened. She smelled of a fresh cigar and cheap perfume. Sadie choked back her revulsion.

Sadie shrugged. "He said he knows what I'm doing. I told him to get lost."

"Details, Sadie, details. How much does he know?"

Sadie narrowed her eyes. What the hell? Technically, Delilah worked for her. When their gig stepped up from stealing jewelry to looted art their roles had apparently changed, but no one had sent her that memo. A cold chill slithered up Sadie's long spine and sent a silent tentacle of fear deep into the recesses of her mind, the kind of visceral warning that had never steered her wrong in the past.

Sadie twisted her neck, trying to shake the feeling. Her mission to learn all she could about a power-crazed man code-named Anubis had sounded easy at first. Another idiot after power. No doubt, his ego would become his Achilles heel. Always did with men like that. It was a story as old as time. The image of Icarus, the prideful Greek youth who flew too close to the sun, came to mind. She knew she could handle Anubis when she got to him. But she needed to get to him. And to do that she needed Delilah. Sadie made a dramatic sigh.

A spook has to do what a spook has to do. And sometimes that meant rolling in the muddy swamps of humanity with scum. In the end, everyone had their price.

Solid intel linked Delilah to Anubis. Since Sadie already knew her from working her cat-burglar cover, she'd been assigned to get close enough to her to meet Anubis. Sounded easy. Hah. Why couldn't people be more predictable?

In her line of business she relied on her ability to assess people quickly, to know their weaknesses, their strengths, the danger they might pose. She'd pegged Delilah as a simple-minded bad-girl who liked money, but Dee was more complicated. A steely edged sense of "something's going effen wrong" gathered at the base of Sadie's spine. In a flash of a false eyelash, Delilah had slid from being a bar-fly with Euro trash humor to something much darker. Sadie stared back at the woman with wariness.

"What does he know?" Dee demanded.

"I didn't wait to find out. I got the hell out of there." Sadie ran a hand through her mane and shook her head. "Then the tall Dutch guy showed up."

Dee's brow furrowed. "I don't like this. How could Jonathon possibly have found out? You only moved one painting last week, a small Rembrandt."

Sadie's insides twisted into a knot. Just *a small Rembrandt! Oh Delilah, what a lost soul.* It was a masterpiece, a priceless painting, a part of European culture, a piece of the world's art heritage, stolen by the Nazis from a Jewish man in Amsterdam at the beginning of World War II. But a woman as rocky-road-hard as Dee wouldn't get any of that.

The well-known painting would be difficult to sell for cash on the black market, but it could be sold to a private collector, or be used as a trading chip in the underworld. Either way it would be out of the world's sight—possibly forever. *Just a Rembrandt!*

Sadie shrugged and took another sip of wine. Moving Nazi-looted art made her feel dirty, but she had to gain Delilah's trust. The wine burned as it trickled down her parched throat. How dirty would she have to get? And how dangerous would Delilah become? The woman reeked of a toxic mix of desperation, determination and greed. Sadie had seen that kind of hunger before. It grew inside people and when it took them over, things never ended well for anyone.

Nodding, she said, "Jonathon looks like a harmless gigolo, but he's not. He's a self-centered bastard who'll do anything to feed his coke habit. Someone must have leaked the information to him."

Delilah's cold black eyes hardened to pinpoints. "Why'd you marry such an asshole?"

"I was sixteen and stupid."

"So he keeps tabs on you, because he wants your money."

"Cocaine is expensive. I guess he's low on cash and decided to hit on me."

"Does he know you steal jewelry?"

"Hah." Sadie looked out the window at the street below. This wasn't something she liked to talk about. A group of young people meandered arm-in- arm along the ancient, cobblestone road singing in beer soaked voices. She looked back at Dee. "He taught me how to do it." And that was the bitter truth. "He said my modeling money wasn't enough. I was young and stupid enough to believe

him. It turned out I was good at it." She hesitated for
effect. "And as you know, I get off on the thrill."

"Does he know I work with you?"

Interesting. Dee should have said, for me.
Sadie hesitated.

Delilah reached over with the wine bottle
and filled Sadie's glass to the top. "No," Sadie said.
"At least I don't think so. Last time we met, I was
working with my old fence Renaldo. But when he
went to jail I found you."

Dee screwed up her mouth as if she'd eaten a
bad olive. "I think I'll pay dear old Jonathon a visit
and introduce myself," she said. "In the meantime I
want you to take this." She put the bottle down,
reached into her purse and pulled out a dark object.

"A gun!" Not just any gun, a Glock 17, Sadie's
personal favorite. But Delilah didn't know that.

"Hustling a little jewelry is no big thing,
sweetie, but you've upped your game." Dee firmed
her jaw like a lawman in spaghetti western.
"Moving looted art puts you in the ring with
dangerous thieves." She lowered her voice to a
whisper. "And organized crime. I've no idea if
Jonathon is working alone or with someone else,
but I intend to find out. In the meantime, stay safe."
She pressed the gun into Sadie's hand.

She released her fingers and let it drop to the
floor. It made a distinct thud when it hit the tiles.
"I'm over my head here." In fact, she was familiar
with many guns and a crack shot, but she acted her
dizzy-dame part.

"Too late to complain, honey."

"What do you mean it's too late?"

Delilah's eyes iced over. They'd always been cold, but now a friggen glacier engulfed them. "In two days, there's a gala event at an art gallery in Amsterdam. You will pick up a package there. You don't need to know what's in it. Your job is simple. Just go there and be visible. That's easy for you. A courier will pass you a parcel and you bring it to me. You'll make five hundred thousand dollars for a few minutes' work."

Excitement coursed through Sadie's veins. This must be an Anubis job. She was finally getting closer to him and the thought made her feel lighter than air.

Dee's eyes bored into hers. "You're already booked for Amsterdam to do a magazine shoot in the central square. This little job at Eros won't take you out of your way."

"Eros?" Why did that name sound familiar? Oh Shit!

CHAPTER 6

*G*odverdomme." Sebastian swore as he entered his Florence hotel room. His fists curled. At least the other guy looked worse. He stripped off his torn tuxedo jacket and blood stained shirt and tossed them into the garbage. Then he grabbed some tissues and pressed them to the cut on his mouth to stop the blood trickling down his jaw.

Grumbling, he grabbed more. It would take a while for the bleeding to stop. With adrenalin still surging through his body, readying him for action, he didn't want to stay still, but he knew he had to. He lay on the bed and put pressure on his cut lip. He needed to slow down, but his heart kept pounding, as if danger lurked around the corner.

Danger. Interesting word. Beautiful women could be dangerous, but this one took the cake. And he didn't even get to lick the icing.

After two minutes, he got up and headed to the mini-fridge. His left eye, swelling to the size of a ping pong ball, ached. He reached for the ice in the freezer. Why did he stand up for her a second time? He didn't even know her name. The ice numbed the pain; at least his physical pain.

On the bright side, he did get a picture of her "ex" and his fingerprints. It helped that the man had been unconscious. Seb would get his identity and with luck the red head's as well.

She had to be in trouble. Why else would she run?

He sent a text message to his friend Xander to meet him tomorrow in Amsterdam where they both lived. Xander ran a private investigation business, specializing in international art crime. He had the connections to find anyone.

There had to be something more Seb could do right now. He couldn't just sit around, or go to sleep. Pacing the cool Italian marble floor in bare feet, he shook his head. A red-headed femme fatale who ran on the wrong side of the law was the last thing he needed in his life. She'd been nothing but trouble from the moment he first saw her. The memory shot a bolt of excitement through his system. *Godverdomme.*

No matter how hard he tried, he couldn't let her go. She pulled him. His gut had never steered him wrong before. But then he'd never met a woman like her before.

She couldn't be all bad. Could she?

***

When Sebastian arrived at his friend Xander's Amsterdam office the next day, the first thing he saw was three-month-old Mauritz sitting in an infant rocking chair, making baby sounds, his tiny fingers wrapped around the handle of an old fashioned rattle. A warmth spread in Seb's chest.

He picked him up and cradled him in his arms. The little guy looked up at him and cooed. A smile spread across Seb's face.

Xander van der Valk, a tall, lean, blond man who'd been Sebastian's best friend since he'd given him a black eye in the fourth grade, sat at a desk watching him. He wore jeans, a white shirt open at the throat and a light blue cotton sports coat. His blue eyes looked tired, but bright like unfailing porch lights left on in the fog. "Angela hasn't had a good night sleep all week, so I brought the baby."

Sebastian gave him a sceptical look. "Don't shit me. You just wanted him with you."

Light shone through the floor to ceiling windows, making the space seem larger than it was. Four desks, and enough file folders to keep any bureaucrat happy, filled the space. The smell of fresh coffee lingered in the air.

Xander's fingers drummed on his desk. "So what's so urgent you got me out of bed in the middle of the night to answer a text message?"

Seb hadn't thought about the time, or the inconvenience a middle of the night text would cause a family guy. Shit. Would he ever get used to having his best friend domesticated? They'd run wild for years. He should be more considerate. The red head made him do crazy things.

When Sebastian didn't say anything right away, Xander's eyes widened. "This is about a woman." His words came out slowly. Leaning back in his chair, he slapped his thigh and his tired face broke into a wide smile. "You're hooked."

Sebastian looked hard at his friend. Hooked? "Hell no. It's just she's in trouble. At least, I think she is."

"A helpless *vrouw*?" Xander rolled his eyes. "Is she hot?"

Sebastian shrugged.

"Got a picture?"

"Of her ex."

"The one who cracked your lip?"

"He looks worse." The baby let out a cry and Sebastian rocked him gently. "I want to know who the asshole is."

The right corner of Xander's mouth twitched. "Well, Sherlock, let's start with her name. She does have a name?"

"Probably."

"You don't know her name?"

"No," Seb admitted, "but she's the one I told you about seeing in Venice."

"The one who landed you in jail?"

"That's the one."

Xander's mouth drew a straight line as he leaned towards him for the phone. "What do you know?"

Sebastian told him the story about the party the night before. Xander nodded through it all.

"You're seriously fucked up, man. You don't know the woman and you keep taking risks for her."

"Look, you can call me an *idioot*, but she needs help." He looked around the room.

With a smirk on his face Xander looked at Sebastian's cell phone. "I'll send the guy's picture and prints through my database. If nothing comes up, I'll run it by Seamus at Interpol and my friends at the FBI. It could take a bit of time to get the results. I'll get back to you later today or tomorrow."

"Thanks, man. "

Seb sang, *"Slaap kindje slap, Daar buiten loop teen schaap..."* to the baby in quiet tones, while Xander clicked keys on his laptop. Baby Mauritz settled into sleep. Time passed slowly, or so it seemed. Seb paced the floor, singing softly.

Xander stopped typing.

Feeling his stare, Seb said, "See, what I can't figure—is why such a beautiful woman would be running from the police in the first place."

"Uh...she broke the law."

"But why?" Seb shook his head. "She doesn't have 'gangster eyes.' And you know I've seen more than my share of them."

"Gangster?" Xander laughed. "You crack me up."

"Yeah, well, I'm not good with words like you, but you know what I mean. The kind of eyes that are fidgety and suspicious one moment and pure evil the next."

Xander stopped chuckling. "And what kind of eyes does she have?"

Silence.

"Seb?" Xander's brows knotted.

Sebastian exhaled slowly. "The kind I want to know better."

"She's a criminal who doesn't want anything to do with you and she has a violent ex-husband. What part of this isn't getting through your thick Frisian skull?" He paused for a moment. "You need to get laid, man."

"Maybe."

"Give me a fucking break. You got me over here on a Sunday morning to search Interpol and FBI records because you think a woman you don't even know needs help?" Xander slapped his forehead with the palm of his hand. "What's in your Heineken?"

Okay, so he sounded stupid. That was the thing with words. They never said what he wanted them to say. He shrugged. "Yeah, I guess I do need to get laid."

Xander pulled his son from Sebastian's arms. "You're nuts chasing after this woman. But you won't let me stop you. You're so bloody stubborn. I'll monitor the searches, ask around and get back to you." He adjusted the baby in his arms. "It's not like you to get all twisted in a knot over a woman. I thought you'd play the field forever."

Seb grimaced. "She needs help. That's all. I've had people help me when I needed it and now it's my turn."

Xander smirked.

Seb gave him a steady smile back. One way or another, he'd figure out what lay behind the woman's mysterious, moss-green eyes.

CHAPTER 7

Cairo

The swishing sound of his office door opening caught Bakari's attention. His eighteen-year old daughter, Rashida, entered.

"I'm busy, child," he said, casting his eyes back down to the papers on his desk before him.

"I am not a child. I study at Unn al Dunya."

The harshness of her voice made him look up at her. She had her mother's warm, almond-shaped eyes that bled into his heart, but beneath their softness hid a dangerous, rebellious streak that worried him. She reminded him of his youngest brother, the one who'd died in a bar room brawl at the age of seventeen. He shook his head to show his disapproval of her tone. She was the only person in the world who'd dare talk to him like that.

Part of him wanted to laugh at her, standing up to him the way she did, but he didn't. He couldn't. She was the golden star in his life. The one who made everything seem worthwhile. It pleased him that she took her studies seriously even though her health was failing.

Part of him wished she would stay home and relax. She hadn't been well. But she had an unquenchable thirst for knowledge. She always wanted to know how things worked and why. She took after him in that way, curious and quick of mind.

He smiled at her. "And I am a proud father. But you must know that in my eyes you will always be a child." He took in her natural beauty: a slim build, thick, black hair falling to her waist, Cleopatra eyes and perfect skin. Thank the gods she took after her mother, his first wife.

"Father, I'm worried about you." She walked up to his desk.

Her scent, a mixture of carnations and honey, made him feel light and warm inside. "Nothing to worry about, habibti."

"First you fast for three days, then you make offerings to the gods then..." She broke off, as if worried she had said too much. "Then you pace. I am not a child. I know something is wrong. I want to help you."

His neck muscles tightened. Rashida saw too much. She could not know the details of his life. Not the past, nor the present, nor even the future. She was the only piece of pure joy in his life, and he could not let anything happen to her. He got up and walked around the desk to stand in front of her. He took her hands, so small and delicate, in his and held them. "You should stay with your aunt for a while."

She blinked. "You would send me away, Father?"

He would fight any man or army for her, but he could not fight his own karma. He had a price to pay for what he'd done. He didn't want to lose Rashida. Sending her away would be hard, but he could feel the winds of time shifting direction, his luck running out. A great change was coming. Djeserit the sorceress had only confirmed what he had already sensed. The good and bad of his life were about to collide and the result would be... dangerous, to say the least.

He needed her out of harm's way. "I don't want to, but..."

"Father?"

"Rashida, I have business problems. I need to ponder them alone."

"Does this have something to do with Safa?"

So she knew. "Safa..." His dead third wife. He stopped to collect his thoughts. "As you know, I reported her missing last month. The authorities told me they found her in the desert a couple of days ago. I didn't want to tell you."

"And you thought I wouldn't hear?"

"I had hoped. Her body...."

"Was found in pieces. Yes, I know. I didn't like the woman, and I heard rumors that she'd been unfaithful to you, but none of that matters now. She's dead. I don't understand why you haven't put a price on the head of her murderer. The man who dared to kill one of your wives."

He nodded. Could she not see the blood on his hands? She loved him, trusted him, too much. "Who says I haven't?"

Rashida's eyes widened.

"That is why I must send you away habibti. You must be safe. I cannot lose you." Ever.

Tears rolled freely down her reddened face. She fisted her hands and stared at him with hurt in her eyes. But she said nothing. Even with her strong spirit, she didn't dare. After a minute she turned and left the room, slamming the door behind her.

***

Five minutes later, the door opened again and Chasisi, Bakari's third brother and trusted assistant, entered. "You want to see me?" He dressed humbly in a peasant's robe, like one of the sellers in the local street market. In that garb, he slid through all areas of town unnoticed, gathering and bartering information for the family. Only his limp, a result of having been born with one leg shorter than the other, set him apart from hundreds of others on the busy streets.

"Rashida must go to her aunt's."

"She heard about Safa?"

Bakari nodded.

"Does she think we had anything to do with it?"

"Of course not."

Chasisi tilted his head. "I will find a likely suspect to pin it on. I would have done that already, but I didn't think they'd find her so quickly and I've been busy helping Hasani with his last shipment of Kalashnikovs going to the Ukraine."

Bakari nodded. "Does anyone know what happened to Safa?"

"No. Her dismembering has them thinking it had to be someone else. Possibly a business enemy exacting retribution on you."

"Just as you said."

Chasisi gave him a weak smile.

It had been Chasisi's idea to bury her body in parts. Bakari hadn't liked the idea at the time, but he appreciated the merits of the plan. He'd let one of his body guards, Gahiji, a man who took a sick pleasure in such things, defile her body, cut her up and bury her deep in the desert.

And now he was losing his daughter. Bakari's chest tightened at the thought of sending Rashida away. Karma could be so cruel.

"Brother, it was self-defence. The bitch stabbed you. You can't feel bad about it."

He looked up at the ceiling. "I have many things I could feel bad about, but not her death. She brought that on herself."

"What's bothering you?" asked Chasisi.

"Djeserit's warning."

Chasisi's eyes widened. "The witch gave you a warning?"

"I must pay for my past."

His brother tilted his head and twisted his mouth. "We must all do that brother."

"But I have done things I am ashamed of."

The room fell silent again. Only the ticking of the clock in the hallway, a present from his last wedding, could be heard.

"Bakari, everything you did, you did for the family. How could you be ashamed of that?"

"I built our family fortune selling guns. I never asked questions about how they would be used. I didn't care. I just wanted money. Now I'm getting older I wonder if I couldn't have been more selective among my clientele."

Chasisi shrugged in his usual way, telegraphing that it wasn't the sort of thing that bothered him. "We would have starved otherwise."

Bakari rolled his shoulders, trying to release the growing tension in his body. An uneasy feeling had been building within him since he last talked to the sorceress. "Yes," he said. "I did it for the family, but now I wonder if our prosperity was worth the consequences that await me. Other families rise with dignity. Ours on the death of others. I chose a bloody trail that will scar our lives through eternity."

His brother's cheeks reddened. "This is what Djeserit said to you?"

"This and other things. I seek her counsel to set things right. There has to be a way. I believe a truly powerful man can create his own destiny. And the ancient texts do not disagree."

Chasisi winced. "I despise Djeserit. I spit on her words."

"She sees what others do not."

"When she's paid well." He looked away. "Have you considered that she's playing you?"

Bakari stood up and walked to the window. Through the opening, he saw the lush palace gardens below, heard the songbirds singing in the lemon tree. The air carried the scent of fresh herbs. If he could only be free enough to enjoy such things. He put his hand on the window sill. "Trust me. I know what I am doing."

"You are a good man and a good brother, Bakari. This I tell you freely. You have nothing to be ashamed of. A man must do what a man must do. We are all chased through life by dark regrets. That is the nature of this world. You are too hard on yourself. Keep Rashida by your side and enjoy your retirement. Hasani will handle the family business and I will ensure that we are all safe."

"But that's just it. We are not safe. There are forces working against me."

"Tell me and I will defeat them."

"If only it were that easy." Bakari took a deep breath. "I must see Djeserit again."

CHAPTER 8

Falling into a fitful sleep after downing a sleeping pill, Sadie wrestled not only with the hotel sheets ensnaring her long legs like chains, but also with memoires that held her captive.

Her mind drifted to the scene of horror in the heart of western Africa.

It didn't matter how many pills she popped, she arrived *there in the sticky heat, surrounded by the fetid smells of wild vegetation, ranging lions and desperate people living in isolation, far from the modern world. Anticipating what she was about to see, her gut twisted and her mouth went dry.*

The terrified cries of a newborn baby echoed in her ears. She wanted to scream, "No," but no one would hear her.

Shaking, she peered through the leaves of the dense jungle, as the shaman strapped the tiny boy to his dead mother with vines.

Only one other person stood by, the grave digger. Once the bodies were rolled into the shallow grave, he shoveled dirt on top of them. The infant cried for his life and kicked his legs, but neither man cared.

The shaman chanted to his spirits in a monotone from hell, while the digger poured more dirt on the bodies. Drums in the village behind them beat on.

She woke up screaming, as if her head had been submerged in hell, which it had been in a way.

Some idiot banged on the door.

"Are you all right," a man yelled first in Dutch, then in English.

There were many kinds of all right, but she was none of them at this moment. "I'm okay," she yelled back. "Just a bad dream."

The pounding stopped. After a couple of minutes of silence, the footsteps traveled away from her door.

Again, she faced the darkness of a strange room, with the same damn nightmare. The ritualized killing of an infant in Nigeria would not leave her, even though she and the baby Jaja, had survived that night. The memory haunted her, coming back to remind her that she'd seen inside the gates of hell. Was it the darkness calling her? She shivered. Hadn't she done all she could? Why did the dream keep coming back?

The CIA had more than its share of shrinks, but she didn't want to see one for fear of appearing "needy." But something wasn't right in her head, heart... life... whatever. Some part of her was out of tune and had been since that night.

It wasn't all bad. After saving Jaja there'd been no turning back. She now had family, and the whole world seemed larger and warmer. The rigid lines of right and wrong, good and evil, faded. Sunrises seemed richer, the air sweeter. The baby had brought joy to her life, but also confusion.

She gritted her teeth. The company didn't want a sappy spook. They wanted a cold calculating master-mind, pulling strings in the shadows.

Pulling her hand over her face she grunted. *Time to focus on the mission.*

CHAPTER 9

Amsterdam

The doors of Eros would open in an hour for the spring gallery show, leaving Sebastian little time to make last minute changes. Not that he should need to. Paul, his new assistant, had spent the last week organizing the event. Still, Seb wanted to check every last detail. The quality of the presentation would reflect on him. Word of mouth was everything in the art world, which could be as emotional as a young girl in puberty. The show needed to be fresh, provocative and, hopefully, a little unsettling. The kind of collection he'd built his reputation on. Looking at each piece in turn he hemmed and hawed.

He'd grown Eros from an idea to a multi-million dollar gallery on the street level of a seventeenth-century canal house in the medieval center of Amsterdam. It featured works that he personally chose, because they reflected the beauty of the human form. Hence the name, Eros. The gallery filled fifty square yards. Seb kept an office in the back for paperwork. He lived in a flat on the second floor and used the third floor space for inventory, supplies and the occasional visitor. The twelve-foot ceilings and enormous windows gave the space an airy, light feel, and the art he treasured a worthy home.

With ten minutes left, he stopped in front of a Taylor Gregory nude done in oil. It looked off. He winced and took a step back, then one to the left, followed by several to the right. The way the light hit the painting irked him. It should shimmer over it, not slice into it, and make the color of the woman's skin alluring. It should pull the audience into her beauty, draw their eyes to her curves and not let them go until they experienced her sensuality with every fiber of their body.

The image of the woman from Venice flashed into his mind and he silently laughed. There was a body to explore. He adjusted the lights. Two minutes left.

Xander had sent him a text ten minutes ago. His research on the red head left him with a lot more questions than answers. Her name was Sadie Stewart. Twenty-nine, American from Seattle. Well-known international fashion model. Jonathon, her shit-head-ex made his living off of rich women. The details were interesting, but none of them explained the way those green eyes tugged at him.

"Boss man." Paul's jarring New York accent dragged Seb's mind away from her.

"Good job," Seb said, turning to shake the hand of his assistant.

"A virgin?"

Seb laughed. "Yeah, it's the first time I let someone else set up a show in my place. It's hard to let go." His mind drifted back to the woman. That's how she made him feel, not like a virgin, but completely alone in new territory. If he were a virgin he wouldn't be thinking about her the ways he had been.

Paul's eyes narrowed. Sebastian recognized the expression as the one he used when Seb's mind had wandered far from the room. "People are lined up," Paul said.

Seb took a deep breath. "You pop the champagne corks. I'll meet and greet. Remember, tonight we talk, tomorrow we sell. Keep the artists sober and circulating." Feeling his pulse elevate, Sebastian headed for the door. The familiar rush that came before a new show surged through his body.

He stopped and turned towards Paul. "And if my Tante Zenneke turns up..."

"Yeah, yeah, yeah. Don't worry. I'll handle her. I'm good with old ladies. I'll put champagne in her hands and make sure she doesn't get lost..."

"Like last time." Sebastian finished his sentence. They'd found her on the street talking to a well-heeled customer about the importance of fiber in his diet. Sebastian had spent most of his life wishing his aunt, his only living relative, would act more normal, but there was no medicine strong enough for that.

He opened the door expecting to see a few familiar faces at the front of the line, like the reporter from Nude Arts, a trade magazine. His eyes snapped to the third person in line, Sadie Stewart. Her long, auburn hair flowed over her shoulders, which were encased in a floor-length emerald-green cloak. Her vixen eyes blinked in recognition and then softened. Her model's smile spread across her face, warming every part of his body.

He cleared his throat. Damn she looked hot. Feeling his professional aura slip as his dick hardened, he smiled at her. Talk about lame. He reached out his hand.

"Sadie Stewart, how nice of you to come." He grabbed her right wrist and firmly pulled her into the room.

Her brows rose at the sound of her name. He wanted to talk to her, but not now. Not here. Damn it. Over her shoulder he could see the crowd pressing in.

"I'd love to have a good long chat with you," –and run my hands all over your body—"but   I must greet all my guests."

"Don't worry about me. I'll enjoy the art." Her eyes relaxed when she said the word "art."

"You like art?"

"Yes, very much. If I were rich, I'd collect it."

"Who's your favorite artist?"

"All time? Van Gogh, no question."

Her words hit him like a spear to the heart. A beautiful woman who loved a Dutch master! She might be slightly crooked, might be a lot crooked...but she liked art. She couldn't be all bad.

"Interesting name you've chosen for your gallery—Eros—after the Greek god of love." She touched his arm. "Tell me, will I be embarrassed by your show?"

"Nothing's embarrassing about love." Did that make sense? It was one of the standard lines he used when people asked him about the Eros name, but it sounded off when he said it to her—more like a stupid pick-up line than an explanation of how he felt about love and art. Her touch made constricted his throat. No doubt about it, this woman had a talent for turning him into a tongue-tied fool.

He firmed his jaw. "I need to see to the event. Please, excuse me." He squeezed her hand and let it go. A connection zinged between them hotter than an open flame.

Sadie's face flushed, but she simply nodded and strolled away in the opposite direction. He groaned. Her scent, a mixture of expensive perfume and fertile woman followed, but not before it stroked his senses into a fevered pitch. Now that he'd touched her, their attraction had become undeniable.

The room filled quickly and the sound of people admiring and discussing art blanketed it. Filled champagne glasses tinkled with the odd private toast, followed by periods of a special quiet, like a collective, appreciative hush as the audience viewed the paintings and sculptures of nudes. Just the effect Sebastian had hoped for.

Seb mingled, welcoming his guests and introducing them to one another and to the featured artists. All the while he kept his eye on Sadie.

Catching his occasional glance, she playfully winked back. The night became a silent prowling dance of I-see-you-but- you-can't-have-me. Not yet at any rate. Time passed slowly.

About ten o'clock he greeted a new arrival and lost sight of Sadie. When he spotted her again, she stood beside his Tante Zenneke. Shit! He looked for Paul and found him tied up in a discussion with one of his best buyers. The young man's face flushed when Seb gave him the eye.

His sixty-year-old aunt wore a long tie-dye turquoise and pink skirt, with a flowing bohemian blouse and layers of necklaces made of multi-colored plastic beads. He'd give her a vintage diamond necklace for her birthday, only to find it later stashed in the toilet paper drawer in her bathroom. Her long, blond and gray hair fell over her narrow shoulders in soft waves. Beside Sadie's simply-stated elegance she looked garish. But the way they leaned towards each other you'd think them the best of friends. They smiled at one another as they talked.

Sebastian marched towards them his cheeks burning. Sweat trickled down his neck.

When he stopped in front of them, they continued to chatter, seemingly oblivious to him, the steaming six foot six Frisian. Normally everyone stopped when he approached them. But not these women.

Zenneke was in full pontification mode. "I like the color pink. You know you can gauge the cost of a painting by the amount of pink in it. I keep telling Sebcha to invest in pink." His aunt's melodic voice spilled into the room, sending sharp prickles up his spine. Hopefully she wouldn't start singing or talking about his wee willie. Both were possible outcomes. He never knew what to expect from her. Did he smell weed?

"Really," said Sadie in a normal voice.

He arched a brow. No hint of sarcasm in her voice.

"Yes, you know creative genius is strongly affected by what the artist eats," said Zenneke.

Sadie smiled. "What they eat? Do tell."

"Yes, a healthy artist will paint with lots of pink tones. Another reason to buy pink."

"I see," said Sadie. "And what about an unhealthy one?"

"Black," Zenneke said, and they both laughed. Not pretty laughter, but the real thing, the rolling kind that infects the atmosphere. Zanneke's body vibrated with the good humor. She put her hand on Sadie's shoulder to keep her balance.

He couldn't be sure if either of them meant what they said, but they were enjoying talking to each other. That was clear. Sebastian stared at them.

"What do you make of my handsome nephew?" asked Zanneke.

"Judging by his show?" Sadie asked, with a twinkle in her eye.

His aunt nodded.

A nasty ripple of anticipation squeezed his gut. Did his aunt have to embarrass him like this? What could the woman say? What would the woman say?

"He's a breast man."

Zenneke burst into laughter again, gales of it, and this time people turned to look her way. He hadn't heard her laugh like that for years. His heart skipped a beat. Someone always shushed her. A tear ran down the side of her face and she swatted Seb on the arm.

"What do you have to say for yourself?" asked Sadie, her megawatt smile warming every cell of his body.

"I like legs too."

They all laughed.

Zenneke pushed him away. "You go do your thing, Sebcha. Me and my new friend will be fine without you."

Sadie nodded. "We are fine," she assured him. Shaking his head, he wandered off to talk with more people. Clearly, the women didn't want him.

An hour later, Zenneke came up to him and kissed him on the cheek. "I'm going home to Leroy,"—her mongrel, flee bitten dog—"but I want to tell you: Don't let that one go."

"What?"

"You heard me. I saw how you looked at her and her at you." She cackled. "Like ravenous dogs catching the scent of ... You know what I mean. If you let her go, you're more of a moron than I thought. Maybe worse than your father." She crossed herself and then swatted him on his arm.

Great! Advice from his wacko aunt. The one who liked the color pink and ... He stopped. She may be as loony as a cat howling at the moon, but she'd always looked out for him, always... loved him. To see her laugh like this made his night. He wondered what she'd shared with the green-eyed vixen. His shoulders tightened as he watched his aunt leave the gallery. His world tilted, but then nothing had been normal since he laid eyes on Sadie.

Through the crowds of people he weaved his way back to her side. She stood in front of the Gregory nude. He smiled at the irony. "Thanks for..."

"Zenneke is a breath of fresh air," she said, not taking her eyes off the nude.

He nodded, feeling a soulful tug inside him. Can souls tug? Anyway, something deep inside felt touched. Quite the woman.

The lights he'd adjusted earlier now shimmered on her as well as the woman in the painting; illuminating flawless skin and full lips, which looked particularly ripe for kissing. Their silence scorched, as they stood close together.

"So you're Dutch?" she said.

"Frisian actually. It's a..."

"Yeah I know. Frisia is an area to the north of Holland and Germany, known for producing tall stubborn men." She gave him a killer, coy smile.

Ouch. She wasn't just hot. She was smart... and funny.

***

Sadie watched how Sebastian's expression changed when he laughed. It was as if he'd removed a mask and let her see inside. The way his eyes shone... the way his cheeks dimpled... the way he looked at her all added up. Part sexy Viking and part modern, sensitive male. A toxic mixture of intrigue and vulnerability.

"Yes, the men from Friesland are the tallest in Europe," he said, "but I won't agree with the stubborn part. I'd say Frisians are strong individuals who believe in holding opinions."

She laughed and his eyes smiled back at her. "Tell me, are you a typical, pushy American woman?"

A wide grin spread crossed her face. She couldn't help it. "I'd prefer to say I'm a free woman who believes in herself enough to be assertive in the world."

He bowed his head to her. "So now can we can move beyond stereotypes?"

She loved the way he opened up and talked so honestly about himself. And his playfulness was fun. But... When did the room get so warm? Desire pooled in her lower belly. She needed to talk about something other than him. She fidgeted. "Your artists are all new," she said. That should be a safe topic.

"Yeah."

"Why?"

***

All Sebastian could think about was kissing her mouth. It was so perfectly shaped... so inviting. He bet she'd taste sweeter than candy. He scratched his chin. Maybe later...

Still, it felt odd to talk art when they had so many other things to discuss. Like, why had she been running from the Italian military police? But being in a public place made such conversation awkward, so he followed her lead.

Art. "Two reasons," he began. "I like modern art and..." he hesitated, "it's less complicated."

Her pencil-thin brows rippled. "What do you mean, less complicated?"

Soft, green eyes implored him to explain, but he didn't feel like lecturing. "It just is."

Sadie grimaced and crossed her arms.

He looked at the light fixture and then back at her. "In the forties, the Nazis looted twenty percent of the best art in Europe. Whenever a piece of art created before the Second World War is sold it has to go through an authentication process and it's a bitch."

"Really?"

"Yeah. I don't know how much you know about art history."

She tilted her head.

"When Hitler was young he wanted to be an artist, but he was rejected by the Vienna Academy of Fine Arts. When he became powerful, he promoted his own aesthetic ideal, which favored classical portraits and landscapes by the old masters. He set up a commission called the ERR, to seize Jewish art. He collected it in Paris. By the end of the war he'd amassed hundreds of thousands of pieces. They haven't all been found, and some are still circulating underground today."

"That's what they call looted art, right?" Her voice carried emotion. She'd dropped the dumb-dame act. Nice. He liked her better that way.

He nodded. "Technically the term refers to any art, pieces of archeology or cultural property taken during a war, natural disaster or riot." God, he sounded like a lecturer. He'd much rather be talking about her or better yet, being with her and not talking.

"Please, go on. I'm interested," she said.

"Mankind's been looting since the dawn of time. Our ancestors considered it the justified spoils of war and all that crap. But today we take a different view."

Her face paled. Was there something wrong with the lighting?

"It's a rape of culture and heritage, totally unethical," he said.

She nodded and cast her eyes about, as if avoiding his gaze. Were they watery? Must be a trick of the light. Her smile, which had illuminated the room moments ago, faded to a shadow. Had he offended her? Maybe she had German blood.

"It's not exactly a polite cocktail conversation," he said and laughed. But his laughter sounded hollow even to him. "I didn't mean to upset you. I wanted to explain why I'm not keen on dealing older art pieces. The provenance checks have to be detailed. I don't want to spend my time filling out forms. Besides, we have great modern artists."

"Your eyes are on fire," she said.

"Excuse me?"

"When you talk about looted art, your eyes get all fiery. There's more to this story, isn't there?"

Shit, she was too smart. A guy couldn't get away with anything around her. He swallowed. "Yeah, my great aunt and her family were Jewish. They were taken by the Nazis..." He hesitated. "And so was their art. It's personal."

"I'm sorry," Sadie said, with a tone that dignified his pain and shot another blasted bullet right through his armor.

He cleared his throat. "So, why the interest in looted art?"

Sadie's eyes widened. Her full lips spread into a picture-perfect smile. "Could be the sound of your voice."

Uh huh. Perspiration beaded on his forehead. Her voice flowed over his manhood with a seductive tone sweeter than syrup, kicking it to attention. Was she playing him? "So why are you here, Sadie? What are you up to?"

She flicked her hair behind her shoulder and scanned the faces around her, as if looking for someone in the crowd. "My friend Mitchell said he'd meet me here. He works with me, but he's late. Must have got tied up." She stepped towards Seb. Her breath tickled his face. "My agent thought it would be good to get a few pictures of us in an art gallery to update our portfolios." She licked her lips. "Tell me again why you chose the name Eros."

Wet lips, seductive voice, a full mane of long red hair and firm breasts moving in. His pulse, which had been running high, quickened. Two could play. Smiling, he gently took her arm and ushered her to a corner of the room where their conversation could be more private. Her body tensed when he touched her, but then relaxed in his hand. Had her husband hurt her? Or some other man? Maybe, that was her problem. Anger simmered in his veins. How could anyone harm such a beautiful woman?

"Oh my," she said, as they neared the corner, "You finding us a wall?"

"Something like that," he whispered into her ear, moving his body against hers to communicate in a more primal fashion.

Her cheeks pinked. Oh yeah, he was back in control.

From the corner of his eye, he could see Paul waving for his attention, but Seb ignored him. He'd cornered her. Sadie Stewart was all his. The rest of the room could enjoy the art. He'd enjoy her, or at least as much of her as she was willing to share in such a public place. She looked up at him. Her full lips trembled in a cover girl pout.

"Spill it," he said.

Her breasts beneath her low-cut dress went up and down as she breathed. Nice cleavage. Feeling her body heat close to his, smelling her scent and watching her lick her lips, yet again, sent his blood rushing to his groin. Damn, she turned him on. He needed to control his desires at least long enough to find out if she was planning on stealing from his gallery or from any of his patrons. It was one thing to flirt with a beautiful thief and quite another to let her take advantage of you.

Taking her hands in his he lifted them above her head and moved in closer. His mouth three inches from hers. "What are you up to?"

She gasped and a torrent of hunger gripped him. He set his jaw. "Sadie, no games. Tell me why you're here."

She tilted her pelvis forward and the lower halves of their bodies met. He groaned and spewed a quiet curse in his head. But he held her hands and her gaze firmly.

"Sadie?"

***

Sadie wrinkled her brow. How could she get rid of this giant? Being this close to him threw her hormones into overdrive. His scent so masculine it tickled her clit and created a primal chain-reaction inside her. She wanted him. No, no, no. She couldn't have him. She couldn't.

She bit her lip. Talk about lousy timing. She couldn't let this incredible chemistry go any further, couldn't let things get any hotter. She bit harder.

And if it did, damn it, she'd be in control. She'd pick the time and the place. His impressive erection pushed into her body, making it impossible for her to think. Please God don't let me whimper.

He nuzzled her neck. "Sadie?"

She sighed. Enough. She stamped her foot on his and pushed on his rock-solid chest. "Sebastian." Good Lord his muscles were hard.

"Ow." He took a half step back and gave her a cocky smile that rippled another wave of lust through her body.

"I don't think we've got off to a good start," she said.

Sebastian started laughing.

She willed her breathing to return to normal. "Don't laugh at me."

"Sadie, leifje, just tell me what you want."

"I'm here to get my picture taken."

"Bullshit."

"And to see the art."

He furrowed his brows. "What else?"

"Why do you think I'm devious?"

"Because you're a crook."

"Sebastian, keep your voice down," she whispered.

"Only if you give me answers. I'm tired of playing games."

"Okay, I admit it. I'm here to see you." She moved closer and gave him a heated look.

He laughed. "Nice try."

She wanted to scream. He could be so annoying. Playing with forbidden fruit was no longer fun. No one in their right mind would hand her an illegal package if they saw her linked to this guy. And she needed that package. Think, Sadie, think. The art show would be over in thirty minutes. She needed to lose him soon. "Is there somewhere more private we could go?" she cooed.

His blue eyes hardened. "Private?"

"I'll tell you anything you want to know, but not here. I feel too... "—she hesitated for drama—"exposed." She ran a finger down his chest to his belt and let it linger just above it.

His breathing quickened and he leaned in.

"You bastard," screamed a woman in the middle of the gallery, shattering the quiet murmur of conversations.

Sadie released his belt. Sebastian turned to look.

Amid a crowd of people stood a tall blond dressed in a black dress and jean jacket, with a snake tattoo on her neck that curled up the left side of her face and ended in the region of her third eye. She swung her arm hard towards a man standing opposite her, holding a cold sneer on his face.

The slap resounded in the now quiet room and the crowd moved back from the pair.

"You screwed around on me," said the dark-haired man who looked like a lawyer. He spoke in a clipped speech pattern.

"You're married for God's sake." She raised her hand a second time.

"Not to you. Thank God." The man put one hand to the red patch on his cheek where she'd hit him the first time, and the other hand in the air to block a second blow. "You bitch." The venom in his voice stilled the air.

All eyes in the room were on the couple.

"You're a lousy lay." The woman's voice rattled with suppressed emotion. Her ample breasts rose and fell so dramatically they bounced.

Sadie scanned the room. All eyes were on the couple.

The man smirked. "Look who's talking. There's a reason I suggested a ménage. You're boring in bed."

"So you're the woman who's been sleeping with my husband." The shrill voice came from a short, dark haired woman approaching the pair, spitting her words into the air. "I'm going to tear your hair out."

"No," cried the man. "Janice, please."

The dark haired, tattooed woman launched her body at the tall blond and they landed on the floor. The man pulled at his wife's arm. "Janice, don't kill this one."

Sebastian shot Sadie a look. "Stay here," he said.

Like she'd listen to him.

People stood transfixed by the spectacle of the love triangle, like flies caught in a sticky strip. Seb ran to the source and pulled on the man's arm. He responded by turning around and swinging at Sebastian's face. Sebastian decked him with one punch. All the while, the women tumbled around on the floor, screaming, biting, kicking and punching—showing a lot of bare legs and rounded asses. Profanity flew through the air like lost ping-pong balls bouncing back and forth. The sound of clothing being torn and screams of pain punctuated sentences. Bare breasts became part of the scene. Bystanders mumbled. Some laughed, but no one interfered.

Sadie headed towards the exit. No one would pass art in the middle of this debacle and she she didn't want to become part of it. Just inside the door a hand nudged her right arm. She turned to find a short, bald man with hazel eyes and a goatee looking intently at her.

"The package," he said, handing her an elegant, brown leather tote. "We'll be watching you." His words slid into her smoothly like a sharp dagger.

Sadie opened her mouth to speak, because she didn't want to look as though she was used to getting a drop pass. By the time she thought of something to say, the man had disappeared into the midst of the mayhem.

As she took the package she watched Sebastian pull the women apart. The husband meanwhile, struggled to his feet, slid between people trying to watch the women and fled out the door. Sebastian restored peace pretty damn quickly. He'd be a good man to have beside you in a fight.

She shook her hair away from her face. Hustling looted art had been a fast way to get to Anubis, a means to an end, but Sebastian's lecture had hit her hard. If only there was another way. If only she could have met Sebastian at another time. If only. Not her chosen way to live a life.

Stringing the long handles of the leather tote over her right shoulder, she put her cape on and re-adjusted her clothing to look chic. People would notice if she looked disheveled and ask questions. People always noticed her. It was the damn cheek bones.

The secret package hung heavy on her shoulder and heavier on her heart. Would it be another Rembrandt? With everything in place she strutted out the front door. She held her chin high like the selfish, self-centered model she pretended to be, a freaking mannequin on parade.

Her gut churned with the acid of self-loathing, but she clung to the hope that somehow everything would work out. They tell you at the CIA that it's all about the greater good. All she needed was a chance to meet Anubis. Moving the looted art would get her there.

Sometimes you get dirty when you fight.

CHAPTER 10

Sadie's pulse raced as she walked quickly down the cobble stone street. Building any speed over the uneven surface was impossible. Her heels each took their turn at giving out one way and then the other. "Ouch," she yelled, as her foot took another side twist and a sharp pain shot up her leg. If only she had a good pair of runners on. Then she'd get her precious package back to Delilah faster than you could say, "There's a sale on designer ruby slippers."

But she couldn't wear runners or go barefoot to an elegant event, so now she had to manage as best she could in her pretty but useless-to-walk-in stilettos. *Friggen five-minute shoes.* She took them off and slowed her pace. Sweat beaded on her lip. Spies with sprains were useless.

Stopping on the next bridge, her breathing slowed. Moonlight slipped through the clouds, bathing the road in a warm glow. A gentle breeze off the North Sea took smoothed the sharp edges of her ragged nerves. The streets hummed with movement. People everywhere, walking, cycling chatting, laughing. Any one of them could be a bad guy—even a truly horrible mobster; but then they could also be a saint. A regular night in Amsterdam—for others.

At moments like this, stolen from her frenetic, double life, she wondered if she'd like to be one of the regular people, have a normal life, maybe a steady man with a dog. Sebastian's rogue smile filled her mind. A man like that could keep her happy for a long time, but would that be enough? Danger and intrigue kept life interesting.

Ten minutes later she entered her chic bed and breakfast. Safe. She needed to gather herself together and be ready for the next step. Maybe a bubble bath... at least a shower. She climbed the impossibly steep, narrow Dutch stairway to her room.

When she opened the door, she had to work hard not to look surprised at finding Delilah sitting on her bed, a cigar dangling from her mouth and a gun in her hand like a tough dame in a film noir. The gun pointed at Sadie and Dee waved it to indicate she should come in. Sadie counted to five for crazy, as in c—r—a—z—y. Then she closed the door. No matter how annoying the woman's new behavior became, she'd pretend it was just hunky-dory.

"Got it?" Delilah's smile trembled and she blinked enough to leave a mascara trail below her eyes. There were some people she'd rather not see the dark side of and Dee had just jumped the line to the top of that list.

Dramatically, Sadie took the package from her tote bag, hidden beneath her cloak. The big reveal. Normally Sadie would take satisfaction in this moment, but not this time. The parcel contained an ancient relic. Trafficking made her feel black like suet inside. As she handed it over to Dee, she cringed.

Not noticing, Dee stubbed out her smoke and grabbed the package. She smoothed its edges with her hands, held it to her heart and strode across the room and back again, muttering words Sadie couldn't quite make out. Just as she considered doing her c-r-a-z-y count again, Dee stopped in front of her. The wild glint in her eyes couldn't mean anything good.

"I'm not supposed to look inside," she said shaking her head to flick her black bangs out of her eyes. "But I have to."

Sadie let her finely threaded eyebrows rise. It didn't seem like a great idea to her, either as a simple-minded model or as a savvy spy. "You sure about this?"

Dee ignored her and unwrapped the first layer carefully, only to find another layer.

"Aren't you supposed to take it directly to your boss?" Sadie asked.

Delilah's feral look grazed her like a shower of acid. "I have to know." She tugged at the second layer and it came away, exposing a white cardboard box about four by six inches, and three inches in depth. "Yes." Dee said.

"I was told to take it to him." Again, the wicked, self-satisfied smirk and a tone of voice that cut into Sadie like a jig saw blade. "But I have a right to know what I'm moving. If I die, at least I know what got me killed." She laughed and the dry, empty sound chilled the already cold room.

Sadie swallowed. "Are you sure you want to cross your boss? He sounds dangerous."

"I can rewrap it. He doesn't have to know." Dee's face shone with a thin layer of perspiration. With a trembling hand she touched the lid of the box and paused. "You only live once." Then she opened it and her face lit up.

Sadie moved closer to see the contents. Her chest tightened. She'd enjoyed the excitement of being a cat burglar, but this was doing something behind Anubis's back was a whole different designer line of intrigue. She stretched her neck.

Dee pulled out three items wrapped in tissue paper and placed them on the coffee table: a silver bracelet, with the Eye of Ra engraved on it, a gold ankh necklace, and a scarab ring inlaid with precious gems. Sadie swallowed and moved closer. "Are they what I think they are?"

Dee picked up the bracelet. "Ancient Egyptian amulets." She turned the silver bangle in her hand, looking at the hieroglyphics etched on the side.

It shimmered in the light. Could she be imagining this? "I've only seen things like this in a museum."

Delilah nodded and smiled. "They have power," she said. "Many have died protecting them."

"Power?" Okay, now she could officially add Dee to the wing-nut list. They were shiny in a weird, ethereal way, but jewels and precious metals did that, and the slice of moonlight coming through the window contributed to the eerie affect. Power? All in the imagination.

Dee lifted the bracelet towards the light. "This one comes from the Middle Kingdom. I know this because you can see drawings of deities on it."

"Ancient Egyptian gods?" A shudder crawled slowly up Sadie's spine. She took a deep steadying breath.

"Yes. The Egyptian civilization started over three thousand years before Christ and lasted three thousand years. They amassed great wisdom in that time and kept their secrets in a library in Alexandria. While many of their scrolls were destroyed, some have remained. They all talk about the power of their amulets." Her voice deepened.

"You seem to know a lot about them."

"I've been researching my new boss, Bakari al-Sharif."

Finally—she had named him.

"He's an Egyptian who made millions in his twenties in the arms trade. He's one of the richest men in the world. His brother has taken over the so-called family business and he lives like a gentleman in Cairo."

A gentleman who beheads his wives. But Sadie didn't say that.

"He," continued Dee, "appears to be a philanthropist, with a passion for learning about the history of his homeland. He's financed the latest dig around the Sphinx. Anyway—I don't believe his interests are academic. Not a man like him. I think he's after power. The power I now hold in my hands."

So Delilah wasn't as stupid as she looked. Sadie nodded. "You've met this man?"

"No, not yet. I deal with one of his people, a guy with weird eyes named Gahiji, which means hunter. He's one scary dude and I'm sure he'd slice my neck if I crossed him."

"Why do I get the feeling there's a 'but' in this?"

"When you know what a man wants, you can make him your slave. And I know what Bakari wants. Even better... I know why he wants it. I have power over him."

"What are you saying?"

"Don't worry your pretty little mannequin head. I'll take care of everything." She picked up the second amulet, a leather necklace with an ankh, and turned it over in her hands. "Look at this one." She held it up to the light. "Do you know what this is?"

Of course Sadie did, but she shook her head. It didn't make the air around it shimmer in waves the way the bracelet did, but it still vibrated with energy. Pulled her? Ethereal energy? Too much champagne.

"It's an ankh," Delilah said with authority as if she lectured to a university class. "The Egyptian symbol for eternity. They used them in their art, and wore them to give them strength. They believed the amulets had healing power."

Her eyes glistened. "I'm not getting enough money for this. It looks like pure gold. The ancient Egyptians believed gold was divine because of the way it shines. They considered it the flesh of the sun god, Ra. What we have here is priceless. And people pay big for priceless."

"So... you're going to ask for more money?" How stupid could she be?

"These amulets are worth a few million and they're paying me thousands, which I then have to share with you. It's not enough." She took a cigarette out of a box in her purse. With trembling fingers she lit it. Within a minute she blew a plume of smoke into the air. Then she shook her hair out of her face, which had paled.

"Do you really think you're in a bargaining position?" Sadie asked. Dee had never talked about her end of the business before. "That Gahiji sounds dangerous."

"With three amulets in my hand I'd say we have all the bargaining chips we need." She chuckled.

"Are you high?" asked Sadie.

"Maybe a little, but not too high to see an opportunity. Look at this scarab ring." She picked it up and put it on her finger. "The wings are inlaid with strips of turquoise and lapis lazuli, the thorax and head with green stone and cornelian. It's exquisite."

Sadie sniffed the air, but she could only detect cigarette smoke. Must be cocaine on top of her regular wine. She'd seen plenty of the white stuff on her modeling tours and all the messes people got into because of it. She needed to talk some sense into the woman. "It's probably safe on Egyptian royalty, but not on you. I'm guessing the boss-man will not be impressed by this conversation about brokering new deals in the middle of a smuggling job."

"You have to keep men in their place, honey. I keep telling you that. You don't let *them* run the show. They couldn't have got these treasure items without our help, and they're going to pay for it."

Sadie touched Dee's arm. "I've got a bad feeling about this." Jeremiah would be pissed if Dee broke their connection to him.

"Stop whining," Dee said, blowing another foul, gray plume of smoke in the air.

"Think about it, Delilah. There's nothing to stop them from marching in here and taking it." A trickle of sweat ran between her breasts.

"That's why we have guns. Guns stop everyone. They're great equalizers. I'll take one of the amulets and give it to them for good faith. I don't think they know there's more than one, anyway. They referred to it as a treasure. You stash the other two and take care of yourself."

Sadie swallowed. "You're not passing them all on?" In her mind, the image of the head of Anubis's wife stared at her with dead eyes. She could taste the sand of the desert. Okay, this was turning into a twisted mission.

"Trust me." Dee stubbed her half-smoked cigarette out on the glass table top.

To get us both killed. Shit. Her op was blowing up in front of her and there was little she could do about it. She didn't need to be stashing amulets from Bakari al-Sharif. She needed to gain his trust. There had to be some way she could get to him. "When do I see the money?"

"Don't worry. You'll get your share. And it'll be bigger now that I know what we're holding. You'll be able to keep yourself in pretty shoes for some time."

Sadie put her hands on her hips. "You said his messenger is dangerous. Let me come with you."

"Bakari al Sharif is wickedly smart. He reads people in an instant. If he doesn't like you, you're dead. Let me handle him. Like I said, you need to trust me. I'll take care of both of us. I'll offer him a fair deal and he'll come across. He is a business man, after-all."

"Dee, I think the cocaine's talking. Give your head a shake." The dead wife's eyes kept staring at her.

"It's not how big you are in this game, it's how smart you are, and I always play smart." Dee looked cockier than a rooster in a hen house.

"Sounding pretty stupid to me right now."

Dee's eyes flared. She threw her half-full wine glass at her. "Shut up, bitch." Without a second look at Sadie, Dee stashed an amulet in her purse and headed for the door.

"Listen to me."

Dee's eyes widened.

"Think about what you're doing. Your plan is too dangerous for both of us."

Silence. Dee's face reddened. "I'm not as stupid as you think. I'll give him the bracelet and barter the price for the scarab. I won't mention the third amulet until we have a deal on the second one. I'll work one treasure at a time. The less he knows the better. Keep them safe." Without another word she grabbed her jacket and left the room, slamming the door behind her.

Sadie watched. How could she stop her?

The door opened again and Dee leaned in. "If you tell anyone about our business, I'll have you killed."

Great! Dee would know the right people to do that. She locked the door.

Sadie put on loose PJs and spread out her yoga mat. After a few easy sun salutations she took a sitting position and grabbed her company phone. She punched in Jeremiah's number.

This op is sooo fucked.

CHAPTER 11

Sitting in a lotus position, Sadie told Jeremiah everything that had happened at Eros, at least the parts he'd be interested in, and all about the crazy scene with Delilah afterwards.

"Interesting," he said.

"What?" She blew air through her nose. "That's all you have to say?" Her cheeks burned. Breathe in, breathe out. Yeah, she got that he had to stay cool, but his Buddha-like calmness made her mere mortal skin itch.

She could visualize him sitting in his pristine office in Langley sipping a mug of Earl Grey tea out of a china cup. His black hair flecked with gray, trimmed so precisely it never appeared to grow. His amber eyes filled with secrets showed no emotion. A ragged scar ran down his neck from below his left ear to his collar bone.

"Did you stash the other amulets?" he asked, as if he were talking about a grocery shopping list.

"Yes." She wouldn't tell him over a phone, but she'd hidden the colorful scarab ring in a concealed compartment in her luggage and the ankh necklace swung from her neck under her T-shirt. Seemed as good a place as any.

"Tell me about Sebastian Wilde."

Could his voice sound any more detached? Her heart stopped for a moment. "He owns the art gallery where the brush pass happened."

"My sources say he's a chick magnet."

She didn't answer, but she could feel his smirk. Damn his sources.

"Sadie, you need to be focused."

She wriggled her nose. "I've never been more focused, but this mission is falling apart."

"Hmm."

"Hmm? That's all you got for me?" Anger rippled through her. She'd thought she'd been lucky to have such an experienced handler, but he sure wasn't much help with this mission.

He broke the three second silence. "Last we spoke, you said you thought Delilah had a devious edge. Now she's proved it. When you play with people who live on the dark side, you have to expect the unexpected. I'm not sure why you're so surprised, unless...."

"Unless?" She pulled her hair behind her ears.

"You're distracted."

"I'm fine," she said, looking at the screaming blisters on her feet. Mostly fine. "Don't play me,

Jeremiah. You know more about Delilah than you've told me. I can feel it."

He grunted.

While she understood the reasons behind the CIA culture of *need to know*, it really burned sometimes. "What now?"

"Stay in place. Don't blow your cover unless you have to. Things will turn in your favor. They always do. Keep your eyes on the target. You have what he wants. He'll come to you. Then you will find out all you can about his plans."

A lot of short sentences. She looked at her cell phone and grimaced. The dead eyes of Bakari al-Sharif's third wife rolled in her head once more like marbles from hell. "I want you to be friggen straight with me."

"As straight as I can be, sugar."

"Okay, Jeremiah. I can do it," she said.

"I never doubt the Mata Hari," he said. That was the nickname he'd given her when they first met and it had stuck like glue and become her code name. Being likened to a World War One era femme fatale was meant to be a compliment, but like everything with Jeremiah; it had a lot of layers. Mata Hari was famous for her sensuality. She loved men and they loved her. Sadie could relate to that. But the poor woman had been framed as a double agent, condemned for being an immoral woman because she liked sex with lots of men, and shot by a firing squad. Not something Sadie aspired to. Not a good fit at all, in her mind. But then other people's impressions of you rarely do fit. She shrugged.

"And, Sadie."

"Yeah."

"Stay away from the Dutch guy. His friends searched Interpol and FBI files looking for you. They discovered only your cover, but Sebastian's persistence worries me. He may not be as harmless as he looks."

Worry? Hard to believe Jeremiah ever gave in to such a human emotion. He was more like a CIA version of Spock. She opened her mouth to argue with him, but he clicked off before she had the chance. She looked at her cell phone. For a man of few words, he sure knew how to snap her bra strap.

Left alone with her yoga mat, she took a deep breath. Something would break soon, or she'd make it break. Straightening her legs she leaned forward into a bend. So Sebastian checked her out. Interesting.

CHAPTER 12

Loud knocking on her door woke Sadie. She checked the radio clock on the table: 3:00 a.m. Friggen hell.

With Delilah's gun in her right hand, she looked through the peep hole. A short, burly man dressed in a black, fisherman-knit sweater, black jeans, boots and a black toque stared back at her. Gahiji? This couldn't be good. *Ugly and mean*—fitted Dee's description. The short hairs on the back of her neck rose. "What do you want?" she said through the door.

"I have something from Delilah."

Great. It probably bites. Leaving the door latched she slowly opened it and peered through the crack. The pungent smell of body odor mixed with garlic hit her nostrils. He had a knife in one hand and something else in the other. Doing her best not to gag, she made a throaty sound. "What?" She took the safety off the gun and prepared for a fight.

His expression, cold enough to freeze a freaking river, sent an icy shiver spiraling up her spine. "This is for you," he said in a voice that would wake the undead. Goosebumps rose on her arms, as he pushed a small, red, velvet jewelry box through the opening.

In a swift, fluid movement she took it, closed the door, locked it, and leaned on it. The sound of his footsteps faded and her shoulders dropped.

The box would have fit a diamond necklace beautifully, but considering the messenger the contents wouldn't be so refined. Gingerly she lifted the top. Her breath stopped. Her mouth opened in a silent scream and her hands let go of the box. As it hit the floor the top fell off and a severed human finger spilled out.

She stared at it. Fresh blood seeped from the cut end. Her throat constricted.

Grabbing her cell phone, she knelt beside the finger and typed a text to Delilah with trembling fingers. "Message received." She hit the send button. Message friggen received. The woman had gone too far this time. What poor person lost a finger because the crazy bitch wanted to make her obey? Delilah had become far too weird.

One minute passed. Then another. No response. Dee always picked up her messages. And she would be waiting for this one. Expecting this one. An icy current ran through her blood.

Sadie sat cross legged beside the box. Damn

that woman. She'd get her out of her life, as soon... as soon as.... she connected with al-Sharif. Perspiration beaded above her top lip. She wiped it away.

The finger was turning a nasty shade of dead. She took pictures of it from several angles, took its fingerprint and sent the data to Langley. Jeremiah would get the information processed. Whose finger could it be?

Still warm. Another freaking shiver ran through her body. Still no word from Dee.

Standing up again she stretched her aching muscles. Someone started pounding on the door! What now?

She walked over and looked through the security hole. Sebastian Wilde. She ran back to the box with the finger and put it on her bedside table. "Coming," she yelled out.

Talk about catching a lady at a bad time! She couldn't blow her cover. How should she play a late night visit from him? How would the model-turned-thief greet him? Maybe she should let her hormones take the lead. That wouldn't be hard.

She slipped the lock, swung the door open wide and grabbed him by his shirt.

His eyes widened.

Pulling him into the room, she threw her arms around him.

Sebastian kicked the door shut.

She liked his style. His muscular arms encircled her body and pulled her close. He smelled wonderful—an intoxicating mixture of expensive French after-shave and the musky smell of a man.

She drank it all in: his strong body holding hers, the scent of his masculinity—him. The fire that had been simmering within her earlier rekindled in an instant.

"And I thought you didn't like me," he said. His baritone voice seared through her senses like a fine whiskey—deceptively calming but knock-your-thong-off potent. She felt heady in a seriously hormonal way.

But she had to stop. It didn't matter how attracted she might feel, the timing sucked. Sadie stepped back. "I don't," she said flatly, "want this right now."

His eyebrows rose and collided in the middle above pale blue eyes.

He must think her a complete idiot. A drop of sweat slid down the middle of her back. She didn't need this Dutch guy with the impossibly high moral code getting in her way. Nor did she need to use or hurt him. She needed to get rid of him. Clearly it had been a mistake to let him in, even if it did perpetuate her cover. What was her sleep-deprived, sex-deprived body thinking?

Sex, you idiot. Good sex with a handsome man. Not astro-physics here.

It didn't matter how he made her body feel, he'd never understand the complexities of her life. Besides, Jeremiah had made it clear she was to stay away from him and Jeremiah was usually right.

He looked down at her with a puzzled expression. "Are you alright?"

Her gut wrenched and she shrugged. "Let's see, my blisters are bleeding and I'm tired. Yes very tired."

His eyes crawled around the room and he walked towards her bed.

"Are Frisians always so nosy?" She followed him. *No, please God, no.* She grabbed his arm to try to control him.

Stopping in front of her bedside table, an arm's reach from the package containing the severed finger, he turned and looked at her.

"I think you should leave," she said, pushing as much indignation as she could into her voice.

His eyes narrowed and his nostrils flared. Damn it all. The man was a lot smarter than he acted.

"Now," she said.

He sniffed the air as if he caught the scent of the dead finger and turned back towards the table.

Edging her body beside him, she prepared to move in front of him, but she was too late. His eyes focused on the box. It had a red stain on the outside. Bloody bloodhound of a man. "Don't touch it." She pulled on his arm. It was like pulling on a tree trunk.

"What is it?"

"Trust me, you don't want to know. Look, it was nice of you to come by to, uh... say hello, or whatever you came by for. Maybe we can have a drink sometime, but right now I want you to leave. Need you to leave." Sweat trickled down her forehead. "I need my beauty sleep."

"You always look beautiful to me."

"Sebastian, please."

He bent over the box and then looked back at her with mischief in his eyes. She pulled harder.

It would be easier to move a mountain.

"Sebastian, no."

Their eyes locked in a tug-of-war. Then his face broke into a roguish smile that made her insides dance.

"Okay," he said. "Tell me what's in the box, then I'll leave."

His rumbling voice sent another warm wave of wanting through her body. The man meant well, but... She shook her head.

"Why can't you tell me?"

"It's nothing." She cleared her throat. "Look, it's late. I'm tired. We can do this another time. Please go."

His lips scrunched up. "There's something in that box you don't want me to see. Did you steal from one of my guests?"

The sound of a group of people passing by on the street singing Abba wafted in on the night air. Stalemate. "I didn't steal from you or anyone at Eros. Honest. What's in the box is... personal."

He cocked an eyebrow.

"Look, why don't we go to your place," she said. "It's noisy here, and I liked your canal house." A dangerous gambit, but she had to get him out of the room.

"My place?" He scratched his chin. His bad boy, baby blues probed her eyes with a glint of playfulness in them. He gave her that killer grin again. "Sure, sweetheart, as soon as I see what's in the box." In one swoop of his long arm, he snatched it up and opened the lid.

CHAPTER 13

"Nooooooo," screamed Sadie, as she grabbed the velvet box out of Sebastian's hand.

He dropped it. What could possibly be in the box to make her so afraid? The fragility in her soft green eyes wrenched his gut. She physically pushed him away, or at least tried to. He took a step back. "What the hell's going on?"

She put the box into the top drawer of her nightstand table. "Nothing." The drawer closed with a thud.

"Nothing?"

"Like I said, it's personal. And I didn't steal it."

Looking down on her, he gave her his best stare. But she didn't even flinch.

"Why are you here, anyway?" she said.

Good question. "You left the show before I had a chance to..." Hmmm. What could he say? A chance to get to know you better? That sounded way too old fashioned, even for the truth. Hook up? Too blunt. He scratched his chin. "Say goodbye."

The light in her eyes flickered as she appeared to be processing his words. Damned if there wasn't a hell of a lot of other stuff happening between them. Whenever he got close to her he wanted her. Badly. Her mane of red hair fell in waves down her arms. He wanted to run his hands through it and pull her closer, feel her curves against his body.

"Good bye," she said with a grin and offered her hand for a shake.

A hand? After she yanked him into her bedroom, she offered him her hand and the door? He took it, and pulled her in for a good thorough kissing. As the warmth of her body moved toward him he heard that wee voice in the back of his head kick in, warning him to slow down.

He pulled back. "Wait a minute. What's in the box? And why is there blood on it?"

"Junk jewellery from my ex. We had a fight."

He put his hands on her shoulders, not wanting to get any closer until he had more answers. She had to be the most sensual woman he'd ever met. It was more than her cover girl good looks. It was the way she moved, fluid and graceful with hips that swayed like a goddess in a sailor's dream. She even smelled sexy. He took a deep breath in, and then let it out slowly. "Bullshit."

She pushed his hands off her shoulders and moved back in front of the table where the box hid. So obvious. "How dare you swear at me?"

"Honey, someone has to."

"Excuse me?"

"Obviously, you've got yourself into a mess and the box has something to do with it. Who did you steal it from?"

Her mouth dropped. "I told you, I didn't steal it."

"You're a thief."

"Look what I am and what I do is none of your business..."

He moved in and kissed her, gently on the lips. They were full and soft and tasted like honey mixed with magic. Fuck. Now, he was done for. "Sure about that?" His voice sounded croaky.

She kissed back, slipping her tongue into his mouth.

He touched his forehead to hers trying to steady himself, feeling his pulse roar. "Look I don't judge people. But why do you steal? You're a successful model." He pulled his hands through her hair. Thick and soft. So soft.

"I didn't steal anything." Her voice, low and shaky, passed his bullshit meter. He considered women complicated, but she blew all the rest out of the water.

"Venice?" He stepped back so he could watch her face.

"Oh, that was an emerald and diamond necklace from a lady with good insurance. She won't miss it."

"But why do it? For the thrill? They have programs for people like you."

"I don't have to explain myself." Now she sounded huffy.

"Then I'll look in the box."

In an instant, the color drained from her face. "Okay. I'll tell you this: I'm turning thirty, my career will be over soon and I need a retirement fund."

"To keep you in designer clothes?"

"They're expensive." She sighed and fluttered her eyelashes.

"I don't buy it."

Her eyes widened. "You, you, you..."

"What?"

Trembling with what he assumed was anger she spit one word. "Bastard."

"Cause I know you're not a flake?"

She growled.

Gotta love a woman who growls. Wonder what other sounds she makes.

"Don't get me wrong Sadie, you look beautiful in your designer gowns, but that's not who you are. There's a lot more to you. Even I can tell that. And I've never been considered the brightest color in the artist's palette."

Her eyes hardened. "I'm not looking for a shrink, or a Dutch cowboy, or... or even a lover. Get out of here."

"Hmmm, not even a lover? Sure about that?" He moved in again and kissed her. A simple kiss. No hands, no bodies touching, just lips. And it was like the finest he'd ever tasted.

She stepped back, her face flushed with arousal. "Look, if we'd met at another time, I really think we could..."

"Have something?"

"Yeah, but..."

"Baby, there's only this moment and what we have is pretty damn fine." He moved in again, but she put her fingers to his lips.

"Stop. You're confusing me."

"I'm confusing you? Tell me about the box."

"Just leave," she said.

"Darling, if I was a sane man, I would." He moved closer again

She picked up the lamp that sat on the nightstand and coiled her arm back to pitch it at him. "Oh no." he said. "No, no." He moved back, away from her towards the door.

She threatened with her arm again and a look of satisfaction crept into the corner of her eyes. Hah, she thinks she's in control.

He took another step back. She looked so hot, like an Amazonian warrior, except instead of a spear she had a table lamp. "How about breakfast?" he asked.

"I don't do breakfast." A small smile started on her face, as if she too saw the humor in their situation. "Too many calories."

With his hand on the door handle, he gave her his most pleading look. "I'd rather stay. I'm house trained."

She shook her head, making her mane of long red curls bounce. He wondered if her hair was red elsewhere on her body. Images of her lying naked before him flooded his mind. "I'll play by your rules. I promise." At least for a while.

"Get out."

He turned the knob. "One last kiss?"

Her stone glare cut through the space between them like a surgical knife.

"I won't ask about the box." He grinned.

That did it. The lamp flew and he caught it with his hand. He put it down on the floor. "It's always interesting seeing you," he said and then he opened the door.

***

What an infuriating man. Why should he care about the box, or how empty or full a person she is? He left without another word.

The door closed quietly behind him and she leaned on it. Her lips tingled from his kisses. Hot kisses. Was he the one? *Oh—come on, woman, this isn't a fairy tale. He's no frog prince and you're no sweet innocent.* You're way too old for girly sentimentality. She grimaced. But is a woman ever too old to believe in true love?

Her grandmother told her that there would be one special man out there for her, and part of her had always believed it. Sebastian wasn't like any other man she'd met. He seemed so...right. Deep down right. It wasn't just that he was so drop-dead handsome he sent her whole body into turmoil every time he came near. It was more than that. His honest blue eyes, his mischievous character... his way of making her feel good about being alive. Sheesh, she sounded like a star-struck teenager.

No, no, no Sadie. It's time to get down to earth—practical. Could he help her out? Not likely. A giant full of moral lectures, he'd get in her way. And she had to face the truth. Sebastian's probably just another guy who wanted what every other man wanted, to own her damn cheek bones so he could show her off around town like a hunter's trophy.

The box. She needed to look at it again. Unbelievable how quickly he zeroed in on it. Like he was a detective.

She needed to get rid of the finger. What if someone needed it? Should she phone the local hospitals and ask? What an impossible situation.

Walking back to the table, she grumbled. She'd seen some nasty stuff in her life as a spy, but she'd never had a body part delivered to her door before. That only happened in movies. She shook her head. Sweat trickled down her neck.

She opened the drawer. The smudge of blood on one side of the box had dried. As she lifted it to her face, her message tone on her regular cell phone rang. She jumped. 4:00 a.m.

"Tell no one about the package," the message read, "or the next body part will be yours."

The screen said source unknown. She screwed up her mouth. Must be Delilah. But her name usually popped up as, "D." Maybe she was using a trash phone. But Dee lacked that sophistication.

"Who are you?" she typed.

"Bring the package to the fountain in front of the American Hotel at noon tomorrow."

Where the hell was Dee? Did she set her up and run off with the merchandise? A stone of worry settled in the pit of her stomach like lead encased with shards of glass. "Message received," she typed and hit the send button.

An emoticon of a devil's smiling face stared back at her. Great, the bad guy had a sense of humor. She took the lid off the box and studied the contents. Definitely a pinky finger, shorter than her own, and the nail had been coated in polish. It had the acrid smell of blood and rotting flesh. With a tissue, she wiped away the blood to have a good look at the nail. Her stomach plummeted. Dee's favorite shade, "Hooker red," with silver stars applied on the tip. Her signature style.

CHAPTER 14

Seb left Sadie's apartment laughing at her lame attempt to hit him with a lamp, but by the time he'd made it down the three flights of stairs a cold soberness had swallowed him up. He felt like he'd been punched hard in the gut. Sadie had to be in some sort of danger. Real danger. He could feel it. Why wouldn't she let him help her?

Sadie'd gotten into his bloodstream like a virus. No, worse than that, more like a damn parasite with teeth like Jaws. The woman came with trouble written all over her. So why the hell didn't he back-off? She was a thief—plain and simple. Getting involved with her would be reckless, stupid, and possibly illegal. But he couldn't deny the pull she had on him.

What hid in the box? Maybe if he knew that, he could make sense of it all. One minute she suggested sex and the next she threw lighting fixtures as him. Whatever was in the box, she didn't want him to see it, and that made him want it--- really bad.

Had she stolen jewelry during his show? No one had reported a theft. He'd check with Paul again in the morning, to be sure there were no complaints. If she had stolen something, that could explain some of her behavior, but it wouldn't explain the flash of terror in her eyes that he caught when she thought he wasn't looking.

Back at his apartment he cracked open a Heineken and checked his messages. Xander had forwarded a document from their friend Seamus at Interpol. The heading read: "LA drop tomorrow, Amsterdam." LA meant looted art. He grumbled.

It was too late to call Xander. He'd already got him out of bed one night this week when he contacted him from Florence. The image of his friend snug in his home with his wife and baby flickered through his mind. Nice image. Tomorrow would be soon enough.

A solid weight hit his right shoulder like a bag of potatoes with a thump. Shit. Rascal, his three-year old Siamese cat had lunged off the top of the fridge and landed on him. Although he knew she excelled at flying leaps, she took him by surprise and he'd never grown accustomed to her claws cutting into his flesh for balance. The suddenness of the cat attack quickened Seb's pulse. It didn't matter how many times she jumped him, it always took him by surprise. "Rascal," he growled with pain, annoyance and affection.

She started talking back to him the way Siamese do, making vocalizations almost as clear as words. Unimpressed by his long absence she had a lot to say, so Seb stroked her long sleek back as he opened a can of sardines—her favorite. Her noises faded into a loud purr. Life with his cat.

The image of Sadie's long red hair crossed his mind. Wonder if she'd like a can of smelly fish. But there were more interesting ways to manage a woman. His body hardened at the thought. Would Rascal approve of her? He threw the licked clean can in the trash like a softball. It missed. He never missed.

Rascal settled into licking her chops, and Seb stretched out on his favorite leather chair with a beer. He looked at his messages again. The rest of Seamus's document didn't say much. "Chatter about an exchange set for tomorrow. Exact location not clear. Stay in touch."

Tomorrow's another day. Maybe he'd help his friends catch some thieves, and learn more about the red head.

The smell of the sardines made him think about how good Sadie smelled good, like fresh flowers in the sunlight. He laughed and took a good swig of his beer. Is that how trouble smells?

CHAPTER 15

Bakari's gut twisted as he descended the rope ladder on the side of Herengracht canal. When his feet touched the deck of the sorceress's houseboat he gritted his teeth. He hated needing anyone, but he needed her.

The green door squeaked open. Djeserit, the Egyptian psychic sat at her table with her tarot cards in front of her, looking like she'd been expecting him, though he hadn't told her he was coming. Kypher incense lay heavily in the air. He could hear the noise of people traveling home from work or school on the street above them. Ancient songs played in the background on her music system. Without a word, he closed the door and took the seat opposite her.

Her dark eyes pierced his. "I told you to never come back."

"I must know more."

"You are cursed."

"Enough." His voice echoed in the small cabin.

Her eyes flinched.

"There must be a way I can free myself from my past. What I did may have been wrong in the eyes of the world, but everything I did, I did for others. Will I be damned for all eternity because I love my family?"

"Do not fool yourself Bakari. Helping your family is second place in your life. You are a man who thinks of himself first and foremost."

"Doesn't every man?"

"You went too far. There's a cost when lives are lost. Balance must be maintained."

His fist banged the table. "You must tell me what you see. That is all I ask. I will deal with whatever is coming my way. You can name your price."

Her face framed with long black hair paled and her hands trembled, but she said nothing.

"What do you see?"

She looked towards the windows as if conferring with a spirit and nodded her head. "It is true there are many paths through darkness and light in this world. I fear you've been in the dark too long. Forces of justice are heading your way."

"Give me a name? A time? A place? Something I can work with?" Maybe, Chasisi was right. She toyed with him for her own gain.

"No," she said, "Chasisi is wrong about me."

His chest tightened. She'd read his thoughts.

"I tell you only what I see."

"Which is?"

Her jaw clenched. "You cannot escape your past. When you pass and Anubis weighs your soul you will be found wanting."

He shook his head. "I'll deal with that when the time comes. I want to know about now. What is going to happen? Why do I keep getting bad dreams?"

She glanced towards the window again. "Your subconscious is sending you warnings. That is why you can't sleep. As you get closer to obtaining the most powerful ankh, you draw danger."

He fisted his hands. Sweat trickled down his neck.

She took a deep breath. "All right. I will read the cards for you one more time." She lit the candles in the ornate golden candelabra snapping the matches with quick angry strokes.

Bakari closed the curtain and turned off the lights. He breathed in the kypher incense and cleared his mind wanting it to be as open as a book for her to read. He sat back down, picked up her tarot cards and shuffled them.

She stood and raised her hands to the sky. "I, coming forth am Amen, the hidden one."

An ethereal lightness flowed through his being.

In her right hand she drew an ivory wand from a pocket in her robe inscribed with hieroglyphs. She waved it once in the air. "I am the keeper of Akashic Records. All of which is, and which shall be. Eternity and Everlastingness. open your portals." She put her left hand on the deck. "May I fly like a golden hawk. May I see the truth revealed." She stood absolutely still. Her eyes lids closed and her body shook. Then her eyes slowly opened.

Bakari forced himself to breath.

Her eyes glazed over like a demon.

She waved the wand once in front of him. "Son of Isis, Searcher of truth. Let your life be revealed."

As he formed his question clearly in his mind, he cut the cards into three piles, and then collected them together. He placed them in a pile in front of her.

Without looking at him, she turned ten cards into the tree of life spread to show his energy moving through matter. "The three columns of the tree represent the three aspects of experience in the physical plane, the pillar of mercy, the pillar of mildness and the pillar of challenge."

He stared intently at the unturned cards.

She turned over the first card, number twenty—Judgement. The card displayed an image of a winged angel blowing a trumpet above people adrift in rough seas.

His eyes widened. The cards confirmed his suspicions yet again. He was hearing a message from his inner self.

Djeserit nodded, "The "Judgement" card. It is a moment of decision for you. But remember the ego travels in the underworld and you must consider the consequences of all your actions."

After a moment of silence she turned the second card, number Eight—Strength reversed.

His lips quivered. Damn the cards. How dare they judge him?

She tisked gently. "The cards never lie. "Strength" reversed in the wisdom position indicates you have a lack of control in your thoughts. You are being selfish and contemplate violence.

He swallowed, tasting acid from the anger boiling in his gut. What right did others have to judge him? Especially now?

She turned over the third card, number Eleven—"Justice" reversed. "The cards know you well."

He growled. "The cards can be wrong."

Shaking her head she met his eyes. "They are never wrong when they are read properly. This card warns that you are thinking about a bad choice and that you are filled with mistrust."

"I can fight that."

"Yes, you can fight it all Bakari. But these first three cards form a powerful triangle. They represent your life energy moving from light into pure consciousness. Only a fool would ignore the warnings."

She turned over each of the remaining card and read their meaning, ending with the bottom one. Four—"The Emperor" Reversed. She bowed her head. "At the root of your activity will be cruelty, confrontation, violence...domination."

He shrugged, "That's all necessary when you want power."

"There will be a price." Her voice held a deep sadness, as if...as if she glimpsed something more than this bad news.

"I know what I want and I know what I must do. Djeserit you know why I seek this power. It is not for me. Does that not make a difference?"

"If you choose to continue on a dark path there is only one thing that may help you. You must reach deeper into the darkness and use the powers of evil."

"The amulets?"

"Yes, to grow your power you must collect them as I have told you. But remember power comes with a price. Every time you steal an amulet and claim it as your own, a piece of your soul dies."

"I have collected ten, as you instructed."

"That is good, but there is one amulet that has more power than all them combined. It's called the Emerald Ankh. It is solid gold, inlaid with powerful crystals and infused with a spell of Kebechet, the goddess of purification. Etched at its center is the Eye of Ra and at its base is an emerald stone like no other. They say when you look at it you look into the secrets of eternity."

"Where is it? At last he could taste hope.

"You will find it in New York." She hesitated for a moment and closed her eyes, "I fear it is your fate to find it."

"It has the dark power I need?" His throat felt drier than the desert.

"It is pure power. When a person of light holds it, it becomes a force of light. When a person with a dark soul holds it..." Her left hand turned palm down, as if saying the words would invoke spirits she didn't want in the room.

"If I have that amulet, will I have the power I need?"

She nodded, not looking him in the eye.

The air cooled and a tingling sensation crawled up his spine. "What are you not telling me?"

She waited a minute and then she said, "You have a worthy adversary."

CHAPTER 16

Tuesday

S*he woke to the sound* of pounding on her door and Mitchell's gravelly male voice shouting, "Get up Sadie."

In the darkened room the neon digits on the radio clock read: 10:00 a.m. The photo-shoot would start in fifteen minutes! Her stupid magazine manager would kill her.

She wanted to run to the door, but after her first step she found all she could only hobble. The blisters on her feet stung. Then the image of the finger came into her mind. This had to be a better day.

Mitchell pushed his way past her and she closed the door behind him.

He turned around to look at her a second time and assumed that obnoxious stance of a boss about to lecture her. Not something she needed now, from him or anyone else. She pushed the air out of her lungs. Sweet Jesus give me strength.

But his sermon didn't come out. Instead he gasped, "Sadie!" His eyes bulged to twice their size as they swept over her body and his mouth twitched.

She tried to smile. "Sorry, I slept in. I'll throw myself together."

"You look awful. He moved closer to her and touched her cheek, "What happened to your face?"

She put a hand to her mouth and then her cheek. "My face?" All she could think about was the gruesome present that had been left at her door. How important could her cheekbones be compared to that. She rolled her eyes.

"You've got no color except for the dark circles under your eyes. Are you sick or something?"

Or something. "Mitchell I'm in a mess."

"Yeah. If you don't get your cute little ass down to the Dam for a shoot in five minutes you can kiss your contract with Extazee magazine goodbye. Need I remind you how much we rely on them for cash."

She soaked in the warmth of his fingers moving her hair away from her face with care and gave him a, "I don't give a flying eff" expression.

"Shower. We'll talk on the way over," he said. I'll text Knickers we'll be a few minutes late."

Knickers, was Mitchell's favorite name for the owner of the magazine who had taken it upon her fat-ass to micro-manage this tour. Knickers—as in knickers tied in a knot, splintered wooden baseball up her ass, grade-A, BITCH. Sadie laughed at the mention of her nickname. Only Mitchell could raise her spirits on such a horrible morning. This wasn't the usual way models were managed, but there was nothing normal about the Lady Knickers.

As hot water streamed over her sore body, the amulets came to her mind. Two left. Did Bakari al-Sharif know that? Delilah had said she didn't think so, but then Dee had a stubborn mind, the kind that liked to believe whatever she wanted it to. It fascinated Sadie how Delilah processed the world. In her head she had her own moral-relativity-slash-reality-bending- warp-machine thing going on. So, if she could believe it to be true, it was true to her. Empirical evidence didn't interest her. Only her own slimy slippery version of the truth. A murky life that now threatened to ooze into hers.

If Sadie gave both the remaining amulets to al-Sharif now, she'd have nothing left to barter. There would be no way to be sure she could get Delilah back with the rest of her fingers intact. No way to meet the infamous arms dealer.

But if she didn't give him both amulets, she'd be toying with him. Only really stupid people pull the tail of a tiger. It was a dangerous game to play with a dangerous man, but unquestionably her best move.

She stepped out of the shower and toweled off. After taking off the amulet necklace; a small ankh made of pure gold attached to a leather string, she put it into the tampon tube she kept in her purse. She grabbed the other amulet; the gold scarab ring inlaid with jewels, from its hiding spot in her luggage and put it in a jewelry case for the swap. Should she put a note in with it? Pausing, she shook her head. Putting anything on paper could prove foolish. She slipped the case into her purse ready for the exchange at noon.

The thought of playing a man as dangerous as al-Sharif didn't settle well. Her whole body felt restless, like it wanted to jump out of its own skin. Damn Dee for creating this sticky mess. Running a hand through her hair she set her jaw. Sometimes you can only go forward regardless of the risks. She'd give the scarab to the courier and tell him she had another amulet, but wanted to give it directly to the boss. Yup, playing the odds al-Sharif would agree to meet her, was her best move. So why did her gut keep twitching?

Ten frantic minutes later she joined Mitchell ready for her day job. They'd do her makeup when she got to the set. No doubt they'd heap it on to hide all her dark shadows. The damned new cosmetician, Jenny who smelled of cheap perfume liked to say, "Our older models need more color, so honey I'll be using a ton of it on you."

Oh hell, screw the Jennys of the world. There wasn't enough blush in Hollywood to make her look good today.

Mitchell gave her another visual once-over and made no comment. Not a good sign. Usually he'd say something like, "Lookin good," or if that would be a stretch, he'd say, "Love the light in your eyes," or if that wouldn't fit he'd say, "The photographers can use filters to bring out your inner beauty." Guess he thought there weren't enough filters on the planet to fix the way she looked this morning. They headed out to the shoot, a five minute walk away. They wouldn't get there any faster by taxi in this busy city, so she had to walk.

As she slipped on her runners, the raw soars on her toes screamed for attention. She gritted her teeth and laced the shoes up. The uneven surface of the road would make walking difficult. She grabbed a couple mild pain killers from her purse and downed them before she stood up.

"So what the hell happened to you?" Mitchell's calm caring voice soothed her soul if not her feet.

"It's a long, long story, Mitch."

"Bad date?"

"Bad life."

He laughed.

A low gray cloud bank hugged the city giving it a moody morning light, fitting perfectly with the fashion shoot and her muddling spirits. She exhaled a long slow breath.

"Sadie, talk to me. You know I'll help you if you're in trouble. I got your back. I've always got your back."

"We don't have much time. But Mitchell, promise me one thing."

"Anything Sadie."

Out of her tote, she pulled out a silver key with a funky Tigger design sticker on the top of it and held it out to Mitch. "Take this. If anything happens to me, this key will open my safety deposit box in the Wells Fargo Manhattan bank. The manager will let you have access to it. Only you." She handed him the key.

Mitchell's puppy dog eyes looked at her. "Sadie, nothing's gonna to happen to you. We're just having our pictures taken. Maybe we should get you some happy pills."

"You have to listen to me. In the box, you'll find a pouch with diamonds, more than enough to cover your costs, my will, and an explanation of..."

Mitchell took her hand, and held it in his. "Sadie, I won't let anything happen to you. If you don't think I can protect you, I'll find someone who can."

"Mitchell listen to me, damn it."

"I am listening to you. We'll work this out, honey. I know you don't want to turn thirty."

"I have a son." Her stomach twisted. She'd finally told him.

"What?" He stopped walking and grabbed her arm.

She continued in the direction of the Dam, pulling him with her. "I have a son and I need to know that if anything happens to me, he'll be taken care of."

He gave her a side glance. "When did you fit that in?"

"Remember, a year ago when I did a shoot in Nigeria? You were busy taking care of your father's estate and couldn't come and I went with that insufferable full-of-himself Henri Bidou?"

He nodded slowly.

"That's when. It's complicated." They were only twenty yards away from the site of the shoot in the middle of the Dam. Knickers, a buxom woman, stood with her hands on her hips. Raw fetid anger shot from the woman's steely glare and punctured Sadie like a hail storm from hell. "I'll explain later," she whispered to Mitch.

"Damn straight, you will." He gave her hand a reassuring squeeze and pocketed the key. His face had lost most of its color. Though he'd never say it out loud, Mitch was worried.

They walked over to their manager.

"Nice of y'all to come," said Knickers, her course voice dripping with sarcasm that hung on her Alabama accent like ice on fire.

"Sorry," Sadie said as she brushed by her to start the shoot.

Knickers grabbed her arm and dug her long fake fingernails into her bicep, which hurt—a lot. Like sharpened razor blades. Up close, the woman smelled of yesterday's coffee.

"Sorry doesn't cut it. You models are all the same. You think because it's your face in the picture you can run the show, but not on my shoot, honey. You're just a stupid model. If you're late one more time, I'll cut you." Knickers sincerity hit like a megaton bomb. "You're not the only pouty smile in town."

Sadie's gut wrenched. She needed this job for her cover. "I said I'm sorry, and I am sorry. I..."

Knickers released her arm and shoved her forward with force. "Save your excuses. I don't need your shit." Her accent faded with her anger.

Sadie started walking towards Jenny to get her blush on.

"You look like hell," Knickers added, the words hitting her back like poorly aimed darts. "You're getting too old for this, honey. No one wants old whores. Maybe, it's time you found yourself a new gig."

The industry had wined and dined her when she was fifteen, and hadn't started using the whore analogy until last year. The certainty that she edged closer to the end of her modelling career left a taste so bitter in her mouth she could choke on it, but she didn't.

Sadie'd liked modeling in the beginning and had grown to love it as a cover for her life as a spy. She spent her days in beautiful parts of the world and her nights taking care of dangerous business. It suited her fine. Stilettoes and stealth. She'd survive this annoying gig and develop a new cover when she needed one for her undercover life.

Ten minutes later Jenny said, "You're done."

Sadie walked over to the set. Time to sell fancy clothes and fantasies.

Mitchell stood, hands on his lean hips, waiting in front of the cameras. The angular lines of his face made him look more like a Renaissance sculpture than a breathing man. His mouth grimaced as he held his usual start-up stance, a let's-get-the-eff-going so we can get the work over. A defiant in-your-face attitude smoldered in his eyes giving him a touch of bad-boy allure. Attitude with a capital A, looked good on him.

She'd never get away with a rebel look. People wanted women sultry, bold, erotic, smoldering...a whole lot of things, but not angry.

Sadie took her place beside him, tilted her head and smiled with her eyes. She needed to dig deeper to make a good picture. Drawing into her mind the memory of Sebastian's sexy grin, the one that made her quiver inside-out her lips spread, and she smiled seductively into the lens with every fiber of her body.

The photographer gave the satisfied groan that Sadie equated with a fat paycheck.

***

Sebastian woke with the taste of stale beer lingering in his mouth. Looking at his clock he did the math. Less than three hours sleep. He stretched his back trying to twist out the fatigue, but he knew stretching wouldn't be enough. Not nearly enough.

His mind had spun most of the night trying to piece together Sadie's crazy behaviour, with the few clues he had about the looted art. Every time he had a thought that might pull it all together, his mind slipped to Sadie's legs—long toned... And then there was the sweet taste of her full lips. They took up a fair amount of his brain space too.

As he drank his morning coffee he sent a text to his assistant Paul to check again, whether anyone had complaints from the night before. He sent a message to Zaneke thanking her for coming to his show and sending his love. His third text message went to Xander to see if any news had surfaced about the looted-art exchange planned for today.

He leaned back with a sense that something was wrong. He paced the floor for ten minutes going over all the details in his mind. Then he sat down again.

The International Herald, his usual morning read, offered little today. The Euro bounced low, Greece continued to tank in every way possible and political scandals in Italy were threatening the government, again. All of this would be easier to read on a full night's sleep. He poured a second cup of coffee from the French Press and remembered his younger days when tea would be enough to get him going. He downed his mug in three gulps and headed for the shower.

His mind relaxed under the pressure of steaming hot water. The tension in his tired shoulder muscles eased. He'd figure things out. He always did.

The doorbell rang. Strange. No one visited him in the morning. No one he knew would be that stupid.

Wrapped in a towel, he checked his security camera. Xander. He let him in.

He'd watched his friend's face age over the last couple of years with the death of both his parents and more than his share of trouble sent his way. He'd seen him pissed off, and hurt. Today his jaw held that stern, Don't-fuck-with-me hardness that brought the memory of all that crap back.

"What happened?" asked Sebastian.

"Here," he said, handing him a gold chain necklace with a pendant on it. It looked familiar. They made jokes about it all the time. Girl stuff. The necklace held a weird place of honor in their extended family. Kat, Xander's wild youngest sister had worn it when she ran around Holland looking for a lost Vermeer a year ago, and before that, Xander's wife Angela had worn it when she chased a psychopath who'd stolen a Rembrandt. He held it carefully in his hand. For such an important piece of jewellery it felt awfully light.

"I remember this," Seb said. "It's the Chinese pendant Angela's friend Lin gave her." He turned it over in his hand, a piece of precious medal the women thought held magical power. "It's the Chinese character for crises, a melding of danger and opportunity." He turned it over once more. Nope. Didn't feel like magic. It felt like metal. He cocked an eyebrow at his friend. "You're giving me jewellery now. Do you want to go steady or something?"

Xander's shot him a frosty look.

Seb stepped back as if hit by a soccer ball in the stomach. Felt like it. "Hey. Just trying to be funny."

"Angela thinks you need it. Don't ask me what I think. When you're married you humor your wife, or your life becomes miserable. Trust me."

"I trust you." Seb tried not to smile too widely. "Never figured you'd end up so whipped." He put it in his pocket. "But can I ask why I need a necklace from China?"

"Got news." Xander said walking over to a chair in the kitchen area. "Sit down."

Sebastian sat.

"The police found a body in the canal this morning."

They find bodies in the canals every morning. "So?"

"This one had no hands or teeth left to make identification easy..."

"Torture?" Seb's gut wrenched. "So another low-life met a nasty end. Why should this interest me?" But the small hairs on the back of his neck rose, as if a part of him knew he was about to care a whole hell of a lot.

"It looks like professionals covering their tracks. The victim, a man by the name of Leonard Bronski, known on the street as The Digger, because he knew where to dig up a good take even in the lean times. The guy was a real orifice, well-connected to everything shady in Amsterdam. The police figure he got tortured for information and then taken out. They identified him by an anchor tattoo behind his left ear."

"Sadie's involved?" That must be what Xander was leading up to. He tried to breathe but all the oxygen left his lungs.

Xander shook his head. "Not directly." He looked away from his friend for a minute. "We have a lead on the art thieves. We have a picture of a well-known fence who goes by the name Delilah Sagwaski. After doing some time in a medium security prison in the states she came over to Europe and appeared to live off of wealthy men. But Interpol kept an eye on her. They thought she might be moving diamonds and other jewels, but they haven't been able to catch her. Then they heard she'd become part of the group moving looted art. She and The Digger were more than associates."

Seb sat straighter. "A lead. We have a lead?"

"It's a start."

"We can look into everyone associated with her, turn over the stones and we're good at that. We'll find the scum hiding beneath the surface." Seb took an easy breath.

Xander shifted his eyes away. "There's more?"

Without looking at him, Xander pulled out his cell phone, keyed buttons, and placed it on the table between them. "This is a picture of Delilah."

Staring back at Sebastian was a picture of a middle-aged woman with black hair. Her arm draped over Sadie's shoulders. They were both smiling for the camera like they... were best friends out for a good time. Shit.

Sebastian scratched his chin, feeling the weight of the world collapse on him. "I can't believe Sadie's involved."

"I told Seamus you'd say that." Xander crossed his arms in front of him. "Are you banging her?"

"No," he grumbled. "But she's ..."

"Dangerous."

Sebastian couldn't argue that. "Look I know she's light fingered, but I can't believe she'd stoop to handling looted art.

Xander looked directly at him, again. "When I told Seamus you knew Sadie Stewart the woman in the picture, he did some more checking around. His information confirms she's a model. But her background is too squeaky clean for someone who spends their evenings with the likes of Delilah. It's suspicious. We want to know more about the woman."

Silence settled deep into the room.

Sebastian had every intention of checking Sadie out, but to do it for Interpol was another matter. What if she were guilty? Like maybe without knowing it. Surely she couldn't be that evil? He swallowed.

He'd have to turn her over. Way too Bogart a role for him. "What do you think?" Seb asked.

Xander's eyes softened. "I think it doesn't really matter what I think. You're the most stubborn person I know. This woman has you under her spell. You'll do everything you can to prove her innocence and you might get your head blown off." He pounded his fist on the table. "Seb, if there's any way I can talk you into walking away from this?"

Seb tilted his head. As if?

"Seamus, my brother Luuk and I can investigate. Trust us. When Interpol and Van der Valk Inc work together we get to the bottom of things. We wouldn't be sidelined by her beauty."

"But I already know her."

Xander winced. "Seb—be careful."

"Where is she?" They'd have her under surveillance for sure.

"Doing a photo shoot at the Dam."

Seb stood up. Xander reached for his arm to stop him from going. "Listen man, Angela made me swear I'd watch you put the necklace on before you ran off trying to save the green eyed lady. That's what she calls her. She said if you won't do it for us, do it for your godson Mauritz."

Seb looked at his friend's hand on his arm and raised a brow. The fact that Xander was willing to physically challenge him over a piece of jewellery amused him, but it also made him feel good. "Okay," he said, grimacing. "For Mauritz." He put the necklace on.

It felt warm on his chest. Had to be his imagination. Had to be.

CHAPTER 17

Sadie's face muscles ached from her trademark pout, the one the world paid big bucks for. Over the years she'd worked hard at perfecting the look to cement her reputation. The mags liked her style, an alluring femme fatale that drew people's imaginations and sold product. She sighed at the thought. They liked her unusually high cheekbones that photographed well. She relaxed her mouth into a tired smile.

The morning had a chill to it that made her long for a good strong cup of coffee. As if he read her mind Mitchell's head broke his pose, bobbed up like a fish jumping for bait. "I need a break," he mumbled.

"Like Hell," screeched Knickers in the background. "We're behind schedule."

Out of the corner of her eye Sadie spotted Sebastian amidst the crowds, fifteen yards away watching. He talked on his cell phone while his eyes danced with hers.

A young athletic man on a bicycle with boxes perched behind his seat moved smoothly beside the set while he talked into a yellow mobile phone. A common sight in Amsterdam, but the way he wobbled caught Sadie's attention. As he neared Knickers he slid into a slow fall.

Boxes tumbled everywhere and their tops became dislodged as they hit the ground. Out of one came a horde of, rats—big rats. Sadie's breath stopped short. At least twenty rodents skittering in all directions.

Knickers screeched. People backed away.

The young man mounted his bicycle and left the scene. Another fallen box burst open and more rats escaped into the busy, city square.

"Rats, rats," screamed a woman in a blood curdling voice. People ran in every direction to get away.

Out of the chaos, the Dutch stud walked right up to Sadie with an irresistible bad-boy grin.

She laughed so hard her eyes watered. "Rodents? I can't believe it. That's quite the entrance."

"Coffee?" Sebastian reached his hand out to her.

"I'm working."

He nodded towards the scene of people scrambling in every direction. "I think you're on break."

She laughed. "Oh hell, why not."

Sending Mitchell a call-me hand signal she hobbled to stand beside Seb and ignored Mitchell's you've-got-to-be-kidding-me death stare.

"This way," Sebastian said.

Smiling she took off her heels and limped with him barefoot across the square to the Nieuwe Kafé beside the late-Gothic, Nieuwe Kirk. Nieuwe meant new, but the church had been built beside the palace six centuries ago. She loved its breathtaking architecture, spires and it's stained glassed windows. It made her feel like she'd entered a fairy tale. The depth of history in Dutch buildings grounded her in a way modern skyscrapers never would. It made her feel like a grain of sand on the beach of time. With a glance she took it all in as she walked with Sebastian..

The air between them sizzled. It just did. Neither spoke.

They sat down outside of the café, near to where the three horse and buggies waited for customers. People milled around them, many of them tourists. The Dam was the busiest square in all of Holland.

When the unspoken heat didn't abate Sadie fumbled for words. "Rats?" She narrowed her eyes at Sebastian.

"Diversions work." He smiled. "But you know all about that."

Sadie shrugged. What the hell did he mean? Did he know about the exchange at Eros? Had it been caught on video? Her throat tightened.

His lips firmed. Something had happened

since she last saw him. He seemed different. Not as comfortable with her as last night. She needed to be careful. "What's wrong with you?"

***

"Everything," he said. Sitting beside her, suspecting she was involved in some way with looted art, but still feeling attracted as hell to her hurt. He had to keep reminding himself she was the enemy, or possibly the enemy, or he'd never get through this investigation. His mind stalled.

But other parts of his anatomy went on overdrive. When he looked into her moss green eyes all he wanted to do was make love to her. *Godverdomme het*. Maybe he wasn't the man for checking her out. Maybe Xander was right.

"Tell me," she said.

He leaned back and looked into her eyes. Clear and sincere. Femme Fatale? Possibly, but his gut kept telling him she was alright. Maybe if he knew more about her he'd understand how she got connected with the thieves. "Are you in some kind of trouble?"

She slid her eyes away from him.

"Look don't deny it. Something's going on around you and it's not good. If you talk to me, maybe I can help you."

***

She looked at the table and sighed. So not like her. Sebastian's directness and willingness to help her hit like a bullet between the eyes. An alarm went off in the spy section of her brain. *Danger: this man is potent* in more ways than one. She pulled a hand through her hair. "Look, Sebastian if we had met at another time..."

"At least tell me about the box."

The damn box. She shuddered involuntarily. She opened her mouth and closed it.

"You are in trouble."

She bit her lip. "More than you can handle my friend." She got up to leave.

"Don't take on a gang of art thieves alone." He took her hand and held it. His had to be twice the size of hers. Warmth and strength flowed through it, melting her resolve. What was it about this man that made her want to open up to him? Damn him. She'd been trained to not trust anyone outside the company. And that suited her well. There's comfort in solitude and above all safety.

But the steely edged fear that her life was slipping close to a dangerous precipice with this op squeezed at her gut. Maybe Sebastian could help her. He certainly knew the town, the art and...

She should ask Jeremiah if she could read him in. But Jeremiah hadn't returned her last call. That meant either he had no information or something big was going down in Langley that pulled him away from her assignment. Knowing her relative importance in the spy chain, she guessed the later.

Anyway, Jeremiah had grown too protective. It was her job to assess the risks and threats and sometimes to act alone. It may break the rules to let Sebastian know what was happening, but it felt right.

They sat in silence for a few heartbeats communicating only through their touch. It steadied her... tempted her. The waitress came and took their coffee order.

When she left, Sadie asked, "What do you know?"

"Interpol's linked you to a ring of criminals dealing artifacts and looted paintings. They think it's the Russian mafia." The left corner of his mouth twitched.

"Bullshit." They couldn't be on to her this quickly. "You're fishing."

He gently brushed a lock of her hair away from her face. His touch sent off a current of desire through her body. "Then you tell me your side of the story. "

She pulled her hand away from his. "Interpol sent you to seduce information out of me?" Shit. She should have known better. A man this kind and handsome had to be too good to be true. Men never really cared. They just wanted women for their own needs.

He blanched. "Uh, not exactly."

"What then."

"I volunteered."

"Someone's got to get the job done, eh?"

"No, no. It's not like that." He gave a false laugh and then turned serious. "I can't believe you're involved." Sincerity flowed out of his blue eyes, as clear as morning sunlight and slapped at her conscience like waves on the shore. If a man ever deserved the truth, this guy did. He wore his thoughts and feelings true as day on his face. His sincerity cut right through her well maintained CIA shields and tugged her heart. What a lousy time to meet a sexy, boy scout.

"Things are not always what they seem," she said. She tossed her hair behind her shoulders. *Sweet Jesus, he opened me up easily.* She started to stand.

"Sadie, sit down and talk to me. I'm your best chance, and I..."

"You what?"

"I care."

She flopped in her chair. *Like we needed that said.* To booster her resolve she thought about her oath to her country and stood up. She reached for her glass of water and threw it in his face. "Leave me alone." A bit melodramatic, but she needed to do something drastic to break the heat growing between them.

Water dripped down his cheeks, but his eyes held hers. He stood up, pulled her to him and kissed her.

His lips, soft, warm and so inviting... She wanted to melt into him, wanted so badly to be with him, but instead she pulled back, lifted her arm and slapped him.

"Sadie," Mitchell called out as he broke through the crowd and jogged over to them. He looked from one to the other. His brow furrowed and the lines of his perfectly sculpted jaw firmed. "Knickers is on the war path."

"I'm done here," she said, nodding at Sebastian.

***

Five minutes later, Xander slid into Sadie's empty seat. Sebastian had dried his face with the table napkin. "Well done buddy," Xander said.

Seb shrugged and took another sip of his coffee.

"In less than five minutes she threw water on you, returned your kiss and slapped you." Xander laughed. "Watching your style is... interesting to say the least. Maybe, you should write dating books."

Seb glared.

"So what did she tell you?"

Seb leaned back. "It's what she didn't tell me. She more or less confirmed my suspicion that what happened at Eros had been a diversion, which means some sort of exchange took place right under my nose at my own fucking gallery." He looked across the Dam to where Sadie posed for pictures. "But I still think she's a victim. She's just too scared to talk. She's wickedly smart. Wickedly beautiful... But I don't think she's evil."

Xander put up his hand. "Wait a minute. Why can't she be evil? She kisses too good?"

Seb shrugged.

"Bad girls can kiss, buddy. Don't get too involved with her. She'll rip your heart right out of your chest and eat it raw."

"Easy for you to say. Xander. She's not like other women. She..."

Xander interrupted, "No she's not like other women. She steals, smuggles looted art and maybe collects body parts on the side."

Seb sent him another shut-up glare.

Xander frowned. "Listen, I know this is not what you want to hear, but you have to be sensible.

Maybe she'll cut off your dick, since that's what you're using to think."

"Fuck you."

"I'm spoken for." Xander looked off for a minute, his face red. "Look, what do you want me to tell Seamus."

"I'm on it, and I'll find out more."

"And how do you propose to do that?"

Seb stared at him. "I have a plan." He didn't but he'd figure one out.

CHAPTER 18

As Sadie hobbled back to the shoot with Mitchell supporting her right arm, she checked her phone: 11:00a.m. Only one hour until her meeting.

The crowds of people milling around the square thickened. Tourists gaped at the scenery while locals hurried to their destinations. Bicycles weaved between everyone ringing their bells to clear a path. The brisk spring breeze made people's cheeks rosy and the glimmer of sunshine had many smiling. She caught smells of cologne, frites and sweat. A busy day getting busier in the Dam.

But she couldn't afford to lose herself in the Amsterdam scene, she needed to be at the American Hotel in the Ledseplein square by noon and it was a twenty minute walk away. "Mitch, how can I ditch this shoot?"

His eyes popped. "Excuse me?"

"You heard me, damn it. I have to be somewhere else in an hour. Unless we can wrap it up in thirty I'm doomed."

His jaw softened and the look in his eyes told her he'd do whatever it took to help her. She didn't deserve such a good friend.

"I'll let them take a few more shots and then I'll complain about an upset stomach," he said.

"Sounds good." She nodded. It should work. No one wanted models to barf over product, or spend too much time in the loo. Knickers would want to kill him of course, but it would take the heat off her.

He leaned closer. "I could say that I'd be willing to try later today. Would that work for you?" Anxiety laced his voice.

"Sure. Whatever." Sweat beaded on her upper lip. Great, now her makeup would start running.

"Tell me about your son, Sadie."

Knickers paced only a hundred yards away from them. Her fiery dragon eyes narrowed to slits ready to slice and dice Sadie when she arrived. The irony of such a cold bitch owning a successful fashion magazine was high on her list of the-freaking-unbelievable in the modelling world. But the witch's rage could not deflect Mitchell's question. "They were killing him."

"Who?"

"The shaman of a remote Nigerian village and the grave digger. His mother died giving birth to him, so they believed him cursed. They strapped his body to his dead mother's and were in the process of burying them both when I heard the baby crying and came to see what was happening. I couldn't believe my eyes. Without thinking it through I took the baby and ran."

"You stole a baby?"

"Had to. There's no 911 in the jungle. I was his only chance."

"Nice of you to turn up," screeched the Knicker Bitch now only five feet away.

Sadie willed her body to shudder and made fluttery eyes, because she knew the woman would like that. "Rat's aren't in my contract."

"Get to work." The muscles in the woman's face tightened distorting it into a melodramatic mask of anger, fit for a Venetian opera.

Sadie put on her sultry pout. Mitchell winked at her before adjusted his own face. His friendship made moments like this easier.

Twenty minutes later, Mitchell complained he felt sick. Damn he was believable.

As Knickers flew into a temper tantrum, Sadie slipped away.

***

The Leidseplein sat between the Museum square and the Dam. Known as the entertainment square it was ringed by popular hotels and restaurants. She headed towards the large American Hotel on the far end. A destination for writers, artists and dancers, it had been famous for well over a century.

Sadie liked to imagine the days when Mata Hari, the famous Dutch World War I spy, held her honeymoon party there, amidst the Art Nouveau decor. The place had a twenties vibe that spoke of clandestine romance and adventure.

Having to meet al-Sharif's man broke the magic. What else in her life would be changed by this op? A chill ran down her spine.

Sadie arrived five minutes early for her appointment in front of the water fountain.

The sound of flowing water usually soothed her, but not today. This op had gone screwy from the outset. First, she had to work the unstable Delilah who partied to the wee hours of the night with cheap wine that gave Sadie horrible headaches, then the woman turned greedy and double-crossed Sadie's mark and now—the finger. The friggen finger.

Dee had never been what she'd call a friend in any real sense, but they'd hung together for the last couple of months and the thought of the woman being tortured hollowed Sadie's insides. Delilah had no idea who she was taking on. A freaking arms dealer who enjoyed violence! No idea.

Sadie felt for the package in her purse and pulled it out. *All this pain over a few old relics.* She slipped the tiny wrapped item into her jacket pocket and shuddered. The deeper she waded into this op, the murkier the people became.

Crowds flowed through the street, along with bicycles and the tram. Amsterdam in the middle of the day hummed like the pulse of a marathon runner, steady and fast.

No one looked out of place. The man who'd passed her the package the night before had been average height with brown hair and tinted glasses. Only his sparse goatee set him apart. He could hide in this throng for days and she wouldn't notice him.

She pulled out her cell and checked the time: 11:59. Still, no sign of that man or any other suspicious looking person. What would a messenger from al-Sharif look like? She kicked at the cigarette butts on the cobble stoned patio. Disgusting, how many got left behind. Where was the bloody messenger?

Her throat dried and her mouth tasted sour. She swallowed but it didn't help. When had she last eaten? She sat at a chair next to the round stone fountain. She smelled the coffee being served at a nearby table and wished for simpler times. Maybe she'd take a vacation after this op and go back to Africa. She'd love to hold JaJa in her arms again. He may not be her son by blood, but he was the only family she had. The only person other than Mitchell she felt a connection with.

A group of American students walked by laughing, teasing one another about their lousy command of the Dutch language. She made a habit of listening to other people's conversations, part natural nosiness, part job requirement. Their gentle good humored gibes reminded her of being young and carefree. How quickly things change.

12:02. A car beeped impatience and a tourist fingered another tourist. Cities, too many people in too small a space and everyone in a hurry to be somewhere. Where the hell was her freaking messenger? The uncertainty reminded her of an exchange that went bad in Zurich six months ago.

They'd lost a good operative that day. She shook her head. Not the time to think about her.

The messenger was late. That's all. Her chest tightened.

She reached into her purse and felt for the gun Delilah had given her. It brought her comfort. How weird could her life get? She didn't usually carry a gun in her purse, because it could easily blow her cover. But it sure felt good right now. This messenger dealt in body parts.

In the many ops she'd completed over the last eight years, she'd only used a gun a handful of times, and then only when necessary. Her job was to gather intel, which usually involved slipping into places and slipping out with secrets. Still, Sadie had been trained to use weapons. She sighed. Shooting a gun would be better than losing a pinky. Anubis and his people played dirty. Dee's finger came into her mind again, sitting in a pool of crusted blood, smelling of dead meat. Sadie shuddered. She'd nail this bastard.

The cool wind off the North Sea chilled her body. She hadn't considered the weather when she ran out of her room for the shoot. She looked up at the darkening skies. With her luck it would rain. 12:08. Damn, he was definitely late. Didn't he have a watch?

The waiter, a square shaped man with a Hercule Poirot mustache dressed in perfectly pressed pinstripe pants and a matching vest appeared. When he lifted an eyebrow in her direction she ordered a café au lait.

Staying relaxed and in the moment during a meet felt like trying to hold on to the trunk of a friggen palm tree in a hurricane. It didn't matter how many ops she'd been on, her nerves rattled. But the elation at the end made it all worthwhile. Minutes passed slower than the drip out of her old espresso machine.

The waiter nodded and said, "Thank you."

"*Et une kafé verkeert*," said a man's voice behind her. *Oh sweet sweet Jesus*. The Dutch hulk had returned. His now all-too-familiar voice grated on her ears like nails sliding down a blackboard. She turned to see Sebastian lope into her space with his long conquering stride. His crystal blue eyes shone like he'd just caught a giant whale by the tail.

"Who the hell invited you?" Her voice came out raspy. This stupid oaf would ruin everything.

"I like the way you kiss." He folded his giant frame into a chair at her table and gave her a devilish grin. The corner of his sensuous mouth quivered as he appeared to be struggling to contain a smile. Either that or he was an idiot. Her vote was on idiot.

The beast. Heat rose in her cheeks.

The waiter raised his bushy eyebrows and fled.

"Sebastian, I told you to get lost." She ran a hand through her thick mane of hair.

"There's something you should know about me." He reached towards her and softly touched her cheek. "I don't always do what I'm told."

"Screw you," she said. But the warmth of his hand on her cold skin felt yummy. Not fair. Her body liked his, way too much; her female chemistry made her a traitor to her mission. Her hormones went on overload.

"Ow. Such language from a lady-crook."

"Sebastian, I swear if you don't leave..." Anger brewed inside her gut like a witch's stew: half lust and half disgust, peppered with self-loathing. She had to get rid of the guy. Not even an insane criminal with a death wish would approach her with this... this... this Dutch giant of a man at her side. She narrowed her eyes at him.

Catching the sudden motion of a man in the crowd from the corner of her eye, she turned to look, but he'd vanished. Shit. Shit. Shit. She faced Sebastian and growled.

"Glad you don't have a glass of water yet," he said.

"Why can't you leave me alone?"

"Cause, you sweetheart, can lead me to some nasty art dealers." The tone of disapproval in his voice dug into her. How much did he know?

Time to barter. "Look, if you leave me alone right now. And I mean *right* now. I'll meet you later and tell you anything and everything. I promise. I'll answer all your questions." She wasn't sure how she'd get approval to do that, but it didn't matter at this point. He had to get out of her way. Now.

It would be easier to move a mountain.

***

Sebastian didn't like the strained look in her eyes, or the lines of tension around them. Desperate people did desperate things. His gut burned. Clearly, the art thieving mob squeezed her. What did they have over her? Maybe, it had something to do with that low-life ex-husband. Seb scanned the crowd, while he made his decision.

"When and where?" he asked. No harm in pretending to agree. He could give her a long leash. Well, as long as she didn't hang herself with it.

Their coffees arrived.

Her face flushed. "Now, Sebastian. I beg you. Go now."

He got up, leaned over and kissed her softly on her cheek. Her skin tasted sweet like apricots. "Be careful," he said. He kissed her other cheek and then the first again, the traditional Dutch kiss for parting. She didn't pull away. He took his coffee and headed inside the restaurant.

Xander and Seamus would shoot him if they saw how he responded to her. Maybe, he *had* been letting his dick do the thinking, but he preferred to think he chose his intuition over facts. Yeah-no he didn't know what that situation was, but for whatever fucked up reason, he trusted her. Was he a fool?

***

Sadie forced a sip of her drink down her throat. 12:20. Had a traffic jam stopped him? She had no idea. He or she probably had a reason. It could be a woman. She shrugged as she watched the snarled traffic.

Thinking about Delilah gave her the heeby-jeebies and she couldn't not think about her. Where had Anubis stashed her? How much pain was she in? Would he ever free her?

A bicycle bell rang close to her and its small sound felt like a big city siren. Talk about jumpy. Another sip. The velvety coffee flowed smoothly down her throat. 12:30.

A black haired man on a motorcycle came to a stop near where she sat. He lowered his aviator glasses and glared at her with bloodshot eyes. She got up and walked towards him putting her hand into her purse to clutch the amulet. He took a box out of his pocket and put it on the ground. By the time she reached the box, he'd roared back into the traffic.

So much for telling him about the third amulet.

Her spirits hit the cobblestones. The box looked the same as the one she received last night. She opened the lid. The insides were dark with blackened blood and in the center was a thumb. She gulped as her fears pushed from neutral to high gear surging a toxic mix of anger, revulsion and hate through her body. She shivered.

Her cell phone buzzed. A text from an unknown source read: "Lose the jerk-off. Meet me tonight outside Central Station 7 p.m."

Sadie stumbled back to her seat. Her whole world crashed around her. Poor Delilah. How long would they keep her alive? How many fingers... The sooner she took down Bakari al-Sharif, the better.

She knocked back the rest of her coffee in a couple mouthfuls. Knickers wanted to fire her. Dee was in danger, or dead. Anubis was severing cutting body parts. Sadie bit her bottom lip. There had to be a way to use the two remaining amulets to meet al-

Sharif face to face. She didn't want to deal with the middleman.

The hardest thing to finesse would be retaining her silly-model image and not letting her seasoned spy side slip.

No one would fault her back home if she pulled out of the mission at this point. Clearly it looked dangerous. She was strictly an intelligence gatherer, not a hit-lady or swat-team type at all. Not even a honey pot like the Mata Hara.

The treasures in the New York City Met Museum of Art were at stake. Besides when Anubis hurt Delilah the op became personal as well.

One step at a time. There's a way out of all of this. There always is. She motioned for the waiter.

She'd take control of things, one way or another.

***

Watching from inside the restaurant Sebastian saw Sadie bend over to pick up a box off the road. He couldn't get a good picture of the courier from this distance with his phone, but he got a partial on the license plate. Probably stolen, but he'd run it anyway. He straightened his back. See—he wasn't just thinking with his dick. Well, at least not all the time.

The box resembled the one in Sadie's hotel room, the one she didn't want him looking at. His scalp tingled, the way it did when danger headed his way. Why couldn't he fall for a nice Dutch girl?

CHAPTER 19

Limping through the narrow cobblestone streets back to her room, Sadie's mind spun through every fix-it option she could think of, like a wacky filmstrip on speed, but nothing looked right. She had honed her spy craft, and she knew she'd find a way to get her man. But a deep sense of foreboding nipped at the edges of her confidence. Bakari al-Sharif's violence went beyond anything she'd experienced. She balled her hands feeling sharp nails bite into her skin. *She hadn't lost the war, only the battle.*

The steady noise and smells of the chaos and clamor of everyday life in Amsterdam enveloped her. Looking ahead, her first crap shoot would be facing the wrath of Knickers. How could she turn things in her favor? Sweet Jesus that woman was impossible to like.

Could Sebastian help her? The image of the strong Dutch man flickered through her mind. Talk about a sexy wild card. If only she'd met him between ops. He made her laugh—plain and simple. That must be the attraction. He made her feel glad to be alive. And womanly.

And then there was the way he kissed. She touched her lower lip. A flood of tingly excitement coursed through her. Damn it. This wasn't the time to go twisting sheets with a man. And, she had no right to complicate his life with her mission. Not if she cared about him. Cared about him? Oh Shit.

The sound of pounding on the door broke her thoughts. "Sadie." Mitchell's voice boomed through the wood.

As if the hounds of hell were on his heels, he rushed past her into the room when she opened the door.

"Okay, spill it," he demanded, his hands on his hips.

Spill? What exactly should she spill? Fingers? Overly protective Dutch men with rat connections? Looted art? Sadie cleared her throat. "What do you want to know?"

"Your son. Tell me about him." Mitch held the muscles in his face so tightly they began to vibrate.

She didn't want to play twenty questions. "His name is JaJa. He's safe for now, but I need your help."

He tilted his head to the right. "Anything."

"I need you to find a woman by the name of Delilah Sagwaski."

"Your fence?"

"You know her?" Sadie felt her stomach fall.

"Of her. I'm not stupid. I've seen you together and guessed your relationship." He reached over and gently squeezed her arm. His mouth firmed into a straight line. "Why are you looking for her?"

"You said you wanted to help." She gave him her no-nonsense look.

"Can't you just text her?"

"That's just it; she's not answering her cell phone." Sadie hesitated, searching for words, "She may be hurt or something."

"How hurt?" A shadow of concern clouded his eyes.

"Mitchell, you ask a lot of questions for a friend who said he'd do anything."

"That was for your baby. Your fence is another matter. You know I don't like stealing."

She turned away from him and walked to the large window overlooking the canal. Outside light rain fell, dimpling the surface of the gray flat canal water. She pulled her sweater closer around her body. "Please Mitch."

"Where would I look?"

"That's the problem. I don't know where she stays. She should have called me. For all I know she lives in a castle, but I doubt that."

"She's the kind of slime that slides out from under a rock when the sun comes out. Probably rents a moldy room down a dark alley," he said.

Sadie's mouth twitched. "You're right. She lives in the shadows and only shows up when she smells money." Sadie tried to smile, but it didn't work.

"Why do you think something's happened to her?"

"It's complicated, but she should have called me."

He moved in and wrapped his arms around her. "I'll ask around," he whispered into her ear.

His hug gave her strength. She didn't like to ask anyone for help, but she needed it. And no one in the world was more trustworthy than Mitchell.

"Thank you," she said, pulling away from him. "Don't let this get to your head, but sometimes Mitch your friendship is all that keeps me going."

He tilted his head again, the way it did when he acknowledged how much their friendship meant to him. She loved the way Mitch could communicate so clearly with her. He didn't need to use words.

He touched her arm. "But I want something from you."

She waited.

"I want you to sleep. The circles under your eyes are growing. Soon they'll take over your face, and no amount of makeup will hide them. I'll tell Knickers we'll do a second shoot at 3:00."

She scowled.

"And while you sleep, I promise I'll look for Delilah."

As the door closed quietly behind Mitchell, Sadie put on a selection of Bach violin concertos. Then she dug out a face mask to block the light. She had to stop thinking about fingers and Sebastian's smile...and sleep. All her problems and maybe some answers would be there when she woke up. Slowly she slid away.

And found herself in the Nigerian wilderness. *The dense humidity made it hard to breath and the little air she managed to suck in came laced with the fetid smell of the jungle, which hit her like a psychedelic drug. Her vision blurred and became distorted. Sounds of the witch doctor chanting and the villagers' drums beating filled her ears. The shaman poured a fluid on Jaja's head marking him for death and picked up the vine to tie him to his dead mother. The smell of death surrounded her.* Sadie screamed and woke up.

***

The blisters on Sadie's feet had grown worse and now exposed raw meat. They screamed as she hobbled along the famous Kalverstraat road and neared the Dam. She ignored the pain, determined to be on time for the shoot. Knicker's warning echoed in her mind. If she was late one more time, she'd lose her job.

The CIA liked her modeling as a cover, and her supervisors would be disappointed if she lost it. They had assured her they would create another cover if they needed to, but this one worked well, and they wanted her to use it as long as she could.

Her company cell phone rang. While cell phones are never totally secure this one used highly encrypted codes. She stepped into a side alley and leaned into a brick wall. No one appeared interested in her. She swiped her password on the top of the cell and pressed her thumbprint into a scanner.

"Jeremiah, what the hell?" she said into the speaker when the connection went through. In her mind's eye she pictured him, the seasoned spy who had done it all and now worked deep inside the company pulling the strings. Women chased him for his body, but she preferred his brain. She enjoyed going for drinks with him and listening to his spy stories.

"You're not the only one out there," he said. While his words admonished her, his tone acted like a tonic on her nerves. It felt good to talk to someone she didn't have to lie to.

"Tell me if I can read Sebastian in. He knows about the looted art. He knows a lot of people in Europe. I think I can depend on him and he could be useful."

The phone went silent for a minute. "You have feelings for him?"

"No." She lied.

Silence returned. "I'd prefer you didn't, unless you absolutely have to. Got your texts. You're getting closer to Anubis. Hang in."

"For what?"

"Chatter on the Internet indicates you intrigue him, in more ways than one. He has a picture of you and his people are asking a lot of questions. Give it more time."

A picture? A chill ran up her spine. "But the fingers?"

"Delilah ran a shady business. A number of people could have cut off her fingers."

"Could have..."

"Yes, I agree it fits Anubis's profile, but hold your hand a bit longer. Tease him out with the amulets. Delilah and her fingers aren't our business. We need to take down Anubis. Remember your target. Stay focused."

The greater good. That's what it came down to. It didn't matter how much collateral damage, how many people were hurt or killed during a mission, as long as they reached their objective. She'd been trained to believe that her job was to execute the plan, not to worry about who would get hurt. She needed to focus.

She swallowed. Ever since she'd seen Jaja being buried alive with his dead mother her insides had shifted. It was like he opened her heart. She did care about Delilah. It didn't matter what the woman had done, she was a fellow human being. Her fingers mattered. Her life mattered. Sadie swallowed. Maybe, she was getting too soft for this job.

"Jeremiah, don't you ever wonder if it's all worth it?"

"Anubis is pure evil. He built the largest arms dealing business in the world. He siphoned money to five different mid-east terrorist groups. Two of them are active in the States. He buried two of our people in the desert last year. We need to take him out. And you are our best bet."

"You're asking me to kill him?"

"No. Just locate him and gain intel. Do what you do best, your *stealth and stilettoes* thing."

"Not too much pressure." The familiar warmth of patriotism flowed through her body. She could do this. She would do this. The asshole had to be stopped.

Jeremiah laughed. "You can handle it."

"Will I have back-up tonight?"

Silence. "Working on that." She knew he wouldn't give her the details on this call.

"I'm late. I've got to get going."

"Enjoy smiling Sadie." The line went dead. Jeremiah liked to tease her about what he called her empty-smile job.

She walked back onto the Kalvastraat clogged with tourists looking at the shops. The rain had stopped, but the afternoon sky remained gray. The mimes who performed at the edge of the square with their elaborate costumes and white faces came into sight. She squared her shoulders ready to take on Knickers's constant barrage of insults. Show time.

And then she ran smack into him. Jonathon, her friggen-ex. Where the hell did he come from?

He blocked her path. "Come with me," he said.

Giving him the evil eye she attempted to walk past him.

He reached towards her arm. Something pricked her flesh. She looked at him and caught his bad-ass gotcha-smile. *Bastard*. Dizzyness swamped her senses. *Damn it to hell. Taken down by a civilian. Jonathon no less!*

Her knees wobbled and her upper-body weaved. Oh no! What had he done to her? Jonathon caught her in his arms as the world went black.

CHAPTER 20

Sebastian shadowed Sadie from a safe distance. Her slow wobbly gait made her easy to spot, so he gave her lots of room. Her blisters made her walk like a drunk duck. Maybe, she'd let him bandage them. The image of holding her foot in his lap and glancing up her long well-sculpted leg slid through his mind hardening his dick. He grumbled.

She deeked into the side alley to take a call on her cell phone. Who did she talk to? Had someone called her? Three minutes later she remerged and made her way down the busy shopping street. Following, he kept a twenty yard distance between them. She didn't appear to notice him, or if she did, she didn't appear to care.

He heard a siren coming from the opposite direction. Then a man grabbed Sadie. Seb hurried forward to see more, but he couldn't get there fast enough. Damn. As he got closer he recognized Jonathon Moore her ex-husband holding her limp body. What the fuck. Something's wrong. Sebastian broke into a run. But the dense crowds blocked his way. "Move. Get out of my way," he yelled at people as he pushed towards her, sweat beaded on his brow.

An emergency vehicle with its siren blaring appeared at the far end of the street. People moved aside and let it in. It stopped by Sadie and Jonathon. Seb increased his speed, but the sheer volume of people held him back.

Loping forward he yelled, "Stop him. Stop him. Don't let him take her." People turned and looked at Sebastian like he belonged in the crazy bin, but no one helped him. Jonathon and another man dressed in a medic uniform loaded Sadie into the vehicle.

"Nooo," he yelled. "Stop them." More heads turned his way but no one understood what was happening. He shouldn't have given her so much room.

The door of the ambulance closed and with the siren shrieking it reversed and motored towards the Dam.

Fuck. Fuck. Fuck. A long list of expletives left Sebastian's lips. But they didn't help. He'd lost her.

***

It took another five minutes to make it to the Dam. The magazine people stood in a circle ready for the shoot. Sebastian jogged over and faced Mitchell, Sadie's friend. Towering a foot above the man, he looked down and let his presence sink in.

Mitchell took a step back, eyes wide. "She's not here yet."

"I know." Seb's heavy breathing made the words come out staccato style, like machine gun bullets. "She's been taken."

An older woman with brittle black hair moved closer to them. "Are we talking about Sadie Stewart?"

"Yes," Seb said keeping his eyes on Mitchell. The man's shoulders drooped and his mouth twitched. He knew something.

The woman exhaled loudly. "That's it, the bitch is fired!" She threw her arms in the air and stomped off.

Color drained from Mitchell's face. "Sadie?"

"Start talking." Seb grabbed the neck of Mitchell's shirt. He'd shake the information out of him if he had to. Awareness that he'd kill him, or any other man to save Sadie, swelled in the chest. He'd never felt so barbarian-primal before.

Mitchell motioned with his head to move away from the others. Seb released his grip and followed him. When they were beyond hearing distance, Mitchell said: "We should go to the police."

"You know she's a thief."

He nodded. "She never hurts anyone. She doesn't deserve this."

"This? What has Jonathon got planned?"

"Jonathon?" Mitchell's eyes bulged. "Jonathon took her?"

"Who did you think?"

Mitchell shook his head dismissing the

question far too quickly. "I know how to find *that* bastard."

The model's words came out way too slowly, for Sebastian's liking. He reached over and grabbed him by the neck of his designer shirt.

"Uh."

Seb stared.

Mitchell put his hands on Seb's arms trying to free himself. Seb kept his hold. "Will he hurt her?"

Mitchell shook his head, and Sebastian released him.

"No. He just wants money."

"He told you that?"

Mitchell's face went white again. He'd make a lousy poker player. "I had no idea the guy'd grab her off the street. Honest, if I'd known..."

Sebastian moved closer to him, staring.

"He needs money, and I..."

"You what?"

Mitchell looked up at the sky. "Man, I didn't expect this."

Seb grabbed his arm this time and squeezed until Mitchell called out.

Mitch put his other hand up in defense. "Look we both want what's best for Sadie. I'll tell you everything."

"Damn straight you will." Whatever this jerk had done had something to do with Sadie being abducted.

"Ow. That hurts."

"It's not the only part of your body that's going to hurt if you..."

"Okay, okay. I get it. Listen to me. I keep

telling you, we're on the same side." Mitchell closed his eyes, when he opened them he made a pained, about-to-step-in-deep-shit face. "Jonathon's been blackmailing me for six months."

Seb narrowed his eyes.

"He has pictures of me, I don't want shared."

Sebastian nodded and eased the pressure on Mitchell's arm.

"He told me all I had to do was keep him informed about what Sadie's up to. I hated myself for it, but he had me by the balls, man. He threatened to release photos to the press of me and shall we say an important married person... in the act. It would have ruined the other man's reputation and I care for the guy."

"What did you tell Jonathon?"

"I kept him in the loop, let him know where we were going, who she spent time with, and when she stole jewelry. For a few texts a week I got to keep my privacy. I didn't like ratting out Sadie. I love her like a sister, but I can't... can't have those pictures get out." He swallowed. "But then I ran out of money to pay Jonathan off."

"So why would the sleezeball abduct her?

"I don't know. But we'll find out."

"No idea?" Sebastian tightened his grip again.

Mitchell swallowed. "Look. Something big's going down. Bigger than her usual jewellery jobs. I don't know what it is, but Sadie's spooked. She told me..." His lips clamped shut.

"Told you?"

"Where her will is."

"Will?"

"Yeah. She's never talked to me about death before and this morning she started talking about what to do if she died."

It made some sense. Sadie must have got in over her head with that Delilah woman and got scared. He released Mitch's arm and the man straightened his back. "Text Jonathon. Ask him what he wants. But don't mention me."

Mitchell pulled out his cell and tapped the keys. He looked up when he finished.

"Let me get this straight." Sebastian eyed him closely. "Jonathon blackmailed you, to keep tabs on Sadie so he could take her money."

Mitchell nodded. "And I feel like a cad. Sadie's ...special to me."

"Will Jonathon hurt her?"

"Nah. She's his source of money. He has a nasty coke habit. He's not stupid."

Unless he's somehow got mixed up with some nasty art thieves. "He grabbed her and then he took her away in an ambulance."

Mitchell lowered his head shaking it. "That must have cost him."

Another reason organized crime could be involved. "Where do you think he'd take her?"

"He's staying at a hotel downtown, the Eerste Klas.

"First class and expensive."

"That's how he hooks up with rich ladies. He prowls in their playpens."

Sebastian nodded. "Room number?"

"I'm going with you."

Sebastian raised a brow. "I don't think so."

"He won't open the door for you."

Sebastian stared at him for a minute. His eyes looked true. "As long as you keep up with me."

***

The Eerste Klas stood majestically over the Amstel River as it had for centuries, but its grandeur didn't faze Sebastian. He nodded his way through the security people. Being known as one of the good guys who bought rounds of beer for others helped. Besides, he played football with one of them on Sundays.

Moments before they gained entry, Sebastian held his breath and visualized how he wanted this to go down. Really, he wanted to kill Jonathon, but he needed to stay focused. Think peaceful thoughts. Yeah, right.

Mitchell knocked on room 257.

"Who is it?" A man's voice.

"Mitchell."

"Go away." Same man.

"You didn't answer my text. Sadie's missing."

"She'll turn up."

"I'll tell that big guy where you're hiding."

The door slowly opened.

Too slowly for Sebastian. He shoved it in, knocking Jonathon back a couple of steps and breaking the security chain. Then he walked forward and punched him hard in the face. He could feel the man's nose breaking with the impact. Blood squirted in all directions.

Jonathon's eyes widened with recognition, then fear, as he crumpled to the ground holding his nose. "Shit, man. Not you again."

"Where is she?"

"I just want to talk to her." Jonathon's voice whined.

With his left hand Sebastian pulled Jonathon up by the front of his shirt and readied his right fist for another punch.

"I need money."

The sound of moaning came from the next room. Mitchell ran past the men towards the sound, calling back over his shoulder. "It's her."

Sebastian followed through with the fist and Jonathon fell to the floor a second time.

***

After the blackness came a slow dawning light nudging Sadie towards consciousness. It felt like surfacing from a deep, dark vat of cold water. What was Jonathon thinking? Why had he taken her? Did he work for Anubis? She heard men's voices. She wanted to call out, but her mouth was taped, so she moaned.

"Sadie?"

She opened her eyes fully to find herself lying on a strange bed. Mitchell who for some reason knelt beside her looked worse than he did after his last hangover. And that was bad.

Looking past him she could see Sebastian standing over Jonathon who lay on the floor. She tried to smile.

Mitchell reached his hand to her mouth and ripped the tape off.

"Oww..." `

Sebastian approached. His sun drenched

blond hair shone in the light streaming through the window. His blue eyes burned with intensity and sweat poured off his body. He looked like a conquering Viking. A warrior no one would dare cross.

Her mouth tasted like a sewer pit. Nausea rose from the pit of her stomach. Damn, she'd been drugged. That's how Jonathon did it. Weren't damsels in distress supposed to look serene and beautiful when being rescued? She swallowed the acid rising in her throat.

"My stubborn friend," she said loud enough to be heard.

A slow sexy smile that held enough heat to melt all the ice on both poles slid across his face.

"I guess I should say thank you." Her voice sounded drugged, kind of warped and hesitant.

He nodded and touched her face with his fingers. How could such a giant of a man be so gentle. "You okay?" he asked as he untied the rope binding her hands.

"Is that Jonathon bleeding on the floor?"

"Yeah."

"Then I'm more than okay." She grabbed the front of his shirt, pulled him in and kissed him with all her heart. Hell, it was a 'conquering moment' after all. He tasted good—strong, virile—Sebastian.

When she released her grip he pulled away enough to look at her. He smelled—manly, primal... Did any of this make sense? Her mind did a woozy flip. She grabbed his shirt again.

"*Mijn liefje,*" he said, his voice low. "You're drugged."

"But kissing you feels so amazing."

Wait a minute. She was drugged. Another woozy moment flowed through her brain. Mitchell stood behind Sebastian. Jonathon lay on the floor. This wasn't a dream.

What was she thinking kissing the big guy? She wasn't thinking. Sebastian had a way of getting into her blood and short circuiting her mind. Of course she could blame the drugs. But that wasn't the whole story and she knew it. She leaned back in defeat. "Sorry."

He gently moved tendrils of her hair away from her eyes. Her stomach churned and she gagged. So much for being an alluring damsel.

Mitchell cleared his throat. "We can't forget Jonathon."

Sebastian got up and moved over to where he lay crumpled, unconscious on the floor. Jonathon moaned and moved his shoulders. Seb put his foot on his wrist, pulled out his cell phone and punched in his Interpol friend's number.

"Seamus, I have a suspect for you to interrogate," he said. He gave him his location and clicked off.

Mitchell looked at him wide eyed. "I don't want to be in the middle of this."

"You should have thought of that when you sold out Sadie."

"What?" Sadie said. What the hell were they talking about? How drugged was she? Mitchell looked pale and guilty. No. He couldn't have. He wouldn't have. "You?"

"I'm sorry..." began Mitchell.

But Sebastian interrupted him. "You two can make peace somewhere else. I'll stay here with Jonathon."

Mitchell's shoulders dropped, but if he thought he was off the hook he was so wrong. When she had him alone, she'd grill him hard.

"I'll take Sadie to her room at the Bed and Breakfast," said Mitchell.

"I'll catch up with both of you later. Take care of Sadie. Go."

Mitchell helped Sadie to her feet. She wanted to walk out the door and leave her treacherous friend behind, but her knees couldn't support the rest of her. Despite her anger she leaned on Mitch for support. "What about the shoot?"

"Forget it. I'm going to take care of you." How could Mitchell have sold her out? Her best friend? She gritted her teeth.

CHAPTER 21

Sebastian let his friends Xander and Seamus into the hotel room and nodded towards Jonathon who sat tied to a chair, bleeding from the nose and mouth. Then he strode over to the window overlooking the river, hoping that the fresh air might invigorate him in some way. He needed a fucking reboot button. A hornet's nest of trouble spun around Sadie. Worry held him in its grip like the talons of an eagle and dug deep. Shit he hated that. Worry never did anyone any good. He liked action. There had to be something he could do to help her.

Seamus, a short wiry man with carrot red hair wore a Scottish soccer jersey and jeans. He took one look at Jonathon and said, "Looks like you got started without us?"

"He fell," answered Sebastian with his back to him.

"Was that before or after the floor came up and hit him in the nose?" Xander's words may have been funny, but his voice held no humor. He wore his usual business casual, chinos, an open necked white shirt and a blue sports coat. His body's abrupt movements when he entered the room telegraphed irritation. Seb could read him like a book. He was pissed. Probably thought Seb was just digging himself into a deeper and deeper mess.

Sebastian smiled to the window pane. "About the same time."

Seamus went to look out the other window as if he expected more company to arrive. Xander walked over to Jonathon. "You abducted a woman by the name of Sadie Stewart?"

Seb turned to watch. Jonathon nodded. Blood trickled from his nose and his right eye had swollen shut.

"Your ex-wife."

He nodded again, but didn't make eye contact.

Sebastian wanted to punch the guy again, but they needed more information from him, and if he were unconscious he couldn't tell them anything. Folding his arms around his stomach he told himself to stay back. He turned and looked out the window again, focusing on the tranquil canal scene below them. He forced his breathing to slow down. All the while he listened to the interrogation going on behind him:

"Who's your boss?" asked Xander.

Silence.

Seamus left his window perch and walked over to stand beside Xander: "We're not interested in you. We figure your boss used you to get to Sadie and the goods. You give us his name and we'll let you go."

"What the fuck are you talking about?" said Jonathon.

Seb stopped breathing. The asshole sounded sincere, but that didn't make sense. Would Xander let him hit him one more time? He could do it in the ribs where the damage wouldn't be so visible. But it would hurt.

"Stolen artifacts. Isn't that why you took Sadie?" said Xander.

"No, yeah, well, sort of. Listen man, she used to be my old lady and I knew she had a new stealing gig that was bringing in big bucks. I wanted some of that money. I need that money." His voice whined like an indulged teenagers who thought the world owed him his heart's desire. Seb curled his fingers into fists. Just one more solid hit.

Seamus said: "Are you telling us you're working alone?"

"I hired some guys to drive the van, but they worked for me. Look I don't know what crazy shit the bitch's got into. I'm not a part of her world."

Crazy bitch? Sebastian turned around and strode over. Xander put his body in his way and gave him the don't-go-there eye.

"So you know nothing about the looted art that's circulating," said Seamus.

"Nothing man. You gotta believe me. Mitchell told me Sadie had stepped up her stealing act and I wanted a cut. That's all."

Xander put a hand on Sebastian's arm. In a quiet calm tone he said, "Not now buddy. Not the time, or the place."

Sebastian grumbled. Adrenalin pumped through his body, making it hard to think rationally. From the moment he saw Sadie taken, he'd been running on over-drive. "He..."

"Get it together Wilde." Xander said. "Face the facts. The woman is connected to the criminal world right up to her fancy eyebrows. Don't let her take you down with her."

Seb shook his head. "All the facts aren't in yet. I don't believe your shit." He pushed past him and walked out the door. "I'll get the real story."

CHAPTER 22

*B*akari studied pictures of Sadie
Stewart. The file folder he'd been given had twenty
shots taken in the last few days and reports about
her escapades as a cat burglar across Europe and
the U.S.. He sipped a cup of tea. Not a typical model.

After three knocks, his body guard Gahiji
strode through the door and came to a stop in front
of him. "I'm sorry," he said as he lifted his empty
hands to show that he had nothing.

Bakari stared hard at him. The man
shuddered.

"The red headed bitch wasn't alone. A big
man sat inside the restaurant watching her and the
street. It looked like a trap."

"What man?"

"I'm gathering information on him. So far all I know is that his name is Sebastian Wilde. He's a well-known Amsterdam art dealer."

Bakari nodded. A collector? "Maybe he just likes the woman. She is beautiful."

Gahiji looked down. "It will take time to find out more about him."

Bakari thumped his tea cup on the table in front of him spilling some of it and swore. "Did you give her the second finger?" Their default plan.

"Yes, and I sent her a text message to meet me tonight."

Bakari could feel his blood pressure rising. He wanted that amulet. "You were right to be cautious. I don't know that we can trust this woman." He drummed his fingers on the table.

Gahiji said nothing.

Bakari got up and walked to the window looking out over a narrow lane. He stood there for a minute. The mysterious allure in Sadie Stewart's green eyes in the photos called to him. Not to mention her firm athletic build. After five minutes, he said, "I want to meet her."

Gahiji had been by his side for twenty years and excelled at his job of enforcement, but he was used to dealing with hard criminals, not pretty ladies. Bakari needed to get a real sense of Sadie and the best way to do that would be to meet her. If she was as breathtakingly beautiful and sensual in person as she was in the pictures and if she could handle danger the way Delilah said she could, the woman would be a good asset for his business.

"It's too dangerous, sir."

Bakari shrugged. "The woman is a good thief. With her modelling career she can blend into many worlds. I could use her in New York." And maybe my bed, but he didn't say that.

Gahiji made no change in his facial expression, but Bakari was used to that. The man had only two looks: tough and obedient. He waited for a command.

"She intrigues me," Bakari said.

Gahiji looking at his feet, groaned. "May I make a suggestion?"

Bakari nodded. This was certainly unusual.

"Something's wrong about this woman. She's too perfect. Let me take something important from her, so that she won't dare cross you."

"Insurance?" Bakari stroked his chin. "A good idea, but not yet. Not until I know more about her." He waved him away and reached for his tea cup. "I will meet her soon."

CHAPTER 23

*O*utside, *the mid-day* sun had become shrouded with cloud and the temperature dropped. But the bustling rhythm of the ancient streets continued. The smell of a *Frites* stand lingered in the air, along with the smell of too many people in a small space.

By the time Sadie and Mitchell made it back to the Bed and Breakfast, Sadie had regained more use of her knees. She hobbled up the stairs to Mitch's room and sat down on his sofa. During the walk home he'd apologized three times and explained in detail why he'd betrayed her. She hadn't the energy to say anything, just the determination to get back to safety.

He handed her a glass of water. The water felt cool and comforting as it flowing down her throat. Her stomach still wheezed.

"You okay?" he asked kneeling in front of her. His big brown puppy eyes implored her for a response.

She winced. "A bit muddled." The image of the second finger came to her mind. Well maybe more than a bit. She took a gulp of water.

Normally he'd make some quip about her being muddle-brained, but he said nothing.

After a few minutes of silence, she said, "I don't know if I can forgive you."

His eyes widened and welled with unshed tears.

"I can't believe you'd rat me out to anyone, let alone Jonathon. You should have told me."

"He said he wouldn't hurt you, and he just needed some money. I gave him what I could, but he wanted more."

"He always wants more. Couldn't you see that. I thought you *got* people."

A tear trickled down his face. "I couldn't have my affair exposed. It would have hurt a lot of people."

"So instead you chose to hurt me. You should have come to me. Talked to me." Tears rolled down her face. Never-ever did she imagine he'd turn against her. Nor him—her one true friend. She slapped him hard across his face. The sound of it snapped through her mind, but it did nothing to mend her fractured heart.

He turned his reddened cheek away.

"You bastard," she said. Then she got up and left his room, slamming the door behind her.

***

Back in her own room, Sadie guzzled two more glasses of water and hit the shower. She needed to get the friggen drugs out of her system. The sooner the better. Tonight she'd meet with Anubis's man. She needed a clear head.

Could the Egyptian arms dealer be as evil as Jeremiah said? She closed the shower door. Nah, no one could be that bad.

She turned the water to hot, then hotter. Steam filled the room and she drank it in. She wanted to wash away not only the drugs but everything else. Like the fact her best friend just betrayed her, her asshole of an ex had abducted her and Sebastian... kept turning up when she told him to leave her alone.

Why hadn't Sebastian called in the police? Those friends of his weren't regular cops. They gave off a Special Forces vibe. She didn't like having a messy personal life and hers had become a super-sized muck up. Dunking her head under the nozzle she water poured over her aching head. She turned off the shower, stepped out and toweled herself dry.

Opening the door she found Sebastian standing on the other side. He turned his back to her. "Sorry, I thought you'd have a robe."

Sorry my ass. She'd caught the mischievous glint in his eye, and his unmistakable rakish grin. "Uh-huh. Turn around."

He complied.

She walked over to the dresser and pulled out underwear, a pair of leggings and a loose top. She'd bike over to Central Station looking like a local, blending in with the scenery. Throwing them on her bed, she said to Sebastian's back, "What did you do with Jonathon?"

"Left him with my friends so I could see you."

"Friends?" She fastened her bra and grabbed the top.

"We go way back."

The cotton top slid over her slight frame and she reached for the leggings. "They don't look like artists."

Seb laughed and started to turn around.

"Not yet."

"The blonde man, Xander Van der Valk is my best friend. He actually is a good painter, but in the daytime he runs a PI business investigating international art theft."

"As in Van der Valk Inc?" Shit, she didn't need *them* anywhere near her op.

"Yeah." He said slowly as if her recognition of Xander's name surprised him. "And Seamus MacIntyre the carrot head works for Interpol."

She growled. Oh sweet Jesus this news sucked. A hot-shot PI firm and a competing agency messing in her op. Too many operatives in her little opera. What if Seb tripped over her real identity?

"Did you just growl? Please, let me turn around."

She pulled up her pants. Jeremiah had to hear this news. How could she lose the giant?

"It's awfully quiet in here."

Sadie walked up to him and ran her hands up his massive back to his lineman shoulders. She inhaled his masculine scent and for a brief moment allowed herself to wonder how he'd look naked... in her bed. Her heart rate rocketed.

Letting go of his body, she said, "Thank you for finding me." The words felt awkward sliding out of her mouth. She wasn't used to being rescued by anyone, let alone a civilian. She would have found a way to escape from Jonathon on her own. Still it had been nice of him to help her out and right now she needed to feed his ego.

Sebastian turned and wrapped his arms around her. "How's the head?" His sapphire eyes searched hers with a warmth that made her feel fuzzy-brained all over again.

"Clearing. Thanks. You're my hero." She stroked his face, feeling the softness of his skin and the roughness of his whiskers. Her lower belly tingled. She didn't need this right now. She wanted to control him.

He smiled that boy-next-door innocent smile. "So if I kissed you now, neither one of us could blame it on the drugs?"

Oh hell yeah. Wait. No. No. She couldn't... She put her hand on his chest to push him away, but oh God it was firm and hard. She bit her lip and pushed gaining at least an inch, but also a boat-load more desire. "Uh, what are you going to do with Jonathon?"

"Really? You want to talk about that now?"

"Sebastian, I need to know." Not really, but it would help ground her and sweet, sweet Jesus she needed something to bring her down to Earth.

He grumbled and then the glint in his eye returned. His right hand came to her face and he gently pushed her wet hair behind her ear, making her tremble with his touch. "We're looking for the people responsible for trading looted art. They're asking him about that."

"He's not involved."

Seb's hand stopped. "We could turn him over to the police, but we'll need you to file charges."

She shook her head. "No. I can't have that kind of publicity. My career is already on the rocks. I'll deal with him my own way."

"And what exactly does that involve? Shooting him with bobby pins at close range?"

She laughed. "Let him go. Trust me, he'll feel my wrath and he'll wish he never met me."

Seb cocked his head. "What are you planning?"

"I'm going to tell his mother."

Sebastian burst into laughter. "His mother?"

"She'll believe me. She knows her son. For him being told on is far worse than jail. He could find peace in jail. She won't give him any and she'll cut off the money she's been sending him, at least for a while. It will be messy and mean and I'll enjoy every minute of it."

He slid his hand down her back to her buttocks and pulled her closer to him. "You are a worthy opponent."

She gasped. Trying to keep her breathing steady, but not succeeding. "Try me."

He leaned in and so did she. When their lips touched fireworks exploded in her body. She'd been kissed many times before, but... not like this.

***

Sebastian told himself 'not to...' Not to like her, not to touch her, not to let her touch him, not to... Fuck that. He had to be with her. He'd figure out her connection to the smuggling later, and if she was involved he'd get her out. Nothing mattered right now but them. The kiss rocked. On a scale from one to ten it soared over the top to Fucking-Fantastic.

He had thought he'd lost her when the man pulled her into the ambulance. He pulled her closer and deepened the kiss. He couldn't lose her.

CHAPTER 24

The sound of a fist pounding on the wooden door broke their kiss. Sadie stepped out of Sebastian's embrace and looked into his blue eyes. She took a breath to regain her composure, but her body felt so aflame it had little effect.

"Sadie let me in. I have to talk to you." Mitchell's voice.

Sebastian squinted. "I wanted to punch him in the face earlier. Now I really want to hit him." He moved a tendril of her hair away from her eyes.

Sadie squared her shoulders and tried to regain control of her breathing. She turned towards the door. "Wait a minute." She turned back to face Sebastian.

He tilted his head. "Don't tell me you're sorry."

She smiled. "No, I'm certainly not that." She touched her lips. "It was..." she paused. "Most interesting."

"Interesting?" He laughed.

"I can't do this right now Sebastian."

His lips pulled into his rakish grin, the one that undid her and was more potent now that she'd tasted him. Damn it. The man grew on her like mold.

"I don't just mean the kissing, I mean—us. I can't get involved. The timing's all wrong."

"Too busy dealing looted art?"

She blinked. "Not exactly. Look I can explain and I will, but not..."

The pounding resumed on the door. "She'll fire us," yelled Mitchell.

"There's nothing like the present moment. Tell me. Are you involved?" The emotion in his eyes touched her conscience. The man kept saving her. She could at least be honest.

Sadie took a deep breath. "Maybe a little, but like I said I can explain."

His face turned grim. "There is no such thing as a-little when it comes to art crime."

"I will tell you all about it."

"Then meet me tonight," he said.

More pounding.

"It would have to be late."

"Come to my apartment above the gallery. You know where that is. I'll be home. Waiting." He walked past her and opened the door.

***

Sadie looked Mitchell in the eye. They stood a foot apart. He smelled of beer. "I don't want anything to do with you. I thought I made that clear."

His torso moved an inch back as if she'd physically assaulted him again. "Sadie."

She threw her hands in the air. "I can't stand looking at you and I can't work with someone who's knifed me in the back."

Her cell phone rang, the tone that meant business. She checked the screen. "Shit it's Knickers."

"That's what I've been trying to tell you," Mitch said reaching for her arm.

She turned her back to him and slid the phone icon. "Yes," she answered.

"Get your skinny ass over here. I'm giving you and Mitchell one more chance."

Sadie looked at her cell. She couldn't care less about modeling, but it was her cover. She took a deep breath. In a sweet girly voice she said, "I'm sorry I didn't make..."

"Look, Mitchell told me everything. I get it. I have an asshole ex myself. Just get over here now."

He told her everything? Sadie couldn't think of anything to say to that. Were they actually bonding over having bad taste in husbands? On another day this would make her laugh.

"Get your ass over here. We need to get some work done."

She turned to face Mitchell who looked at her with his big brown eyes. Whatever story he made up, it had worked. A text message scrolled across the top of her screen, "Stilettoes on sale," Jeremiah's code for "contact me NOW." She hit the key to acknowledge the info.

Sadie spoke into her phone to Knickers. "I'll be there as soon as I can. But I don't want to work with Mitchell. He's ...we're...not getting along."

Silence.

"Did you hear me?"

"I don't have anyone else on hand. Mitchell can do the job." Knickers clicked off.

Sadie turned around to look at him.

"We can do this," he said.

"Give me five," she said. "I'll meet you on the street."

***

After Mitch and Sebastian left, she pulled out her company phone and punched the code for Jeremiah.

"I don't have much time," she said.

"Interpol is looking for more information about you. Did something happen to blow your cover?"

She exhaled slowly and then gave him a quick summary of how Jonathon had abducted her and she'd been freed by Sebastian and his friends. She wrung her hands as she told him about Jonathon, knowing how much he hated the man.

"You want to abort the op?"

"No way."

Silence.

"Anubis wants what I've got. He...Wait." The beep noise of a text arriving on her street phone stopped her. She pulled it out of her pocket.

"Remember- tonight 6pm in front of Central Station."

She exhaled. "Jeremiah," she said into the phone. "I just got a text message confirming the meet tonight."

"Proceed with caution."

"Back-up?"

"George is on the train from Brussels. He'll watch from a distance unless you signal him to move in."

"Good." She'd been through many difficult situations with George and she could trust him.

"Before you hang up."

"I gotta go." She started hopping on one foot as she peeled off her leggings.

"There's more to Sebastian than meets the eye. He may act like a regular guy, but he's a sharp business man and street wise. Don't underestimate him."

More than meets the eye? Tell me about it. She looked at the phone waiting for more. Jeremiah clicked off.

CHAPTER 25

Five minutes past five, she headed down to Central Station to meet with the man from Anubis. With each step, she reviewed and refined her plan, visualizing the exchange going as smoothly as possible. Brown elm blossoms floated in the soft spring breeze to the ground clustering in piles on the narrow cobble stoned streets and forming clouds on the surface of the canals. Everywhere she looked she saw the blossoms that looked like leaves. They call it Amsterdam's spring snow.

People walking and cycling home from work filled the medieval streets. Bicycle bells rang and groups of friends chatted on corners with relieved end-of-day look on their faces. The smell of fresh baked bread wafted from a bakery and the sun reappeared to warm her face.

George hadn't showed up yet, but she counted on him getting into place in time. She scanned the horizon. The crowds thickened as she neared the station. She checked her phone—5:30. Almost there.

Sebastian would wait for her tonight. The image of the man with his sun streaked hair and wicked smile flickered through her mind making her world tilt. Their chemistry couldn't be denied. She'd read him in and then see how he felt about her after that. Most men would run, but there wasn't anything ordinary about Sebastian. He might just have the balls to stay.

Maybe he'd still want to see her, maybe he wouldn't. If nothing else, the information would keep him out of her way. Jeremiah hadn't given her the green light, but she'd do it anyway.

A pigeon flew by her shoulder and she stopped for a minute. She'd never broke protocol before. Never dared. But Sebastian needed to be dealt with. The intensity of whatever it was connecting them deserved that.

Then, she'd have to figure what to do about Mitchell. After the shoot, which went without a hitch, he left to sulk in his room. She never did learn how he talked Knickers into giving them another chance. Eventually she'd forgive him, but she didn't see how their friendship could ever be the same. She smiled as she remembered the last time they'd gone to a comedy club together and laughed the night away. He'd been such a good companion for so many years and then Jonathon got to him. The bastard.

Jonathon. She hadn't heard anything from Sebastian's friends, but she didn't expect to. As soon as the op ended she'd be on the phone to Jonathon's mother and that would be a conversation she'd remember to her dying day. She smiled.

Still no sign of George. She walked on.

When she crossed over the bridge to the station, which sits on three man-made islands on the river Ij, she saw him. George, a man who looked to be in his mid-twenties, but was at least a decade older, stood on the west side of the entrance in a casual hanging out stance holding a well-used longboard, looking like one of a million young American tourists. Tall and gangly, he wore a Led Zepplin shirt and faded blue jeans ripped in the knees. His long black hair had been pulled back into a pony tail and he hadn't bothered shaving for a couple of days.

She checked her cell phone. 5:45.

Nothing and no one looked out of place. A quarter million people passed through this station every day and as she could feel the throb of the crowd like a pulse that increased with proximity.

The enormous building was made of red and yellow bricks, a neo-Renaissance structure with impressive spires. The outside looked a bit like a castle, but inside its formidable walls was a sanctum of Dutch efficiency and business.

A pick-pocket slid through the tourist groups. She tightened her grip on her purse. The smell of people sweaty from a day of work or travel stifled the air. Sounds of car horns from frustrated drivers trying to negotiate the heavy traffic behind her and people talking filled her ears.

Would Bakari al-Sharif send the same messenger? She checked her cell again, 5:50.

He hadn't been punctual the first time. Could be his thing. Her chest tightened. Two fingers...two of Delilah fingers. Anubis was not a man to be toyed with.

"Lady." The voice came from behind her.

Turning she saw the man she'd seen on the motorcycle the day before. She stared at him for a moment and then took a deep breath. "I want to talk to your boss," she said.

He lowered his aviator glasses and stared over them. Only once before had she seen such cold flat eyes. They had belonged to a ruthless mercenary. He laughed at her, and the sound held a menacing tone that iced the air between them. A distinct odor of garlic assaulted her nose.

Her heart froze for a second. Pulling out of her bag the package with the Ancient Egyptian scarab wrapped inside, she said, "Here it is."

He reached for it, but she pulled back. "I need more work." And I sure as hell don't want you to be my go-between.

"Give me the package and we'll be in touch."

She handed it to him. Without another word he turned and vanished into the thick crowds. 6:05.

As she walked back to the town, that inner-trembling she experienced after a critical moment in an op when so much is at stake and so many things could go wrong eased. Staying alive in her business depended on wise planning, good eyes and a hell of a lot of luck. She lost sight of George following her after the first five minutes.

Time to go home and wait. The hurry up and wait game had never been her favorite.

***

Sadie turned on the hot water and jets in the hot tub. She may as well enjoy herself. Carefully she took off the ankh necklace and placed it on the shelf beneath the mirror. Delilah's Glock sat beside the tub with her two phones covered by a hand towel.

The heat of the water eased her worries as she climbed into the tub. Her aching feet and fraying nerves relaxed.The last remnants of that cloudy-drugged-head feeling drained out of her. She sat back and listened to Puccini's La Boheme. After twenty minutes she checked her cell phone. 8:00p.m. and still no text. Looked like her gambit hadn't worked.

Time for a new plan. Jeremiah expected her to call in five minutes. With great care she stepped onto the small mat on the shiny white tiled floor. She'd slipped the day before. The floor tiles matched the white tiled walls and white tiled ceiling. Clean and efficient, and so Dutch. Some of their tile work she liked, but these white ones gave her the feeling of being trapped in a sanitized sanatorium waiting a big, burly guy in a white uniform to arrive to scrub her back. She laughed.

She'd been so focused on her bath tub exit she hadn't heard him coming. It was the change in air temperature as the door opened that caught her attention. She stood naked on the mat.

It wasn't the big, burly guy.

Bakari al-Sharif, code name Anubis, strode into her private bathroom as if he owned it... and her. Taking in her nakedness, a slow smile spread across his square face. A lion of a man, he bristled with intensity and purpose befitting a general in an inter-galactic war. She took a snapshot of him in her mind: stocky build, five-ten, middle-aged with raven black hair graying at the temples, olive skin and a mole on his left cheek. Anubis. Dressed in an expensive designer suit he oozed power. His exotic cologne had a potency she'd equate with danger for the rest of her life.

A chill ran up her spine. No escape. Clenching her teeth, she willed her body to ignore the adrenalin rushing through her system and focus on him.

He feasted on her curves with hungry eyes as black as the night. She thought she'd find him ugly and disgusting, but his conquering demeanor held a peculiar, erotic charm. She felt appreciated more than violated.

But totally owned. Yuck. How could she play this one? She motioned with her hand for the clean bath towel on the rack beside where he stood. "Please," she said.

He picked it up and handed it to her. Another man stood in the other room. She caught only a glimpse of him behind al-Sharif's back. Probably the messenger. Trapped.

She waited until the cold black eyes of Anubis were back on her body and then she slowly wrapped the towel around her body and pulled her waist length hair away from her face. Her hand itched for the gun on the floor. Maybe she could end it all right now.

He watched seemingly mesmerized by her movements and said nothing.

"Are you my new boss?"

"Call me Bakari." Perfect English with a touch of a BBC accent. The demanding tone of his voice made the hair on the nape of her neck quiver. Now that she had a towel wrapped around her, his eyes left her and scanned the room.

Shiiiit. Her gut clenched. Despite the cloud of steam that hung in the room, it wouldn't take him long to see the ankh. She reached towards him and offered him her hand, letting the thick white towel slip exposing her right breast. Hell, he'd already seen it anyway. The cold air hardened her nipple. "Sadie Stewart," she said.

A tentative smile returned to his face. He took her hand, but instead of shaking it, brought it to his lips and kissed her. His touch, weirdly tender, sent an icy tingle through her body. Not what she expected. But then nothing about this scumbag was what she expected.

She took her hand back and repositioned the towel drawing his eyes once again to her breasts.

"When I said I wanted to meet you Bakari, I didn't mean like this."

"I spend too much time in the office. I enjoy the occasional field trip." He smiled. "And this one has been most interesting."

She fidgeted with her towel feeling his desire heat the space between them. "No more fingers?"

A shadow crossed his pupils. "Not unless you disappoint me." His mouth twitched. "And then it will cost you more than fingers." His eyes shimmered with power. "Such a shame to harm a pretty body."

The look of cold pleasure in his eyes shook her confidence. An icy feeling gathered at the base of her spine. This asshole might enjoy watching her body being dismembered as much as he'd enjoy raping it, maybe more.

Jeremiah's warnings echoed in her mind. She'd met many assholes in her life, heck even married one of them, but this one made the devil look angelic. Her blood ran cold. She tried a smile, but under the circumstances even the trained model part of her couldn't muster one.

He laughed as if he'd followed her train of thought. "I'll leave you now. But you will be given instructions and money."

She pulled her famous pout until his pupils dilated and his nostrils flared and then she said, "Okay."

A whole-lot-of-weird left the room with him. She wanted to jump back into the tub and wash it off. The spot on her hand where he'd kissed her burned, not in a good way. At least he hadn't spied the ankh. She folded it in a washcloth, and pocketed it in a robe before throwing it on.

***

Bakari closed the bathroom door behind him. He had expected a simple minded model. She had the requisite high cheekbones and perfect skin, but she'd faced him with rare bravery and... she glowed with an animal sensuality. She could be very useful to business.

He imagined her long red hair spread over his pillows and her firm round breasts in his hands. He smiled at the thought of her arching her back beneath him, begging for more. With his wealth and power he could have any woman he wanted, but this one pulled him. He exhaled slowly.

Gahiji stood by the door watching him with his usual grim expression.

Bakari shook his head. "Tell the woman she's hired. Tell her you will contact her when we need her. Give her the five thousand in Euros not dollars and then give her an extra thousand and say it's for her hospitality. Tell her she will earn much more."

Gahiji nodded.

Bakari swallowed. "Have Chasisi find out more about her, and don't tell her anything about me."

Gahiji nodded again.

"With her looks and daring, she will be a great asset, but until I know for sure that I can trust her..."

"Want me to take some insurance?"

Bakari hesitated. "Not yet. The fingers have scared her enough to get her cooperation. If I use her in New York, then maybe."

As he walked down the long narrow staircase his need for sex eased. He hadn't been with a woman since the night Safa stabbed him. He'd see a prostitute tonight and sate his physical needs. But that wouldn't end his desire for Sadie Stewart. A slow tingling awareness that this woman would mean more to him worried him. An American! He laughed out loud.

It wouldn't matter how many women he slept with he'd still want her and he knew it. She had a magic all her own, a sense of her own female power. To have such a woman. The image of her full lips begging to be kissed crossed his mind, along with the thought that she'd be the death of him.

CHAPTER 26

At a fast don't-think-about-what you're-doing clip Sadie strode along the Herengracht towards Sebastian's place. Once the most important waterway in Amsterdam, its name translated to the gentleman's canal. Lined with seventeenth century houses built by rich merchants and businessmen, the medieval brick road was impressive even now. The original owners of the houses invented capitalism, started the world's first stock exchange and the Dutch West India Company, which connected the world in a way it had never been connected before.

The canal houses looked like scenes from a story book, each unique and full of character. Tall, narrow and built side by side; outlined with dramatic gables and shutters; they possessed a sense of dignity and elegance of a by-gone era that made Sadie wish she could time travel.

If she went back to Holland's Golden Age, she'd not only get to meet some really interesting men with big floppy hats who changed the world, she'd also get to avoid facing Sebastian, or worse her feelings for him. She kicked at a pebble on the road. Never had she had to wrestle with such strong feelings for a man.

The light of a crescent moon lit her path as dusk settled. The soft spring breeze warmed her chilled nerves. People gathered at cafes on the street corners and music wafted onto the street, the Dutch enjoyment of life, what they call *gezellig*, spilling into the night. She breathed in the atmosphere.

Was this the right decision? Maybe she shouldn't meet with Sebastian. This was a matter of the heart, not the mind, and no matter how many times she beat herself up about it, her feet kept walking in his direction.

Tired of wrestling with her conscience she pulled out her phone and called Jeremiah. He'd said he would do more research for her. "What about Sebastian," she asked.

"This is what I've found out about your Dutch Romeo. He's a successful art dealer, well liked and well-connected. His best friend Xander Van der Valk runs a business..."

"I know all that."

"He's helped Xander van der Valk and his friend Seamus McIntyre at Interpol with some investigations, all having to do with looted art. They took down an Italian mob guy six months ago, but he wouldn't take any credit for it. He doesn't like publicity. Wilde told a reporter, and I quote, 'We need to slide through the shadows to take down the scum.'"

Sounded like Sebastian. "Can I trust him?"

Jeremiah went silent. Something had his shorts in a twist.

"Tell me," she said.

"People say he has a wild streak. In his twenties he got into trouble with the law, but he appears to have straightened out. He likes to drink, play football and chase women. He's known for having a new lady on his arm every week."

Didn't sound that wild, though the part about women gutted her. "So I can read him in?"

"Why would you want to do that? Are you falling for him?" The concern in his voice irked her. He'd been concerned before, but his voice had never held such a worried tone. If Jeremiah's new found paternal instincts started to compromise her work, she'd have to request a different handler. The very thought nauseated her. Jeremiah, the master spy, rocked. Who could be better at saving her ass than him?

Her chance to chew the silence. She needed to sift fact from emotions.

"You did get the part about other women?" Jeremiah said.

"I'm not...well I don't think I'm falling..." Hell. She'd already fallen, but she wasn't about to share that with him. She cleared her throat. "I think he could be useful. He knows this city and he's good at..." *Kissing* came first to her mind. When his lips touched hers she lost all sense of time. She chose not to share that fact either. "...having my back." The niggling sense Sebastian was *her man* wouldn't leave her. She'd sound like a silly romantic moron if she said that to Jeremiah. He was maddeningly logical at all times.

Jeremiah grumbled. "There's a hell of a difference between taking down your ex and taking down Anubis. Sebastian's not a trained operative. If you don't think George is enough backup, I'll see about bringing in more. I'll come myself if you like. Listen to me Sadie. Anubis is a brutal man. Pure evil. Remember his wife's dismembered head."

She rubbed her temple and turned the idea over in her mind. Jeremiah had never offered to help her in the field. "No," she said. "When too many spooks gather, they give off a smell. And I can't afford to raise anyone's suspicion. I need to work solo. You can send George elsewhere and thank him for me."

"Whoa Sadie. George is a good man; he could be your silent deadly shadow." One of Jeremiah's favorite lines.

"No, I can do this better alone. And it will be safer for me." Her hands felt clammy. "Will you give Sebastian clearance?" Why did this feel like a daughter asking her father's permission to go to borrow the family car?

After a heavily pregnant pause, enough for quadruplets to be born, he answered, "Your call," and clicked off.

"Good bye to you too." She stared at her phone. Definitely not a happy man.

***

Sebastian buzzed her into his building and she took her time climbing the narrow winding staircase to his apartment. How could she explain herself? She could state the facts: "Hi, I'm an American spook." Too weird. She smiled. How about, "I'm not really a thief, or a smuggler. I'm just your run of the mill James Bond." Her stomach clenched as she supressed a giggle. Nah, sounds too much like a television commercial for a silly show. She could say, "I didn't want to lie to you Sebastian but..." That wouldn't work either. They both knew she meant to lie and was damn good at it. That's why she'd come, to clear through the lies and see where that left them.

With no prepared line, she took a deep breath and raised her hand to knock on his door, when it opened.

Sebastian's broad shoulders filled the space of the doorway. His soft blue eyes met hers and caught. For the first time in her life she understood the phrase 'her heart skipped a beat'. In that moment she knew with certainty it didn't matter what cover she hid under. He'd find her. His truth shone in his eyes. It didn't matter to him if she were a thief, smuggler or spy. None of that mattered. What they had went much deeper. Her insides quivered.

A warm smile spread across his face making her body hum. He simply and completely cared for her. His sincerity hit her like a mega-ton bomb and her stomach dropped three floors back down to ground level.

"Maybe I shouldn't have come," she said.

Again her feet did the thinking and she walked into his apartment. With a glance she took it in. An eight foot statue of Eros stood by the door. Modern paintings spread across the far wall. Leather furniture. Restored old wooden flooring. The smell of espresso. She turned back to face him.

"I'm glad you came," he said. "It's time we were honest with each other."

"You've been honest all along. It's me who hasn't."

"Tell me you had a good reason." He placed his enormous hand on her back just above her butt and guided her to the sofa. His strong and confident touch sent a tingling current of pleasure through her body. To be cared for by a man like him, would be like a dream she'd never dared dream come true.

She sat down and he sat beside her. "Tell me your story," he said.

"You can't tell anyone what I'm about to tell you, or I might just have to kill you." She used a flat voice.

He started to laugh, but then stopped when she gave him a no-nonsense stare. His eyes widened and the skin around the corners crinkled with concern.

"I've never been an ordinary girl." Scratch that. "I would like to be normal for you, but..."

Sebastian took her hand in his. "I never liked normal."

That's a good thing. The warmth of his touch calmed her. She took a deep breath. "I grew up the skinny daughter of a single alcoholic mom in Seattle, won a modelling competition and landed in New York at fourteen. I met Jonathon, married the louse at sixteen and then divorced him six long months later."

"It's hard for me to imagine you with him. But then it's hard for me to imagine you with any man other than me."

The certainty of his voice stilled her. How could he be so sure of his feelings when they hardly knew each other? Yet she felt sure too. She took another breath. "I liked my life as a model, but it never really satisfied me. You know, like an artist without paint thing." She figured he'd get that analogy.

He nodded. "So you decided to spice up your life by stealing?"

"No, not exactly. When I was twenty I was approached by the CIA and became..."

"The CIA?" he interrupted her. His back straightened and he peered down at her.

"There is only one. Anyway. Nine years ago I began to work for them. Modelling is my cover."

The smile started on the left edge of his face and spread right across. "I knew you were one of the good guys."

"I love the work. I get to do some good in this fucked up world. As you know, there's a thrill to taking down a bad guy that's hard to explain."

"And you excel at it."

She nodded.

"But it's dangerous." The crinkle lines around his eyes deepened.

She shrugged. "The way I figure it, the better I do my job, the less danger I put myself in. Mostly I'm sent in to watch someone, or gather information. Sometimes I'm told to steal something like a flash drive. I'm no assassin or big time spy. I'm just one of a large number of small operatives used to gather intel. But I'm good at it."

Sebastian traced the side of her face with his fingers sending a current of heat through to her toes. "And how are you connected to the looted art ring?"

"Bakari al-Sharif, CIA code name Anubis, is collecting ancient Egyptian amulets. He's a power hungry maniac. Chatter on the Internet suggests that he has a big heist planned for New York's Met Museum of Art. My job is to find out all I can about his plans, so we can stop him."

Sebastian cocked a brow.

"I've made some progress." Sadie gave him a brief rundown of her relationship with Delilah and how she was getting close to her target.

Sebastian didn't comment, or stop her as she told him the whole story.

"So that's why I lied. I'm sorry I deceived you," she said. For whatever reason, she wanted to be honest with him.

He took her hand in his and the room fell into silence. Deep and loud silence that echoed in her heart. She implored him with her eyes to say something. Anything.

After a moment that felt like a century he said: "I don't know what to say."

"Well," she paused trying not to get lost in his eyes. Sweet Jesus he had the bluest eyes. "You could tell me how you feel about what I just told you."

His full lips pulled into his rogue smile, the one that made her clit tingle.

"I'm not so good with words," he said. "They always fail me. And in English it's worse." He exhaled slowly. "When I look at you I feel pulled. It's a deep primal feeling like a tide or current that can't be denied. It's like you... touch my soul." He leaned in and covered her mouth with his.

With the touch of his lips on hers, her body ignited with passion. Her locked-away desire for him broke through her defenses. Her mind could not comprehend how she'd developed such deep feelings for a man she hardly knew, but her heart knew she had.

Her mind shut down. She wanted him, and she wanted him now. Her pulse quickened as he pulled her closer into his embrace. She pulled on his back in response and with one quick twist he lay her down beneath him. Looking up at him she laughed. He'd taken her by surprise again.

After a long slow kiss, he sat up and tugged on the bottom of her sweatshirt. It flew over her head. A second later her bra fell to the floor. The cold air tightened her nipples. Her breathing increased. His hands reached for her. Her heart thundered.

She didn't think anything could pound louder than her heart, but the loud banging sound coming from Sebastian's door caught her attention. She froze. He stopped and looked at his entrance way.

"Sebastian. I've got to talk to you." A man's voice came through the wood.

He looked at Sadie with apology written across his rugged features. "It's Seamus, Interpol."

By the time Sebastian made it to the door, she'd thrown her shirt back on, tossed her hair back over her shoulders and squished her bra as best she could between the cushions in Sebastian's sofa. Any dolt would know what they'd been up to, but that didn't matter. Panting and hot all over she got up to stand beside Sebastian. She needed to know what Interpol had to say.

Seamus strode into the room, Xander at his heels. Great a convening of the three Muskateers.

When Xander saw Sadie he hesitated and then turned around to face Sebastian. "A body turned up in the canal."

Her gut clenched. Bodies turn up in the canal all the time. She knew the stats. Most of them were men with their flies open, having fallen into the canal half-baked when they took a leak. A dead body didn't have to have anything to do with her or her op. It didn't. And she certainly didn't want it to. All the same, she swallowed hard, not wanting to follow where her gut wanted to take her. She waited.

"It's Delilah Sawatski and she's mutilated." He turned to look at Sadie.

Going on auto-pilot she didn't blink. She walked up to Sebastian, kissed him gently but meaningfully on the lips and walked past him to the door. "I'll be in touch."

***

After Sadie left Seamus showed Sebastian pictures of Delilah's bloated body. "You have to tell us what you know about Sadie and let her go."

Sebastian looked Seamus in the eye. "Trust me, I've got this one."

"Are you fucking out of your mind? She's got you by the balls. Do you think I don't know what we interrupted? She's crooked right down to her pretty polished toe nails and her partner in crime just turned up missing body parts."

"She's not dangerous." Well not in the way Seamus meant.

"Seriously man, you've lost all sense of reality."

"I...I do like her, but..."

Xander spoke up: "Like? I think we all know it's more than that. You need to stand back and let us follow her."

Sebastian's chest tightened. No way in hell he'd let any other man protect her. "No."

"It's not a suggestion buddy. I'm ordering you to stay out of this," Seamus said. Interpol and the Amsterdam police will take over. We need to get to the bottom of this mess. I bet that woman is up to her pencilled eyebrows in stolen art and deception. I don't want you hurt."

"You want me out of your way." Seb's gut churned. By nature, he was slow to anger, but when it happened the world had to watch out. His face heated up, his pulse roared and his fists clenched.

Xander's eyes widened. "Buddy it's for your own good. Her friends play too rough for a civilian like you. If you'd seen the woman's body...."

The caring in his best friend's voice steadied Sebastian's temper. But he couldn't tell him all he knew about Sadie. He couldn't tell him that she fought on the same side as them. He'd die before he'd betray her. But he could let them think he would stand aside.

After a heavy silence he said, "I know what I'm doing."

CHAPTER 27

Could she have done something to help Deliliah? The question played over and over in her mind like a broken vinyl record. The buzz of the street enveloped her as she meandered through people like a goldfish in a bowl darting to avoid collision, but never making contact with anyone, even with her eyes. The stale smell of the air added to a feeling of emotional suffocation. But she wouldn't give into it.

Her old mantra, "*the world's fucked, but I can survive,*" popped into her mind like a lifeline, a resonance that went back to her early years at home with her alcoholic mom. After her funny bone wore down by the gristle of life, she clung on to that one truth. It gave her distance from the ugliness of the world. It kept her emotionally afloat. "*The world is fucked*..."

Did Delilah have to die? And worse did she have to be mutilated? Sadie held back the tears threatening her eyes. She could still remember the zany woman's high pitched laugh, her love of rot-gut wine and her bawdy sense of humor. Sadie's fists clenched. One more reason to get Anubis.

Once she'd secured her room, she pulled out her cell phone and punched in Jeremiah's line.

After he picked up, she said, "Delilah's dead."

He paused. "The report just crossed my desk. This op is getting too dangerous."

"Like hell. I'll get this asshole, if it's the last thing I do."

Silence. Her heart thundered in her chest and sweat trickled all along her spine. Her face heated up. One of the reasons she'd excelled at being a spy was her ability to shut down her emotions and get ruthless. And now was the time she needed to do just that.

But the emotions weren't going away.

Silence.

"Jeremiah?"

"What's going on with you? Is there something I should know? You seem... different."

"I'm not quitting."

"I didn't think you would, but for the record, I advised you to do so, and..."

"I didn't tell you everything about Bakari's visit," she interrupted.

"Tell me now."

She told him about being nude, needing a towel, watching the man's eyes hunger for her. "The asshole's pants showed an erection when he left. I can get close to him. I know it."

"What are you suggesting?"

"Whatever it takes."

"Sadie, you've never slept with a mark before. Anubis is not to be toyed with. You won't be able to tease and run."

"He's a man. I can handle him." She wiped away the perspiration beading above her top lip.

Jeremiah sighed. "I don't like the looks of this end game. The pieces aren't covered. Too much is at risk."

Sadie had made up her mind, so she said nothing.

"You know in Cairo, where he grew up," Jeremiah talked slowly annunciating every syllable carefully for some reason, "eighty percent of girls are castrated before they become women—eighty percent. It's not a law. It's a custom that girls willingly succumb to. It is a barbaric belief. Most women there are treated like brood mares and nothing more. His interest in you is purely..."

"Erotic, carnal... whatever," she said. "I can handle him."

Silence. "You're my best operative."

"Look Jeremiah. You need to listen to me. I'm your protégé and I know you care about me like a daughter, but you need to stand back and let me do my job. Male operatives don't stop at seducing their marks. I can do this. I can give that beast a night of pleasure like he's never seen. Trust me. I know my way around a man. I'll have him begging for more. And I'll cuddle up to his side like a sweet little kitten and show no mercy." The same cold chill that had grabbed her when she'd met Bakari returned, but she shook it off.

"Keep me posted."

"Hold on... I'm getting a text." Her other cell phone jingled. She read it out loud so Jeremiah could hear it: "Tomorrow noon. My man will pick you up and bring you to me." Check. This meeting could be safe and informative. She knew Jeremiah couldn't pull her back from it, not when the CIA wanted Anubis so bad.

"Sadie." Sadness saturated Jeremiah's usually inscrutable voice. "You seem hell bent on getting this guy. I want you to think before you jump into bed with him. Sleeping with a man like him is not something you can wash off with soap. It'll slither into your pours and lie deep beneath your skin. Inside you. Trust me, I know what I'm talking about. Sex is never just sex, especially for a woman like you."

"The Met Museum." That's all she needed to say.

"I'll give you forty-eight hours. If you find something in that time, you can stay in place. Otherwise, abort the mission. I don't want him toying with you."

"Oh don't you worry. It will be *me* playing *him*." She thought of Delilah again and her anger rose so quickly she could hardly stay on the phone.

Jeremiah went silent for a moment. He didn't appreciate her humor today. "If you go into his lair in Amsterdam, New York, Cairo or wherever, I can't protect you. His defences are too thick and there are," he hesitated, "political considerations that stop me. "You'll be on your own." He hung up.

CHAPTER 28

After Jeremiah clicked off, Sadie pulled her suitcase out of the closet and filled it with her things. She needed to move fast if she wanted to stay out of Sebastian's reach. He'd want to see her after the news his friends gave him. He'd want her to stand down.

And she couldn't.

Maybe it was a damn character flaw and one that would get her killed, but she just couldn't walk away from this op now. A man as evil and cunning as Anubis had to be stopped and she had the skills and power to do it. Even Achilles had *a heel* and she was determined to find Bakari's.

No, she'd never slept with a mark before, but she wasn't a virgin. She could do this. That *damn cold chill* flowed through her body again, but she stopped it with her anger. The image of the

Egyptian exhibit at the New York City museum floated in her mind. Half the collection had been donated by private collectors; half had been taken in archaeological digs in the first half of the last century. The beauty of the ancient art work was breathtaking and irreplaceable.

Unzipping her bag again, she took the ankh out of its hiding place in the lining. Holding it in her hands gave her an odd sense of strength. She had something al-Sharif wanted. The ancient Egyptians thought amulets had magical power.

She'd never been one to believe in dead rabbit's feet or any other hokey metaphysical crap, but she had to admit this *thing* made her hands warm. It probably connected in her mind with her fear of Anubis. Yeah, that was probably it.

She turned the carefully sculpted piece of gold over in her hands. The ankh shaped like a cross with a loop handle represented the ancient Egyptian belief in eternal life. She never wanted immortality or power here on earth. All she ever wanted was a full and good life. Her breathing slowed as she pondered the symbol and her heart flooded with longing for Sebastian. She wanted him too. Time to get moving.

She put the ankh necklace around her neck. It would be safest there. What harm could it do? She smirked at that thought. A hell of a lot of harm. If Bakari found out she'd hid it from him he'd skin her alive. But she'd talk her way out of that scenario. Goose bumps beaded on the skin of her arms and she gritted her teeth as she closed her suitcase and wheeled it to the door.

***

Mitch's eyes looked like saucers when he opened his door, bloodshot saucers. "Sadie?"

"I need a place to hide."

At lightning speed he opened the door wide and she walked in. Normally, he kept his surroundings organized, not obsessively neat like people think all gay men do, but well-sorted. Today his clothes were sitting in heaps on the floor, his bed hadn't been made and the air smelled like stale coffee, beer and weed. "I'm so sor..."

"Don't start." She'd turned to face him and held up her hand. "I'm not ready to forgive you. Yet. But I need your help." Watching his eyes soften she continued. "I need to disappear."

"Who are you hiding from?"

"Sebastian." No friggen way in hell could she see him again before she moved in on Anubis. Her feelings for the man were too strong and Jeremiah had been right, he—distracted her. Besides, he would go ballistic if he knew her plans.

Mitchell's eyebrows rose. "Seriously? The giant hunk with the blue eyes?"

"It's complicated. What I need from you is total trust and loyalty. Can you do that?"

He nodded, but his face looked sadder than when he opened the door.

"I'll throw my stuff in the closet. No one can know I've stashed it here. If anyone asks about me, tell them you don't know where I am. I already sent a text to Knickers saying I can't work tomorrow." She paused. "I'm heading out for a big date at noon.

I may or may not..." Her voice caught. "Return to sleep here."

Mitchell said nothing, but his puppy dog eyes did their magical thing. Her resolve melted under their caressing scrutiny, but she couldn't tell him more. Not after the whole ordeal with Jonathon. She couldn't trust him completely. At least not yet. Flicking her long hair behind her shoulders she walked closer to him feeling her smile turn playful. Time to toss him a bone. "There is something else you can do for me."

"Name it."

She couldn't help but smile. "Phone Jonathon's mother."

CHAPTER 29

Asleep, Sadie's mind drifted back to the scene of horror in the heart of western Africa, far from civilization.

The oppressive heat hung in the air making it hard for her to breath. Her hair stuck to her face with sweat. The smell of the wild clung to her nostrils. The sound of wild animals moving behind her in the bush sent tremors up her spine. She was back in the center of it all, feeling helpless and alone—again.

The drums beat loudly with a hard rhythm that would haunt her till her dying breath. Her awareness floated above the scene unable to stop it. The shaman dressed in a robe of vibrant oranges and red, bound JaJa to his dead mother's body. He danced and chanted to his spirits. The grave digger stood beside him saying nothing.

Every detail of the dream was the same as all the others, until the shaman turned his head and looked directly into Sadie's eyes.

Sadie screamed, but knew no one could hear her. The drums were too loud and help was far away. Why had she strayed away from the others? Why had she thought herself invincible?

Three black holes tore open on each of the enchanter's cheeks. Worms slithered out of them crawling through his blood to mount the surface of his eyes. He spat words at Sadie. "Do not think you are safe."

Sadie stared at the transforming figure of the witch doctor. A scream of horror caught in her throat.

"Help Bakari, or the vengeance of the gods will fall upon you."

She woke up screaming as if her head had been submerged in a pond of black water. Mitchell shook her by the shoulders. "Sadie, Sadie," he said.

She snapped to wakefulness and pushed his hands off her. "Just a dream." Her whole body, drenched in sweat shivered from something much more malignant than the chill of the night air. She felt violated, like she'd been touched by...

Mitchell sat on the side of the bed and reached for her hand. She let him take it in hers and they sat in silence as her body calmed down.

"I think someone or something is trying to warn me," she said.

Mitchell's puppy brown eyes probed hers. "I've felt nervous before a big-date before, but you sweetie take the jitters to another level."

She laughed.

"You know," he said pushing her sweaty hair away from her face. "The ancient Egyptians had a thing about dreams. I've seen their Dream Book in the British Museum that dates twelve hundred years before Christ. It's the first document in human history that talks about dream interpretation and it dates to more than a thousand years before Christ."

Of course. The missing piece in her mind fell into place with a solid thump and she felt like her lungs filled with lead toppled into her stomach. Somehow Bakari and the amulets were affecting her mind. She didn't think that could happen if she didn't believe in their power, but maybe it could. Superstitions had their own power. She bit her lip.

Mitchell not picking up on her response continued. "They thought dreams were messages from the gods, omens that could help you predict and prepare for the future. They believed that when you dream your eyes are opened to a larger reality."

Great. She shuddered not wanting to accept any of this happened to her, the skinny girl from Seattle who liked to play football with the guys on the weekends. Oh my God, now she was thinking of her childhood. What had gotten into her? Why wouldn't the damn dream go away? Why did it choose now, of all times, to change and become more... more horrific? "Could they manipulate their dreams?" She had to ask.

Mitchell's eyes widened. "They thought so. They believed in conscious dream travel. The initiated communicated through dreams. They could cross time and space and shape shift to do so.

Would they choose to be worms? That sure as hell wouldn't be her first choice if she could shape-shift. She shuddered as the image of the shaman's disfigured face appeared in her mind. Dream walking? Hocus pocus gobbly gook ... She took a deep breath. It didn't matter how many silly words she strung together to try to diminish what happened to her, the dream had got to her, like a warning. In every cell of her body. Could her unconscious really be trying to speak to her? Or someone else? When had the room become so cold?

"They would chart their dreams," Mitchell continued.

Sadie put up her hand. "Enough," she said. "My head hurts and I need sleep."

Mitchell kissed her on the cheek and left. Over his shoulder he said, "I'm just outside the door."

Sadie didn't think she'd fall asleep again, but she did. Like a rock. And this time she didn't dream.

***

When she woke, sunlight streamed through the bedroom window warming the top sheets of the bed, giving Sadie a delicious cocooned feeling. It would be so nice to hang out all day and enjoy it. But Dee would never again see the magical morning light of Amsterdam that inspired so many painters over the centuries. She owed her.

As she stretched, a lingering feeling of horror seeped back into her mind from her nightmare, like a sticky mental residue. Gritting her teeth, she forced the memory of the last time she saw Jaja into the forefront of her mind, a healthy boy laughing with his new brothers and sisters. Her pulse beat steadied.

Time to focus on work. The sensible thing to do would be to stash the ankh necklace not with her stuff, but somewhere else, somewhere no one would expect it to be. Ideas scrolled through her mind. A safety deposit box, the Bed and Breakfast front desk, the mail... None of them felt right. An inexplicable attachment to the damn thing had grown in her heart. She didn't want to part with it and a small voice inside her, the one that had saved her ass on many occasions, whispered, *Keep it.* It didn't seem like the right time to question her intuition, so she put it back on.

She had to focus. What do you wear on a dinner date with one of the most evil... scratch that... *the most evil man* in the world, a bastard who sells guns to anyone with cash, knowing some would end up in the hands of child soldiers. A man who chopped up his wife, Delilah and who knows how many others.

She took a deep breath. He was still just a man and she could handle him. She'd been graced with good looks for a reason, her calling was to work with the CIA. Her face and fame got her into places other people couldn't go.

And now it had got her a dinner date with Barkari. She'd learn his plans for New York and pass them on. The CIA would work with the FBI and stop him. Her gut no longer clenched when she thought of the man. Worse, it hollowed out like a void. And the *damn chill* that liked to visit whenever she thought of him crossed her body once again.

Enough already. One week from now this would all be over and she could be... She stopped, aware of exactly where she wanted to be. In Sebastian's arms.

Bakari had told her they'd be dining, but didn't say where. She assumed the restaurant in whatever fancy hotel he stayed at, or worse his hotel room. What would a man like him want her to wear? A man who could pretty well have any woman he wanted.

She smirked at the thought. He wouldn't want her to look cheap. And she couldn't do exotic. Her face was far too all-American girl next doorish. Her strong card had always been a classic look. Yves St Laurent, Chanel... That's what she'd do. Wear some classic designer knock-offs. She had lots of them.

Starting with Italian black lace lingerie to outline her finer points, she checked herself out in the mirror. It didn't matter what clothes she put on, to her she still looked like the skinny kid from Seattle with no ass. But she knew the rest of the world saw her differently. Women envied her cheekbones, men—other parts.

She stepped into a pencil skirt over her head, navy with classic pinstripes that would hug her curves and look demure at the same time. Sliding into a matching blue V-neck blouse she'd picked up in Florence, she enjoyed the sensation of the smooth silk flowing over her body. How long would he let her stay in her clothes?

Studying herself in the mirror, she shrugged. The clothes weren't expensive, but comfortable enough. They'd fit the "stylish but hungry" image she wanted to present. She stepped into the highest and most expensive heels she had to complete her femme fatale ensemble. Men like stilettos and with her long legs she looked good in them.

Putting on a thick layer of lipstick, the one she called her Mata Hare Red, she assessed herself in the mirror like the run-way model she was. This would do. But the most important part would be a cloak of confidence she'd have to hold in place.

Could she go through with it, if he wanted sex? Her heart rate increased as she picked up her hair brush. Of course he'd want sex. The thought of his hands, covered in black hair on her body made her shiver. She'd close her eyes tight and think of the flag. She laughed at her own sick joke.

Taming her long hair into a French bun took some time and a lot of bobby pins. She kept her eye and cheek makeup light, but effective, accentuating her high cheekbones and almond shaped green eyes. When she looked in her face in the mirror one last time, she made a weak smile. A woman going to battle. Good enough.

***

In the bright noon day light, Deadeyes waited for her at the entrance of the Bed and Breakfast, a half-finished cigarette in his mouth. He smelled disgusting and this time it was more than garlic. Sneering, he gave her a once over that would have chilled molten lava. He motioned to the waiting taxi.

Sadie didn't waste a smile on him, but she did wiggle her nose. At least she didn't have to wear

a bag over her head. Been there done that. She got
into the back of the car and the bulky bodyguard
took the seat beside her. "How long have you
worked for Bakari?" she asked.

His eyes focused on the back of the driver's
head. His hand stayed in his pocket, probably
holding a gun. "No talking," he said in a thick accent.
His breath reeked. Did the Neanderthal not know
toothpaste had been invented? She let herself have
a momentary fantasy of putting him in a
mouthwash commercial.

Smiling at her own humor, she leaned back
and looked out the window. The amazing scenery of
Amsterdam normally enthralled her, the canal
houses, old shops and the comings and goings of
millions of people. But not today. Numbness settled
into her bones making them heavy with a
foreboding that wouldn't let go.

The car crossed through the medieval part of
town and kept going. Jeremiah's blood pressure
would be climbing about now, as he followed the
GPS in her cell phone on his own maps. She smiled
at the thought and concentrated on keeping her
breathing steady. She needed to stay calm and
professional.

Where would you take someone to butcher
them? The outskirts of the city seemed like a good
idea.

No, Bakari wouldn't hurt her yet. She trusted
the look of wanting on his face. He wouldn't be so
quick to dispense of her, not when he wanted to
play... She gritted her teeth and glanced at her
companion.

Deadeyes held no love for her. He could do anything.

They stopped at a small private airport. That, she hadn't expected.

***

A beautiful, petite woman with Cleopatra eyes dressed in a maroon suit welcomed Sadie aboard a seventeen-foot private jet, built for four to six people. She'd flown in one before during a secret mission in Brazil. Hell she'd even landed it after the captain went and died on her. She liked the plane.

"Please take a seat and make yourself comfortable," the woman said in perfect English. Sadie took the first seat. Deadeyes who had followed the women into the plane, walked past them to the pilot's cabin. He entered and closed the door behind him. The sliding sound of a heavy-duty lock slipping into place echoed in the small space. The engines started up.

"Would you care for a glass of wine, or perhaps a coffee?" the flight attendant asked.

"Where are you taking me?"

The woman smiled at her. "Cairo, of course."

Of course.

"My name is Eboni and I am here to make your flight as comfortable as possible. Perhaps a magazine?"

Sadie matched her smile. "No, thank you, but—" She hesitated for effect. "Flying makes me nervous." Not really, but she hoped she sounded believable. "Could you sit with me?"

The woman took the long chair on the opposite side of the aisle and fastened her seat belt.

Sadie did the same, crossing her fingers that old Deadeyes wasn't the pilot. "Have you worked for Bakari for long?"

"Our flight will take four and a half hours. Once we're in the air, I can serve you a snack or a drink perhaps."

"You don't want to talk about Bakari."

She didn't say anything, but the look in her eyes telegraphed her answer: *No one talks about Bakari.*

When the wheels were up and Amsterdam had faded into the distance, Sadie said, "I think I'd like a drink now. Perhaps a glass of white wine and some cheese if you have some."

As the attendant poured the wine, Sadie asked, "Do you live in Cairo?"

"Yes. I am very fortunate to have this job, which allows me to see other parts of the world." Once in the air, Eboni undid her belt. "I'll pour the wine."

"I do hope you'll join me." Was this woman one of Bakari's lovers? She wasn't one of his wives, because Sadie hadn't seen her face in the dossier on Bakari she'd been sent at the beginning of the mission. How much did this woman know about the man and how much would she be willing to tell her?

They drank and nibbled on cheese for four hours talking travel and girl stuff that didn't matter. The price of the leading nail polish kept rising. Geraldine Lake, the highest paid model in the world, looked awful on the front of the last issue of Vogue. Maybe the rumors that her celebrity lover left her were true. But Sadie steered the conversation back to their present. Didn't Deadeyes need a fashion consultant and mouthwash. They laughed.

But the woman wouldn't talk about her boss. When Eboni seemed relaxed and bonded in a girl to girl kinda way, Sadie tried a new tact. She said: "I'm scared of Bakari."

Eboni's black eyes widened.

"His take-charge manner turns me on, but..."

"But?"

Sadie laughed. "I know about Safa." The image of the dead woman's eyes roamed through her mind.

Eboni nodded and leaned back. A shadow crossed her face. "Safa was kind hearted. I never thought he'd hurt her. Not her." She put her hand to her mouth as if it could catch the words that had fallen out.

"That's all right," Sadie said quickly. "I'd guessed it might be him. But why? Why would he kill his own wife?"

Eboni shook her head. "I don't know that he did. But... it's possible. You know how it is. Some men can be gentle one moment and cruel the next. Balari's moods fluctuate by the second."

The door to the pilot's cabin opened and Deadeyes stepped in. He cast an angry look at both of them. Had he been listening? "We are about to land." He took a seat in their cabin.

As she disembarked from the plane Sadie thanked Eboni for her companionship.

The woman nodded and held out her hand. When Sadie shook it she felt a slip of paper pass between them and smiled. Sometimes help comes from the most unexpected places. It was the sort of serendipity she counted on.

***

Bakari's home had been built to impress, in an age when the wealthy went all-out. Large elegant and solid, surrounded by lush gardens, it had a dreamlike quality. Sadie made her doe eyed cover girl look. "Wow," she said.

Bakari standing at the open door nodded his head. Dressed in a black suit and tie befitting Wall Street more than a tale from the Arabian Nights he looked powerful. His eyes took her in with a warm glance and he smiled. "Good evening," he said.

"Oh my goodness. This place... this palace is amazing." She blinked.

Deadeyes who stood behind her grunted and then disappeared somewhere into the ancient stonework as they proceeded into the centuries old estate. She took Bakari's arm and let him escort her in. "I've never seen such a beautiful palace," she said in a breathy voice.

"I wouldn't call it a palace," he said putting his cold hand on top of hers.

"Marble floors, marble columns, winding staircase to the next floor reminiscent of *Gone with the Wind*, glittering chandeliers... I call it a palace." Enormous bouquets of flowers in crystal vases sat on tables that dotted the long entranceway. The sheer opulence of the place had its own allure. The exotic Arabian luxury reminded her of the homes of the sultans and pashas of old.

He laughed at her words. "It is my home."

"I live out of a suitcase." She snickered. "But it is made of the finest Italian leather."

He grinned. "To me you are a breath of fresh air." His eyes raked hers leaving no doubt his intentions. "Tonight we'll dine on one of the smaller terraces. It's more intimate."

Intimate. Great. She kept her awed smile in place. "That sounds wonderful." Had she slipped into a southern accent? Must be that damned staircase. She couldn't overdo it.

The stone terrace turned out to be the size of her bedroom in the Amsterdam Bed and Breakfast. It overlooked a lush garden with a pond in its center. Four pink flamingos and two white swans swam amongst the water lilies. A pair of loons called to one another in the distance. The warm night air smelled of verdant vegetation surrounding her with a feeling of fecundity.

If she were with the right man this would be romantic. Sebastian's honest face flashed through her mind. She couldn't think of him now. But it was impossible not to. The guy had got into her DNA. Talk about a mismatched protein!

The round table covered in white linen had been set with the heavy silverware and fine china. Even knowing his financial net worth didn't prepare her for this display of wealth. How many children beyond his estate walls could be fed for life with the money it must take to keep this place clean? She bit her lip. He held out the chair for her and she took her seat sending him a hot look.

He poured her a glass of white wine. "Eboni told me you liked white."

The man left nothing to chance. She took a sip and leaned towards him letting her leg touch his. She knew her wine. This one would've set him back more than a thousand American bucks. "What do you want me to do?"

His smile widened. "Let us eat first."

A petite woman in a white uniform brought the first course, a cucumber salad. Sadie smiled at her, but the woman avoided eye contact. Her face remained a frozen mask. Another reminder she'd landed in a foreign land. Oddly, the warmth of the ankh hanging around her neck comforted her.

Picking up her fork, Sadie said, "I didn't realize we'd be eating dinner in Egypt. I will need to get back."

"Your next shoot is planned for Lucci, Italy in a week."

Sadie's chest tightened. She nodded and did her best to look impressed and not annoyed or... imprisoned. "And unless you can offer more money than Extazee Magazine..." She bit into the cucumber and the fresh flavors exploded in her mouth.

Laughter skittered across his dark eyes. "Money? Is that what you're about?"

"You can laugh, because you have lots. The rest of the world..."

He held up his hand. "You will be well paid. And I promise to deliver you to your next job on time if that's what you want." He made the word *job* sound more than plebeian, more like vulgar.

Her shoulders dropped with drama and she dug into her salad.

Tilting his head as he watched her eat, he smiled. "I wasn't always rich. My father was a merchant and he made enough for us to manage, but he was murdered by a petty thief. He'd used up all his savings to take care of his parents in their old age, a common problem in our country."

Sadie tilted her head to encourage him to continue.

"My mother was left penniless with three young boys. She did laundry for the neighbours and we lived on other people's charity for years, until..." He stopped and looked out at his garden.

She shook her hair behind her shoulders.

His eyes returned to her and she gave him a coy smile. The room warmed.

"Until I reached sixteen and sold my soul to the devil." He took a long drink of his wine and leaned back watching her all the while. Some sort of amusement twinkled in his hard eyes. He hadn't touched his salad.

Sadie stared at him. His honesty cut into her. She hadn't expected that. Anything but that. She gave him a bawdy laugh. "The devil? Do tell."

He smirked. "I got work in the arms business and discovered I was good at trading guns for money."

She made herself look suitably surprised.

"I sold guns and explosives to anyone with money."

"African states and..."

"Oh don't get holy on me Sadie. Half the time I worked for the CIA."

Her breath caught. "That can't be."

"Still is." He swirled his wine and took another sip. "My brother runs the business now, but I know he maintains close ties with the Americans. I've retired."

"Why would the CIA hire you?" She swallowed suspecting the answer before it came.

"Because they can't deliver arms around the world on their own. If they did, they'd be accused of funding wars."

Goosebumps rose along her arms. So Bakari was in bed with her own agency. She tried not to smile at this. She thought she'd left her naivety behind years ago with training bras, but once again life surprised her with its twists. The evil man she'd been sent to spy on, worked with the company. *Sweet Jesus.*

"Would you like a shawl? You look cold?"

She gave him a wan smile. "Just... surprised, that's all."

The tiny woman reappeared and cleared their dishes, giving Sadie time to consider her next move.

"So you built up a successful business, which made you a fortune. Your family is now well taken care of. Why are you interested in collecting artifacts? Did you meet another devil?"

He laughed. "Yes, I have made money and amassed power, more than any normal man needs in this world, but I still need more."

Okay now the crazy's coming out. She nodded and looked demure.

"My oldest daughter Rashida battles a rare form of leukemia."

Sadie's mouth dropped.

"She is the light of my life. I want the power to heal her. At any cost." When he spoke his daughter's name his black eyes softened. He reached for Sadie's hand and encircled it with his.

All the disgust and hate she'd built up for the man drained out of her. Who could fault a father for wanting to save his daughter? "So you think the amulets will help her?"

The second course came: Koshari considered by many to be the national dish, a mixture of rice, lentils and macaroni. She took a sip of her wine feeling it hit her blood stream. In the candlelight Bakari actually looked handsome in a mature, exotic way. His square jaw and soft olive skin drew her. The maid left them.

"All ancient Egyptian amulets have power," Bakari said. "But I search for *the one* that has the healing power to cure her."

A chill ran up Sadie's spine.

"A gold ankh on a leather string."

CHAPTER 30

Amsterdam

S*ebastian,* *Seamus* **and** Xander drove to the morgue to check on what remained of Delilah's body. Looking at her corpse on a slab of metal chilled him to the bone. He'd need to wash his memories away with scotch later when he had time. This was far too close to Sadie.

He breathed through his mouth and made a mental checklist: head, severed forefinger and thumb of left hand missing. They must have got her identity by fingerprinting the remaining fingers. The canal water had bloated her body, but not enough to hide the signs of torture: burn marks along the inner thighs, cuts near her breasts, broken arms and ribs. The woman had died a horrible death.

Sadie. Her image flowed through his mind, her moss green eyes and sensuous smile. Sadie. He couldn't let this happen to her. A lump formed in his throat. He wanted out of there, but he stayed to hear the official report.

As the medical attendant went over the details, Xander gave Sebastian meaningful looks throughout. Worse, he kept shaking his head.

But Xander didn't know the whole story. Seb didn't like keeping secrets from his best friend, but he'd promised his silence to Sadie. A man is only as good as his word.

Seamus cleared his throat and said, "...tortured, mutilated, beheaded and left in a canal." He gave Sebastian a hard look, "Your girlfriend keeps interesting company."

With his gut churning, Seb headed for the door. There was nothing he could say to his friends.

"Seb," Xander called after him. But he kept walking.

Sadie hadn't returned any of his text messages. He didn't want to interfere in her op. He admired the hell out of her for taking on Bakari al-Sharif. But damn it all, he wanted to protect her, wanted to be with her. How do you fit that into a text message?

He returned to his apartment at two in the morning hoping she might be there. She wasn't. But her scent still hung in the air. He thought about having a scotch or a beer... or twenty, but wanted to stay sharp. She knew where he lived. Surely she knew he'd come to her side any time she asked. Anytime—Anywhere—

If she'd ask. Would she ask? Dating a she-Rambo could get complicated. He fell asleep in his chair with his cat Rascal purring on his lap, wondering how best to stay out of her way and yet make contact with her. Oh how he'd like to make contact with her. His mind drifted.

The morning sun arrived and still no news. He pressed coffee, ate fresh local cheese on a baguette and scowled a lot. He wanted her safe and with him.

Was he being old fashioned? He grabbed hold of the Chinese pendant on his neck and made a silent wish, but no magic resulted. "Fuck-it." He couldn't sit around holding a pendant and hoping she'd call. Not when she could be in trouble. Especially since she could be in trouble. Anubis was ruthless, a deranged lunatic who liked to collect pretty things. And he thought nothing of killing anyone who stood in his way. The image of Delilah's mutilated corpse flickered through his mind and the taste of acid rose in his throat. Unable to be a still a moment longer, he went into his bedroom threw on jeans and a sports coat, grabbed his passport out of his safe and headed out.

Sadie didn't answer the door of her room at the Bed and Breakfast. Where had she gone? Was she alone? He called Xander for help and his friend arrived within minutes with tools. When they opened the door they found the room swept clean. No sign of her remained, except the scent of her perfume.

"What the hell." Sebastian paced the empty space with clenched fists.

Xander shook his head. "She's gone, buddy. Maybe it's for the best."

"Like hell it is."

"There's no signs of trouble. She left on her own accord."

Sebastian stretched his neck. "Look, thanks for helping me out. One more thing."

"Yeah I'll talk to the Seamus and the police. Are you going to search for her on foot?"

"Something like that."

They parted outside her room. Xander headed down the stairs to the street. Sebastian ran up to Mitchell's room two steps at a time. Sadie'd been furious with the man, but he was like family to her. He might know something.

Seb knocked. No answer. His gut churned. He had to do something.

Flying down the stairs he hit the road in record time, jogged through the tourist crowds on the Kalverstraat to the Dam and went looking for a photo shoot, but there was none. Sadie's soft green eyes filled his mind. She had to be safe. Had to be.

He jogged back to the Bed and Breakfast and tried Mitchell's door again. Still no answer. He went back to his apartment used a search engine to get information on Extrazee Magazine and after a few clicks and one phone call discovered where the owner stayed when she visited Amsterdam, the Orange Tulip. When he got to her hotel, the front desk told him she'd left to do business in Rome.

Rome? Is that where Mitchell and Sadie had fled? But then why didn't she tell him that? Why didn't she answer his texts? His chest tightened. It felt wrong. He had to be missing something. Sadie sure had a lot of secrets.

He went back to Sadie's Bed and Breakfast. This time Mitchell answered his door a crack, and Seb pushed his way in.

"Where is she?" He scanned the room, noting its tidiness, which didn't lend him to thinking Sadie had been there. No girl things. Then he caught a lingering scent of her.

"Not here."

Seb squinted down at the smaller man. "Where is she?" He'd beat the answer out of the asshole if he didn't offer information.

Mitchell put his hands up. "Chill man. She went out on a date, said she might not come home and hasn't. I thought she was with you."

Sebastian's gut wrenched and he exhaled slowly, sweat beading on his brow. "No, she's not with me. And she could be in trouble. Did she tell you anything more?"

Mitchell shook his head.

"Godverdomme het." Sebastian grumbled as he turned and strode out the door.

"Let me know..."

Sebastian didn't wait to hear the rest. He made it down the stairs and out the door in a few seconds. Yes, he probably should trust Sadie to handle herself, but no, he didn't, because his gut told him something was wrong—very wrong. And what the hell was she doing on a date with Anubis? It had to be him, had to be part of her op.

Sadie'd told him the man pulled women apart. He sent a text to Xander, "Need to know location of Bakari al-Sherif."

CHAPTER 31

Cairo

The hair on the nape of Sadie's neck rose. He wanted the golden ankh! The one that hung around her neck!

Sadie breathed in the night air laced with the sweet smell of lotus blossoms. The amulet lying beneath her blouse burned. How could she explain it to Bakari? Slowly she adjusted her hair behind her shoulders, taking in the way his eyes widened in response.

She leaned across the intimate table towards him. His male scent mingled with an exotic cologne. The candlelight softened his hard features. Yes he was definitely handsome.

"Didn't the ancient Egyptians make lots of ankhs?" she said. "Why is this golden one so special?"

She willed her thundering heart to steady. She had no illusions about the man. If he knew she had it, he'd be enraged. What despicable things would he do to her for her treachery? She hoped he'd take the color of her burning cheeks as a sign of attraction, not horror.

"I'm sure you've seen pictures of ankhs in many ancient Egyptian tomb paintings. They are often held by gods or goddesses. They symbolize eternal life."

"Like the image of the number eight on its side?"

"They are more than symbols, they are active magic. My people carried carved ankhs as amulets to give them strength and good health."

"And do you believe that?" Breath in... breath out. Sweat beaded on her top lip.

He looked away from her for a moment, as if the question cut too deeply for comfort. Then he turned back, his dark eyes filled with emotion locked on hers. "Yes."

She gulped.

"Do not be frightened. When I find the amulet I will use its power to do good."

"To heal Rashida?"

He nodded.

"So, how does that work? How does a hunk of gold create power?"

He laughed. "You are so modern. You believe the world is only what you see," he paused and waved his hands in the air. "It is so much more." A bird called to its mate in the garden seemingly punctuating his words.

She leaned closer and touched his hand. It felt cold and lizardy, but she retained the connection. "Like Shakespeare said, 'There are more things in heaven and earth... Than are dreamt of in your philosophy'."

"Exactly. There are sources of power in this world tapped only by a select few. Those sources affect the natural laws which control all we see before us. There is magic in the world Sadie. Believe me, I have seen it."

Again with the deep chill. It crossed her body quickly and settled at the base of her spine. "Is there not a cost for such power? Or is that a myth to keep us behaving."

He grimaced. "Yes, there is a cost. There is a cost to everything we do in this life. But I will do whatever it takes to save Rashida."

Sadie needed to gain his trust to get more out of him. Right now he considered her one of his many pawns. A pretty one, but still just a pawn. She needed him to think of her as more than that.

"I... I understand," she said lightly squeezing his reptilian hand. "I don't have any children of my own, but there is a little boy I care very much about, and I would do anything for him." The image of Jaja playing with other children filtered through her mind and tears welled in her eyes. "Anything." In one swift motion, she reached for the leather strap holding the ankh around her neck and pulled it over her head. She looked at it once for good luck and then offered it to Bakari.

His mouth dropped. The way his carefully constructed demeanor shattered confirmed her suspicion. He hadn't known she had it. He stared at the ankh and then at her face. "Explain."

"I lied to you and I don't want to lie any more. Not when I know why you want the amulets. It's not about money."

"Not at all." His solemn voice echoed in the night. The maid returned and he waved her away. "Not now." His voice thundered.

"Delilah gave me two amulets to hold. I told you I only had one, thinking I could make extra money on the second one." She swallowed slowly. A tear fell from her left eye." I need money. I hope you can understand."

"So why give the ankh to me now?" His voice edged with heavy, hard to read emotion.

"For Rashida." She kept her tone light, but she could tell by the shock in his eyes, the substance of her words hit him hard. If his silence could be said to gasp, it did just that. His stilled amazement echoed off the walls.

Firming his mouth into a straight line, he took the ankh from her hand and examined it. A wave of light crossed his dark expression and then he placed it on the table between them. The quiet in the room felt heavier than an iceberg. Finally he spoke, "Thank you."

"Is that the one?"

"It is a very fine amulet. I sense power in it, but no, the ankh I seek is about twice the size and possesses many times its power. It is known by our people as The Emerald Ankh."

"Can I help you get it?"

The intensity of his stare made her think for a moment that he saw beneath her cover. Her heart stopped. Hell, the world stopped.

Bakari held the smaller ankh in his fist. "It is in the Metropolitan Museum of Art in New York, amongst as you put it, 'a lot of other ankhs'."

Her eyes popped. Bingo.

"My men will break into the museum and grab a collection of amulets. You will fly The Emerald Ankh back to me. That is if you want the job. You will be well paid."

"You want me to smuggle it?"

"Name your price."

"I have to go through customs like everyone else," she said straightening her backbone and shaking her head.

"Yes, but your passport shows that you travel a lot and you are so beautiful and charming the border guards don't check you closely. I will give you luggage that will help you conceal it."

"Just the one piece?"

"Just the one. The others I will have returned to me in other ways. You Americans have no right to keep Egyptian treasures. But I will have replicas made and sent back to the museum." He rose and walked over to her extending his hand.

She took it and stood up. "I... I'll think about it."

He smiled, probably because people rarely thought about taking orders from him. They just did his bidding. No thinking involved. But she didn't want to appear to be too easy. Hmmm. Too easy. On that subject... She leaned towards him and watched his eyes widen. "I'm so sorry about Rashida..." She brushed his lips with hers.

He stared at her as if he needed to assess the situation, as if she were a bank statement.

That chill that had haunted her since the first moment she met him settled deep into her her bones. Could her body respond to him or was she about to perform an award worthy performance. Screwing him would strengthen bond, seal the deal, further her mission. Hell it might even give her control.

He cupped her face in his hands and kissed her softly. If Sebastian did that she'd be flying to the moon. Instead, she felt emptied. She stepped back. "Good night." She didn't want him to think her too easy. It might make him suspicious.

"You must be tired," he said as he gallantly took her hand and kissed the top of it.

She smiled like a cat about to purr.

The corner of his mouth twitched. She could feel his hunger, but also his self-restraint. A man didn't get as far as he had without being able to control himself. "It is better that we keep our relationship business-like until you return with the ankh. You are..." He paused. "Distracting."

He called for the maid and she appeared. "Show my guest to her room and make sure she is comfortable."

Bakari picked up the ankh from the table and handed it back to Sadie. "To keep you safe, Habibti."

CHAPTER 32

Bakari stood on the private stone balcony off his bed chambers sipping a glass of fifty year old single malt scotch, as he looked over his gardens. The gentle night breeze softened the spring heat, but not his ardor. It would take more than a perfect glass of whisky to rein in his feelings. The American woman possessed a toxic she-magic. Could she be the worthy opponent Djeserit had warned him about?

What a woman. Her image, perfect features and luscious body burned. A man could get lost in her moss green eyes, her flawless velvet skin, her long shapely legs. He wanted to run his hands all over her body to see if every curve felt as good as it looked. Tasted. He swallowed. He'd seen many beautiful women in his lifetime. Laid with them.

Married four. But Sadie Stewart drew him in a way none of the others had.

She shone so brightly all other women faded in his mind. Demure one minute, overtly sexual the next; smart and spirited. The woman's refined good looks and feisty spirit made her exquisite.

He may as well admit it to himself. She'd done what no other woman had ever done before, though many had tried. She'd touched his heart. Up to that moment he wasn't even sure he had one.

The intent way Sadie listened to his story about Rashida warmed him, and then when she offered him the ankh, she blew his mind. Surely, she knew she risked angering him, risked her own life, and yet she did it anyway. Because it was the right thing to do. The woman had courage, honor and heart.

What would it be like to spend time with a woman like her? To not be alone in the darkness with her. To be truly cared for by her? She could be his equal. A voice inside him whispered, *She could also be the worthy adversary*. He shook his head, not wanting to believe that.

Still, he had to be careful. So much was now at stake. Her beauty alone made her dangerous. She could be an instrument of his karma manifested on this plane to exact justice on him, the obstacle Djeserit had warned him about. He exhaled slowly and pulled out his cell phone. She would never forgive him if he did this. But did he need her forgiveness? He texted Gahiji: "Take Mitchell."

***

Sadie's bedroom with its floor to ceiling windows and dark wood panelling looked modern. She had expected cobwebs, stone and mould like the House of Usher, because of the age of the castle, but the room surprised her. A gorgeous vanity table made of polished mahogany on the far side caught her eye first. Made for a queen, it had a four foot mirror with side mirrors that folded out and could be adjusted, a velvet, cushioned chair to sit on and drawers for cosmetics and brushes. She ran her hand over the polished wood and sighed. Everything about this castle seemed surreal.

In the center of the room sat an enormous king sized bed. Her eyebrows rose as she approached it. A dark green silk negligee and robe lay on the pure white quilted cover. Did that mean Bakari intended to visit her? A calling card? Goose bumps rose along her arms.

As she put on the fresh clothes, she enjoyed the softness of the silk against her skin. Then she scanned the room noting one camera facing the bed, which probably meant there were others. Undoubtedly there would be mikes as well. She pulled out her cell and sent a coded text message to her friend Chloe, aka Jeremiah. "Coffee, next week." Which meant, I'm alive and busy. Why did Bakari let her keep a phone? Did he think her that harmless? Maybe, she'd gained his trust. Maybe. She wouldn't bet her cheekbones on it.

Time to check-out the privy. In the large well-appointed bathroom, she re-read the telephone number Eboni gave her and flushed the piece of paper down the toilet. Throwing cold water on her face woke her up a bit.

She returned to the main room and started her three Salutations to the Sun, a practice she did every night before she slept. Her muscles stiff from the flight stretched out slowly.

As much as she tried to lose her mind in her yoga, it kept slipping back to her situation. Even the evil scum of the earth have reasons for what they do, but never in a million years would she have guessed Bakari's. His willingness to embrace any karmic retribution to save his child melted her. No longer could she consider him simply a mark that needed taking down. Whatever else he'd done in the world, at his center he was a caring father and her heart bled for his misery. She could only imagine how horrible it must be to watch your child die slowly and not be able to do anything about it. She lay down on the floor for Shavasana.

But she couldn't relax enough to hold the pose. Her lower lip slipped between her teeth. He had to be stopped. Time to focus on the mission. No matter what his reasons were, he had no right to steal from the Met Museum, no right to snatch a heritage piece from the world's view. She got up and stretched once more.

Sliding the negligee over her head she felt the finely woven silk caress her skin. She ran her hands up her sides and brought them to her breasts teasing whoever manned the camera. Bakari might take a look. Then she doused the light and crawled into the gigantic bed. If only Sebastian could be here to share it with her.

Her eyes were almost closed when the bedroom door opened. She stilled her body and listened. One intruder rustled to her bedside on light feet. After considering her options she sprang up and turned.

Eboni dressed in a black silk gown looked down at her with a hesitant smile.

"I thought you might like company."

Company—with cameras rolling. Interesting. Sadie sat up with a straight back and pulled the cover to her breasts. "It's late."

"You've had a long day." Eboni sat down on the bed and traced Sadie's cheek lightly with her long delicate fingers. The invitation in her eyes could not be mistaken. Funny, Sadie hadn't picked up on her interest on the plane.

Sadie pulled back. "I'm sorry if I've given the wrong impression. I like men."

Eboni nodded. "We don't have to have sex. I could give you a massage, ease your tension, help you sleep."

"Uh, no... thank you." Were the men in the security room getting off on this? She leaned closer to her and whispered in her ear. "Did Bakari send you?"

Eboni smiled and whispered back as she trailed light kisses along Sadie's neck, "He believes all women are bi-sexual."

"And let me guess. He likes to watch."

Eboni licked her skin. "Yes, and then he likes to participate." She leaned back and their eyes connected. Her trembling smile looked both wizened and sad.

Sadie leaned back and turned to face the camera. "Not tonight."

Eboni nodded and with the elegance of a queen stood up and left the room. Okay, her experience with Bakari had been floating along on her personal creep-meter scale at eight out of ten, now hit fifteen. She may have to sleep not only with Bakari, but with selections from his harem. Orgies really weren't her thing. The stakes kept going up.

***

Several hours later, the sound of Sadie's door opening woke her. Dazzling sunlight streamed through the window. She sat up with the cover wrapped around her. The maid from last night walked in with a tray of food. Again no eye contact. Did the woman ever look at anyone? She took the tray from her. One boiled egg, dry sourdough toast, a bowl of strawberries, juice and coffee. Very American, and one of her preferred breakfasts. Bakari had a good research team.

The woman stood beside her bed for a minute as if waiting to be excused.

"Thank you."

She nodded, her eyes locked on the floor. "You are to be ready to go in and hour. I will bring you more clothes." That said, the woman turned and scurried away.

***

After eating, quickly showering and slipping into her new clothes Sadie descended the grand staircase at the designated time, feeling like a teleported Scarlett O-Hara. Ready to make her grand entrance with her designer suit, she hesitated at the landing. It wasn't Bakari waiting for her.

Deadeyes stood at the bottom with an ugly leer on his mouth, smelling foul. Did they serve garlic at breakfast? "Follow me," he said.

"Where are we going?"

He turned back to look at her and mumbled, "To work."

Talk about a man of few words. He took the role far too seriously. She looked down at her clothes, a vintage Chanel suit in navy blue. Not her color, but definitely her style. "New York?"

He grunted.

CHAPTER 33

Sebastian borrowed a private jet from his friend Joos. Not having the time to explain himself, he took the keys from the hangar where he knew they'd be and claiming to be the owner notified the airport authorities of his flight plans. He had his pilot's license and often flew with Joos. But never alone.

He'd smooth over the borrowing details with his friend later, preferably before the police were called in. Chances were Joos would stay in the French Riviera another week with his new lover and be none the wiser. It might cost him a painting, but it would give his friend a good story.

Once he got the plane cruising at a good altitude and had the wings level, he let himself breathe normally. He'd catch up with Sadie. Four hours later he landed safely in Cairo. All in all, a successful flight.

He grabbed a taxi and headed to Bakari al-Sharif's palace. The friggen place looked big enough to house an army. Morning sunlight glowed on its stone pillars. Definitely the kind of place to impress a woman. He grumbled. Somewhere inside this cavernous monolith Sadie would be trying to wield her spy-magic. He didn't like her odds, not one bit. The man was a seasoned criminal and as dark as they come. The thought of him touching her body wrenched his gut.

In the early morning heat, he walked the perimeter noting cameras and guards everywhere. Guess that's one thing about being in the arms business, guns came cheap and easy.

When he returned to the entrance, the gate opened and a black suburban with tinted windows motored through. He stared hard at the windows, but could see nothing, until one rolled down and Sadie looked out. He caught her gaze and held it like a precious gem. Her eyes glanced off him and looked into the distance. He was being dismissed. Or warned.

Watching the rear end of the car motor down the road, he firmed his jaw. He couldn't just let her go. He phoned Xander.

"Tell me you're not in Cairo." His friend's voice sounded flat.

"Have you learned anything more about Bakari al-Sharif?"

"Like I told you last night. He's supposed to be in his home in Cairo." Xander stopped talking and muttered to someone else. Then he said, "Seamus wants to talk to you."

The Interpol agent's thick Scottish accent rumbled through the phone. "The man is in the international arms business. He's deadly and unpredictable. Don't mess with him."

Nothing new. "Do you know his itinerary?"

Silence.

Seb twisted his stiff neck. "An asshole like that must have someone watching him. Tell me. Do you know what his plans are for this week? Can you find out?"

"Sebastian, I know you like this woman."

Jezus Christus, the mighty Seamus had turned on his therapist voice. And it sucked big-time. Tall burly guys who drink a lot of beer and made loud farts shouldn't try such shit. Interpol must have made him take a sensitivity course. "Seamus, a little help would be nice."

"The guy rips people apart. Seriously. The severed head of his third wife was found last month in the dessert. And they say he liked that one."

Seb's stomach twisted. Sadie had left out that detail. She'd told him the man had a violent and volatile nature and that people got hurt around him. She'd mentioned severed body parts, but not his wife's fucking head. What else had she not told him? Her long list of secrets could get irritating. Through clenched teeth he said, "All the more reason to take him down."

"On your own? Buddy you're out of your mind."

"I have reason to believe he's collecting

ancient Egyptian artifacts. I want grab the asshole."
Seb's anger rose like molten lava burning through
his system. Sweat poured off his face. He wanted to
bust up something bad. The rising heat of the
Egyptian day didn't help.

"Artifacts? You didn't mention that before."
Xander was back on the line. "What aren't you
telling us?"

"A lot. He's a *geten neuker*." Sebastian looked
down the empty road. He needed to keep calm for
Sadie's sake. Needed to be focused. The heat of the
sun made the air shimmer.

"Goat fucker," Xander translated for Seamus,
though the man probably knew how to say the two
words in every European language.

"Seb how can we help you?" Xander said.

"What the fuck," Seamus swore in the
background. "It's suicide. If you're truly his friend
you'll tell him to come home."

"Seb?" Xander repeated.

"I'm in Cairo and I'm heading to New York.
Don't ask me how or why. I'll call you when I land. If
you learn anything about the man and his
connections in that city, forward it to me."

"New York?"

"The big apple." Seb clicked off. Enough
words. He needed to move.

His gut churned. Could he get to Sadie in
time? He could fee danger heading her way like a
wave about to engulf her. That feeling came all at
once with a certainty he couldn't deny. You could
call it a sixth sense. Whatever. He just knew he had
to get to her, and he knew he'd follow her to the

ends of the earth if need be.

    Damn the *Geiten neuker.*

CHAPTER 34

New York

B*akari paced* back and forth in his New York City apartment. He couldn't sit and listen one minute longer.

His brother Chasisi sat in a white leather chair smoking a foul cigarillo that stunk like bad cabbage. He'd replaced his peasant robe with an Armani business suit. Below his furrowed brow he had the same black eyes as his brother and they watched him closely. "Bakari you must listen to reason."

"You want me to kill Sadie."

"For your own good. She's trouble. You don't have to do it yourself. Just say the word and it will be done. You do not need to watch her die."

"You say this because she is beautiful?"

"Be reasonable. There are many women in the world. You can take your pick. You don't need this one."

"You must have some reason you want to get rid of her." Bakari walked up to the window and looked down at the busyness of Manhattan, cars and people filled the space below, all in constant motion between the tall, gray and glass skyscrapers, like ants in a modern anthill of concrete. His fists clenched. His brother was right, the American had gotten into his blood.

"She's too good to be true Bakari." Chasisi blew smoke into the air. "Beautiful, smart, sassy, willing to do anything you want and... here is" He paused as if he wasn't sure he should continue. "What I really don't like about the American—she turned up just as you are about to pull off the most daring art heist of the century."

Bakari kept his eyes on the streets below. "Many women are willing to do anything I want. I am rich and powerful. I am no fool." A light rain fell outside and people put up umbrellas to protect themselves. They scurried with haste never looking up to see the sky or the people who watched them, all intent on their own little worlds.

"But no other woman has affected you like this. I can see it in your eyes; hear it in your voice. You trust her and you shouldn't."

So that was it. Bakari walked over to Chasisi and sat down in a chair opposite him. "What if she's innocent?"

"I shouldn't have to tell you about collateral damage. The museum raid will take place tomorrow afternoon. Let me take her out before then."

Bakari put his head in his hands. Sadie. For the first time in his life he'd glimpsed what it would be like to have a modern relationship. His four wives had never made him feel like she did, not for a moment. They acted more like obedient slaves than true lovers. He could see the fear in their eyes and could taste their hatred for him on their lips. Prostitutes could amuse him for hours at a time, but they had worn out hearts. They made him feel like he was fucking a black hole.

Sadie Stewart. She could be his woman in a very real way.

"Are you listening to me Bakari?"

He must have zoned out and missed something. "Yes, yes of course I'm listening. I just don't agree."

"Was she that good in bed?"

Bakari stood up and strode to the window again. Normally he thought nothing of discussing such things with his brothers, but it felt wrong to talk about Sadie. The sky had turned a darker shade of gray and the drizzle had hardened into rain. "I didn't sleep with her."

"Sleep?" Chasisi's voice rose, indignant, and he shook his head. "Maybe, that's your problem. Screw her. Screw her until you no longer have a need to screw her. Then maybe you'll have your wits about you again."

"No. The raid on the museum is planned for mid-day. Sadie will fly out of New York on the Dutch Airlines at six for Amsterdam. I have no time to..."

"Make the time Bakari."

He shook his head. A quick indulgence wouldn't satisfy him. When he had sex with Sadie for the first time he would relish every moment of it, take her slowly and deeply. He didn't want to bang her as the Americans say.

His brother sneered.

"I have insurance. He pulled out his phone and showed Chasisi a picture of Mitchell tied to a chair with today's Amsterdam newspaper sitting on his lap. Blood trickled from his mouth. "At the first sign of trouble with her, I will show her this. He is her best friend, her only family that I know of." The memory of Sadie's tangy perfume and moss green eyes swamped him for a moment and he stiffened. If only there'd been another way.

"I still think you should kill her."

"Not unless I have proof she has betrayed me. Find that and then I will let you do whatever you want with her."

His brother stubbed out his cigarillo and stood up. "I will hold you to that Bakari."

***

Sadie updated Jeremiah through another coded message and waited. She loved New York City, its diverse culture, its busy-ness, its speed. When she was fourteen she'd lived in a model's apartment with a bunch of other teenagers. At sixteen having made her first cover on Vogue, she moved into a studio apartment of her own. She married and divorced Jonathon that year. She sighed. The CIA recruited her here when she was twenty. In many ways the city felt like home, even though she grew up on the rough side of Seattle. In New York she could be anybody she wanted to be. The largeness of the city gave her the feeling there were no limits to her life.

Stretching out on the leather couch in the hotel room Bakari had arranged for her, she travelled down memory lane for a few stolen minutes. A sharp disinfectant smell made her sit up. Bed bugs? Had the hotel been infected? Damn she hated those biters. They crawled into the best hotels in the world. She checked her arms.

No signs of bites. How silly could she be? Frightened of itsy bitsy bugs, when she'd chosen to take on a major international criminal. She laughed. The scales in her life never balanced. But the thrill of the chase was worth it.

Thrill. Her thoughts flowed to Sebastian. He'd been leaving messages on her phone and she had been ignoring them. She'd told him to stay out of her way, told him she needed to do this alone, but the stubborn giant with the big heart didn't seem to listen. When she saw him in Cairo, she automatically opened the window of the car. It wasn't a wise thing to do. It could have blown her cover, but she couldn't help it. She wanted him to get the message to stay back, to stay safe. But one didn't take subtle hints. In fact if they both survived they'd have to have the talk about him listening to her and taking her seriously.

In the background, a John Wayne western played on the television. Any minute now he'd say, "Well shucks mam," and plant a big kiss on the mouth of the heroine. The lighting would fade and cheesy music would play. If life and love could only be that simple. She changed the channel to a cooking show, figuring the people who monitored her could make whatever they wanted of that.

No sign of Bakari. Had he changed his mind about her? She thought she'd hooked him, but she hadn't seen him since their dinner on his terrace in Cairo over twenty four hours ago. Her only company, if you could call it that, had been Deadeyes. She tapped her foot. The waiting would drive her crazy.

Whatever Bakari planned, had to happen soon. That's why he'd brought her here. His time frame was short. Otherwise he couldn't fulfill his promise to return her to Italy next week.

The blond on the big flat-screen whipped meringue to top of a very-yellow lemon pie Must be nice to have such a safe job. If she lost all her modeling contracts, would a TV show like this take her on? Although she regularly burned her morning toast, her practiced smile might help the ratings. Lucy from I Love Lucy came to mind, being goofy but lovable in the kitchen. She could ham it up if need be...

A discreet knock sounded on her door. Show time?

Looking through the safety lens she saw Bakari holding a bouquet of roses. She undid the top button of her silk blouse and pushed her breasts together. Taking a deep breath, she opened the door.

Bakari handed her the roses and walked into her room as if he owned it, but then in a way he did. He scanned the room. "Nice to see you again Sadie."

A shiver slithered up her spine leaving a residual trace of dread along its path. It squeezed her throat and froze the words on the tip of her tongue. She couldn't afford to freeze-up now. She'd have to work with her body responses, not fight them, if she wanted to look authentic.

She took the roses and held them to her nose giving herself the time she needed to regain her composure. "They're gorgeous," she managed. And of course they were. Large red roses with long stems. Each one absolutely perfect. Must have cost him a couple hundred. But that would be pocket change for him.

"I thought we'd talk about your next job," he said as his eyes returned to her.

She'd only met Bakari twice before and each time he gave off a strong aura of being in command, not only of himself, but of everyone else, so strong an aura that it sucked the air out of the room and pulled everyone in. Even though she'd put up her mental defences to counter his charm, she'd felt his pull. Like a freaking undertow.

He was a lion of a man. Meeting him made her understand how people could follow Hitler. Bakari had that kind of charisma that challenged and took charge.

Once again the full force of his charm descended upon her, flooding her senses with his strength. Touching the ankh around her neck, she smiled at him.

Strong men fascinated her. His characteristic air was a finely meshed cloak he'd perfected to get people to do his bidding. His atrocities were probably overstated too, so that if his charm didn't work on people his evil reputation would. But today he didn't wear his evil warlord mask. Today, he seemed almost human, but shadowed by an extraordinary sense of who he knew himself to be and his purpose in life. His confidence and determination glowed from every pour of his body and its power sucked her in. Or at least tried to.

"Are you worried about the heist?" she asked.

The sound of busy of the busy hotel came through the open door. He closed it and walked over to the window. "Rashida's doctor called this morning."

Holding the roses, she waited for him to say more.

"The cancer is growing quickly. He says we have to tell her, but I can't..." His voice hitched.

Sadie put the roses on the coffee table and walked over to him. She put her hand on his shoulder. His body shuddered at first and then stilled. They stood like that for a while, Bakari stared out the window as if the answer might be out there, but of course it couldn't be. There are no answers to painful times. There's only the going through it with people you love.

Bakari turned around and looked at her, tears welling in his eyes. "Life's so cruel," he said.

"Go back to Cairo and be with her."

Light flickered across his black eyes and the air in the room grew colder. Her chest tightened. She'd met many bad guys, but none like him. He had an uncanny ability to change the mood of a room in a second. The hair on the nape of her neck rose sensing a darkness approaching; fearing his next words. Needing to act, she reached out to him and wiped a single tears from his cheeks. "Bakari."

His eyes softened for a moment and he took her hand in his and kissed it. "Sadie you are an enchanting woman."

Oh oh, here it comes. The friggen bell's tolling. She had to act. Stepping closer to him, she said in a soft voice, "Bakari I like you too."

"In another place... in another time, we could have been lovers."

"We still can be."

He exhaled slowly. "Why is it Americans think they can change everything? Have everything? Some things habibi you cannot change. Our paths have crossed, but we are not destined to be together."

"How can you say that?"

"After I show you something, you will never want to talk to me again. This is the last time you will see me."

She put up her hand to stop him from saying more.

"Fate is pulling us apart."

And a hundred other things like the fact she had a thing for a crazy Dutch guy and she didn't date evil men, but she wouldn't argue with him. She waited.

He swallowed so hard she could hear it. "Let us have one kiss, one kiss before I show you."

There are many things a spook can prepare for, but kissing a man like Bakari wasn't one of them. Her stomach dropped. Of course she'd anticipated this moment, but there was no way she could be prepared for it. Her heart stopped. Stay in cover. She leaned in and he kissed her.

His lips felt cold and rubbery. Her mind detached like a boat leaving the shore.

Softly at first, and then deeper, he kissed her, his tongue exploring her mouth. His whiskers rough on her skin.

Her body felt ice cold, frozen in the grip of darkness. She moaned softly and made her breathing increase. He ran his hands through her hair. How long could this damn kiss last?

His hands roved down the sides of her body and came to a rest on her ass. Oh great! He pulled her closer and she could feel his full, very full erection. She moaned more loudly in response and prayed for deliverance.

Stepping back, he took moved his hands to her face. "I am sorry Sadie. I wish we could have had more." Sorrow and regret shone in his eyes.

"Bakari, we could get together after the raid. We have the rest of our lives."

His lips firmed into a straight line. "It's time for me to show you." He pulled a cell phone from the inside of his suit jacket. "I don't want to hurt you. I hope our kiss proves to you that I truly care about you. But you left me only two choices. Either I have you killed, or I take insurance to ensure you do as you're told and don't get in my way. I cannot risk my plans being damaged by you. Not when Rashida's life is at stake"

Her chest tightened even more.

He punched keys on his mobile phone and turned the screen towards her, so that she could see it. Mitchell sat tied to a chair with today's Amsterdam newspaper on his lap. His eyes were black and swollen disfiguring his face. Blood trickled from his nose and a weeping cut marked his handsome left cheek.

Her knees gave out and she sank to the floor. Bakari reached to steady her, but instinctively she hit his hands away. She crumpled like a broken Barbie onto the carpet. "How could you?"

"If you behave, I give you my word, that you and your friend will be released unharmed."

She glared at him. Now she had tasted evil. "What do you want me to do?"

"Give me your cell phone and promise to not contact your people at the CIA"

She swallowed hard. Tears welled in her eyes but she refused to cry in front of him. He knew... and he had Mitchell. Her end game was screwed. She headed down the final runway alone. No point in arguing with him. Either his men had broke her cover or he'd read her. A man like him didn't get as far in the underbelly of the world without being able to read the nuances of every face and every heart. He knew her true identity.

Ah to hell with that thinking. Red hot anger burst through her fear, swamping her body like a tsunami. She'd find a way to take him down. She stood up and stared at him for long minute. He was only human, and humans could be destroyed.

She grabbed her cell phone from the table and handed it to him. "How did you know?"

"I didn't," he said looking at her with sad eyes. "Not until you confirmed it this minute." He stared at her and continued. "You are too perfect. My people warned me about you, but I wouldn't listen." He shook his head. "But I worried. A beautiful smart woman with so much courage spending her days modeling clothes. It didn't add up. I guessed and am so sorry to be right. Good bye habibti." He turned and walked out the door closing it quietly behind him.

CHAPTER 35

Bakari entered Djeserit's hotel suite ten minutes later. Sitting in the middle of the outer room on a posh New York City sofa, she looked up at him. In front of her a spread of tarot cards lay on a purple cloth she'd put on top of the glass coffee table. He didn't want to disturb her concentration. Her face looked pale and a single tear ran down her left cheek.

"What is it?" he said.

Her hands darted out and pulled all the cards together into a pile. He hadn't had a chance to identify the cards, but it didn't matter as he didn't have her vision to understand them. To him they were rectangular pieces of cardboard cards with elaborate images on them. They didn't speak to him the way they did to her.

Still, it was interesting that she felt the need to hide the cards from him. He made a mental note to have Chasisi review the camera tape. She wiped away the tear. "I don't like being bossed around, Bakari. It interferes with my energy. I cannot see all that I need to see."

"I'm sorry Djeserit. I know you don't like leaving Amsterdam, but I need you here. I am about..."

"To do something very foolish."

"You saw it in the cards?"

"No in your eyes and in your heart." She waved her right hand dismissively in the air.

"I want the amulet."

"Sometimes Bakari a man needs to let nature take its course. To interfere..."

"Yes, yes, yes... so you keep telling me. I tempt the wrath of the gods. I break the balance of life. I threaten the karmic rules. There will be a grave price to pay. I get it."

"But still you go on."

"I must save Rashida."

Silence filled the room.

"And the other woman?"

"What other woman?"

"The American who seeped into your heart. Did you think I wouldn't see her?"

Bakari grimaced. Why did he ever try to hide anything from this woman? He smirked. "Her name is Sadie Stewart and I am attracted to her in a way I haven't experienced before. Perhaps it's what people call falling in love, and for me it would be for the first time in my life."

"Then abandon your stupid plan. Be with the woman and allow Rashida to die with grace."

"No." Bakari hadn't meant to shout, but he had.

The sorceress's head moved back an inch as if she'd been slapped. She held up her hand for him to stop.

"I must save my daughter. She is my flesh and blood." He took a seat opposite Djeserit and looked at the stacked card. "And you will help me."

The air grew still and cold. The seer's eyes flickered to each side of the room and then came back to rest on his. In the olden days she would have been considered a holy one, one of the initiated. Later she would have been called a witch. He thought of her as all of that and more. He counted on her vision to steer him to the amulet.

"If you insist." She lit the single candle on the table and gave him one last searching look. "I will not use the cards for this."

His jaw firmed. At last she admitted her gift. He had to know what she saw.

Slowly she stood and raised her hands to the sky. Her red silk robe looked out of place in the pristine hotel room with its white plaster walls, but he knew from experience that otherworldliness would take over her and she would be beyond time and place. Her wizened face turned colder than a stone statue. "I, coming forth am Amen, the hidden one."

A breeze ruffled through the room as the spirits gathered. Her words reverberated through his being. His chest expanded and he felt lighter than air.

In her right hand she drew her ivory wand inscribed with hieroglyphics from her pocket. She waved it once in the air. "I am the keeper of Akashic Records. All of which is, and which shall be. Eternity and Everlastingness. Open your portals." She put her left hand on the deck. "May I fly like a golden hawk. May I see the truth revealed." She stood absolutely still. Her eyes closed as if as if she listened to distant voices.

Bakari breathed deeply.

A wave of calm flowed over him as he looked at her transformation. She had opened her eyes, and they were glazed over, no longer her own.

She waved the wand once before him. "Son of Isis, Seaker of truth..." She faltered and the candle flickered.

Bakari swallowed.

"I see a storm."

"Tell me."

"A violent storm will ravage your life, all that you care about, all that you know..." Her head fell backward, her face looked to the ceiling. "You are at a turning point. You could still turn around and go the other way. You could dedicate your life to helping others, heal your Karmic path." She stopped for a breath. "If you go forward this storm will gust and swirl around you until the world as you know it comes to an end."

Bakari stilled the shiver coursing through his body. "I must have the amulet."

"You want power that is beyond your reach. It is not meant for you." Her voice no longer sounded like her own, or the one she usually used during readings. This voice was male and menacing. "Do not go against the gods." Djeserit's whole body trembled.

Bakari fell to his knees. "I must save Rashida." Sweat ran from his every pour of his skin. It dripped off his face and down his back. His shirt clung to his body.

The sorceress reached over and touched his head. Her hand felt like liquid fire. An electric jolt ran through his scalp and down his spine. When he looked at her ethereal eyes the power behind them at first humbled him, then diminishing him into a million broken pieces swept-up by the river of eternity. Its relentless current dragged him through his own sins, like a kaleidoscope... into darkness.

He put his hand in front of his face to protect himself. "Let me save her. I beg of you."

Sounds of lightening, thunder and crackling fire flooded his ears. The smell of smoke burned his nostrils. The currents from the otherworld pulled harder until he thought he would not survive. He held on to the one and only thought that mattered: his love for Rashida. "Please Djeserit, let them know my heart."

The sounds eased and then eased some more. He took a deeper breath and waited.

"If you are prepared to pay for upsetting the balance of all that is, and all that will be, if you are prepared for the cost to your soul and the souls of your descendants then this is what you must do.

Take the smaller ankh you gave the woman and use its power to guide you. It will be stronger now that it has been lying next to her pure heart. Use its energy. Go to the museum and take the Emerald ankh. Let no one get in your way."

The words flowing through the body of the sorceress echoed in the room. He felt the floor beneath his knees shake and the candle went out. He closed his eyes. He had his answer.

***

After he left, Djeserit said a prayer for Bakari and one for herself. Her body trembled as tears flowed down her face. It didn't matter how much she cared for the man, she could not change his destiny, or hers.

CHAPTER 36

*P*acing the carpet hadn't helped Sadie. Nor had taking a shower to wash off the memory of Bakari's disgusting touch.

Time to lighten up. But how? The crazy idea of camp letters nudged her memories.

If she had the luxury of writing a camp letter home to the perfect suburban family she never had it would begin: *Dear Mommy and Daddy, I suck. My best friend has been captured, I've been mauled by a maniac (not by a bear) and I am about to steal a fancy rabbit's foot because said maniac thinks it will heal all his pain. Don't count on seeing me soon, if ever. I really really suck. Your devoted screwed up daughter Sadie xo.* The thought made her smile.

Then there would be her star-crossed Dear John letter to Sebastian: *Hey Sailor, I got a thing for you. But love is not enough. At least I think I may possibly love you, or am falling in love with you. Never really felt like this before. I get all lightheaded whenever I think of your wicked smile. And other parts.* <friggen hell> *But 'we' weren't meant to be together. I screwed up and am now working for the evil side. I know you, the righteous boy scout guy, would never approve, but it can't be helped. Wish we could have met at another time. I will always remember you.-* ~~Love~~ *...* ~~Hugs~~*...* ~~Kisses~~*...* ~~Affectionate grope~~ *the lady from Venice.* Not sure he'd like that note, but it made her laugh.

There was Mitchell to consider. *Dear Mitch...* The words wouldn't come. How do you apologize to someone who will die because of your stupidity? Maybe it was her pride and not her sorely lacking IQ that got her into this mess. Even after all the warnings Jeremiah tossed her way, she thought she could take Anubis down. Why did she think she could? Reality really sucked. *Dear Mitchell, I'm sorry... eternally yours, Sadie.*

Her quirky sense of humor usually buoyed her spirits, but not today. Dressed in jeans and a sweatshirt that had been delivered to her door, ready to do Bakari's bidding she waited.Uggh.

Picturing the insides of the hotel and the museum, she recounted the number of exits in each and their locations. There had to be a way to turn things around. She considered and weighed every friggen fix-it option she could conjure up. But the brutal fact remained that if she succeeded in escaping, Mitch would die.

But he might die anyway. Stalemate? She could get information to Jeremiah, but then again she'd be signing Mitch's death certificate.

Time laced with regret ticked slowly by.

Two insufferable hours later, she heard a knock on the door.

Old Deadeyes did not disappoint. He strode into her room smelling of garlic dressed to kill. Literally. Black work boots, black pants, black jacket. Monochrome dressing taken to a sleaze ball lethal extreme. Probably had rubber gloves in his pockets. Above his Grim Reaper duds she found his scowling leer. Above that, his deader-than-dead eyes. Rushing in, he slammed the door behind him, grabbed her by the arms and threw her against the wall with surprising force.

Her back hit first and then her head in a whiplash motion making a thud that rang in her ears. Air rushed out of her lungs.

"I want to kill you."

She spat in his face.

Wiping the phlegm away with his beefy hand, he hissed, "*Qah'ba*." He grabbed the amulet that hung from her neck and ripped it off her body. Then he put his forearm up to her throat and pressed hard, cutting off her breathing.

Her well-aimed knee got him in the groin and he doubled over. His dead eyes came alive with rage.

Sadie put her hand to her throat and gasped for air. "Bak...Bakari would not like this."

"Dead women can't talk," he muttered. Sweat beaded on his forehead. Sweet Jesus, he smelled worse up close.

"You think he won't find out?"

His lips curled like he wanted to say something, or do something, but couldn't.

"Bakari gave me his word. If I keep my end of the bargain, he will release me unharmed."

Deadeyes grunted. Not a pretty sound.

"Bakari would want you to treat me well." She pulled the hem of her top down. "I must look good when I go to the airport with his treasure. I'm guessing he said something like that to you." She spoke slowly not knowing how well he understood English, or how well his synapses connected. Her neck throbbed with pain, but it probably wouldn't bruise because of the way he'd exerted the pressure. Maybe, he hadn't intended to hurt her. Maybe, he wasn't as stupid as he looked. Nothing in Bakari's world turned out to be as it appeared. Why should Deadeyes be any different? She exhaled the breath she'd been holding.

"So cut the shit. You don't scare me. Just tell me what to do." She turned her back on him and walked to the sofa like she was the queen of some foreign land. She made it all the way there before he spoke.

"You are flying out on Egypt air flight 986 leaving at 6:30 tonight. Pack your stuff in the new luggage I brought you and be ready to leave here at 4:30."

"The package?"

"I will bring it with me and put it in your bag when I come to pick you up."

"And Bakari?"

He shook his head. "Be ready for my return."

After he left she went back to pacing. The heist would happen today, this afternoon. How could she get word to Jeremiah? Should she get word to him? Her fingers tingled as her mind weighed her options.

She picked up the remote for the TV. She'd see if she could access the Internet from there. But the remote didn't work. It must have been tampered with. Crossing her fingers, she picked up the hotel phone, but it didn't work either. Her luxurious hotel room lost its elegance. It was a prison, the place she'd be stuck while Bakari's men broke into the Metropolitan Museum.

In broad daylight? How could he hope to pull that off?

CHAPTER 37

Sebastian looked out the side window of the commercial plane as the wheels left the tarmac. He didn't want to tempt fate by taking Joos's private jet for another ride. The last thing he wanted was to be thrown in jail.

His mind fixated on Sadie. One good thing about beauty is it gets noticed. Her strong independence, love of life and raw courage drew him, but there was no denying her physical beauty. Even in a city as big New York, people would stop and stare at Sadie. Some would recognize her face from magazine covers, all would respond to her sensuality. So finding her shouldn't be that hard. The hard part would be convincing Sadie to let him help her.

Women. Why did they feel the need to act so 'kick-ass' these days. Why couldn't they just accept that they're weaker? Well physically, that is. Sadie had the balls of a Navy SEAL. He'd giver that, but she was no match for the kind of men Bakari al-Sharif would hire. Hopefully she continued to hold the upper hand by using her brains. He didn't like to think of her in bed with the *geiten neuker*. Didn't want him to put one finger on her. His jaw clenched.

No matter how much he tried to decipher his undeniable attraction to Sadie he came up with the same simple, but devastating answer. This must be what it feels like to fall in love. Sweat beaded on his forehead. Tante Zanneke had said Sadie was *the one*. How could his aunt have known? Sadie's ballsy spirit pulled him like a fucking magnet.

She wanted him too. He could feel it in every fiber of his body. If she wasn't so patriotic and determined to take down that asshole...

But, he'd never try to change her. Her she-warrior thing was sexy. He just wished she'd let him help. He looked out the window again. Cairo shrunk into the distance. It would be a long flight.

Once through customs, he picked up a text message from Xander: "Sadie last seen at the Central Station Hyatt."

Forty minutes later he walked up the wide staircase at the street entrance of the Hyatt hotel by the monolithic white face statue to the lobby. Sounds of the busy Manhattan streets faded inside the old hotel.

If only he could strangle someone. He couldn't seem to breathe properly. His body had gone into a fucking, permanent fight or flight mode. The dark haired woman in a hotel uniform at the desk smiled at him, but then the delicate corners her lips quivered and her eyes started darting around as she took him in.

He knew the signs. Being an angry six foot five guy scared the shit out of people. Normally he hid his agitation because he didn't like to be looked at as a monster.

"Hotel security please," he said with an affected Dutch accent to emphasize his Europeaness. "I'm with Interpol." The fact that he sounded a bit like his crazy Aunt Zeneke made him wince. That he lied didn't bother him.

"Do you have identification."

"Call security. Now." He let all his anger vibrate through his body.

She blinked once and picked up her phone with trembling fingers. Sebastian turned around and scanned the enormous lobby filled with chairs, sofas and hanging banners. People of all nationalities and races wandered about. There were Arabs in the mix, but evil comes in many colors and Bakari could hire anyone to be his henchmen.

Two minutes later a man dressed in a well-tailored suit appeared on his right side. He looked like the younger cousin of Schwarzenegger on extra strength steroids. "I am Leandro Laiche, head of Security. Can I help you?"

"Where's your office?"

After ten fucking-yada minutes with the Security guy, Sebastian took the elevator to the ninth floor, where he found a short stocky man dressed in black walking the length of the hallway. The man looked up and reached inside his jacket when Seb emerged from the elevator. The burly guy's eyes held a violent determination to kill. Seb had seen that look before. Time stood still.

Seb would have taken on a fire breathing dragon at this point. Gritting his teeth, he willed his legs to saunter down the narrow carpeted hallway even though he wanted to run. When he came alongside the man, he turned and gave him one hard punch in the solar plexus. The man's eyes bulged and he folded over. Seb hit him in the head and then hit him again for good measure. The guard fell to the floor unconscious. Seb used the key the Security man had given him and opened the door.

Across the room, Sadie's with her unbelievably long legs stood on the window ledge. Her right hand attacked the edges of the window seal with a butter knife. She stopped when he entered and turned to look at him. Their eyes met.

***

How the hell did Sebastian find her? She shouldn't be surprised. He always found her. A warm glow flowed through her body. She never thought being rescued would feel good.

She jumped down to the floor. "What took you so long?"

Sebastian strode across the room and pulled her into his strong arms. His familiar scent and rock hard body made her want to pull him to the floor and take him right there, but the clock was ticking. She let her body sink into their embrace and the long deep kiss that followed. Panting she stepped back. "Got a phone?"

Sebastian pulled a hand through her hair and studied her face. "Only you would let me kiss you like that and then ask for my phone." He reached into his pocket and handed his over to her. Meanwhile, he scanned her body she guessed for injuries, but his scrutiny made her hot.

Sadie turned her back to him so she could concentrate. He kept his hands on her shoulders. Her heart beat wildly. She punched in Jeremiah's number and on speaker phone told him that Sebastian had rescued her and Bakari was hitting the museum right now. She knew they'd heightened security there because of the threat, but she doubted anything could stop the determined Anubis.

"I'll notify the FBI, send in a SWAT team and the police. You can stand down."

"Yes sir." *Like hell*, sir. She turned to Sebastian. His blue eyes filled with compassion as he traced her jawline with his long fingers. His 'rough skin - soft touch' melted her.

After a couple minutes of silence Jeremiah came back on the line. "Do you know what his plan is?"

"The man is brilliant. I don't know how he plans to pull it off, but I have no doubt he'll succeed if we don't stop him."

"Sadie, you need to get to a safe place and stay there. The last thing we need is for Bakari to use you as a hostage."

She blew out a long slow breath. "He already has Mitchell."

"Where?"

"In Amsterdam. He threatened to kill him if I didn't help smuggle the Emerald Ankh, the piece he's most interested in, back to Cairo."

She could almost hear the sage spy nodding his head while he reached to knock over a pawn on his chess set. Collateral damage. Damn it. Maybe, she shouldn't have phoned him. It could cost Mitchell his life. But her training told her she had to let her handler know the situation. He would help her. He had resources. He was on her side. He... She bit her lip. Bottom line: he didn't care about Mitchell.

"Sadie, I'm ordering you to find a safe place. Take your friend with you and wait for my call. We'll handle the museum heist and find your friend."

"But..."

"The best thing you can do is stay out of the way."

Being the queen on his chess board, she could see the logic of his decision. But the heart knows no logic. "Will you send..."

"Yes, I will have a team of operatives look for your friend and alert the Amsterdam police as well. Trust me."

Trust? She'd always trusted him. The fact that he'd asked for it made her wonder. There was a hollowness to the tone of his voice. Mitchell could be sacrificed for the greater good. And all that bullshit. She couldn't swallow it anymore.

A horrible coldness clutched her. Mitchell didn't have a chance without her. A tear slid down her face. "Yes sir..."

Sebastian reached in and turned the phone off. "Let me contact my people in Amsterdam. They'll find him." He wiped her tear away. "Don't give up hope." He took the phone from her and walked away.

Sadie listened as he phoned his friend Xander and set things in motion. He clicked off and turned towards her. "What now?"

"We go to the museum."

"That's my woman."

She punched him lightly in the stomach as she brushed past him. "I'm nobody's woman, but my own."

CHAPTER 38

As the taxi dropped Sadie and
Sebastian off on the street in front of the Met
Museum of Art, a scene of pandemonium was
unfolding. Hundreds of people flooded down the
cement stairway heading in every direction, frantic
looks of fear etched on their faces. Fire alarms
blared above their confused cries.

Stunned, she stared at the colossal pillared
building, the largest friggen museum in the country
and one the ten largest in the world. Hard to believe
it had been broken into in broad daylight. Bakari
had balls of steel.

Seb grabbed the arm of a young man who
flew down the cement steps and asked what
happened.

"Smoke man. Smoke. I ran and so did everyone else. Something big's going down. Probably terrorists."

A growing line of black and white police cars lined the curb and the sound of a fire engine siren approached. Ten uniformed city policemen pushed their way through the crowds to the enormous doorway, while twenty more struggled to manage the chaos of the fleeing crowd and prevent a stampede. No sign of the SWAT team. They were either already inside or not on the scene yet.

Seb grabbed her hand and pulled her towards the steps but the crush pushed them back. Black smoke billowed out of the doors. Its pungent odor stung her nostrils and made her eyes tear.

Where were Bakari's men? She couldn't see anything in the middle of the sea of people. She let go of Seb's hand and let the crowds carry her back to the street. He turned and looked at her. "Sadie?" His voice barely registered above the din.

Once free of the building some of the people gathered on the street to see what would happen next. Ambulances arrived and paramedics walked through the masses offering assistance. The last group out seemed to be limping and coughing. One elderly man had blood running from his mouth. All of this because of Bakari and his superstitions.

Seb made his way back to her and they stood together holding hands watching the debacle.

"I hate feeling useless," she said pressing her lips together.

"You're not useless. You got the cops here. We turned the tables."

"Let's hope they got here in time." Her breath hitched. She thought of Mitchell. "Give me your phone."

Seb pulled it out of his pocket and handed it to her. The crowds were thinning. She sent a text to Jeremiah with a picture of the steps and the chaos.

He responded, "Get out of there."

She shook her head. "I don't know why I bother."

Another text came in: "I ordered you to get out of there."

She wrote: "Mitchell?"

"Working on it."

Sweet Jesus.

Seb put his arm around her and pulled her close to him. His embrace calmed her nerves a bit, but her feelings were like hot lava ready to erupt. The thought of Mitchell dying filled her with self-loathing and anger. Why did she ever become a spy? Did she really think she could change the world? Too many assholes—too many. If Mitch ended up hurt, she'd kill Bakari herself. She pushed air out of her lungs and leaned into the warmth of Sebastian's body.

Sebastian squeezed her shoulder and spoke into her ear so he could be heard above the noise of the chaos. "Come on. Let's get out of here. We don't want to get in the way."

"But..."

"I don't want you in danger."

"Retreating sucks." As she spoke she spotted a familiar face in the crowd. She froze. A tingling sensation ran over her skull. Eboni, the flight attendant on Bakari's plane, wearing a loose black dress that fell to her calves and a black hijab moved through the crowds. She looked different in the traditional dress, but her exotic dark eyes were unmistakable. They could not be hidden.

Sadie pushed through people towards Eboni, shoving and elbowing a path that would meet up with the woman. Eboni carried a large shoulder bag. Bingo.

Seb followed. She didn't have time to fill him in, but he must've known she was up to something, because he stayed on her heels. When you have a giant at your back no one complains about you rudely making your way. It took five minutes to get near the woman. Seb had fallen behind by only a few yards.

Two minutes she estimated. Two minutes and she'd have Eboni. The Emerald Ankh had to be inside her bag and possibly other artifacts. Sadie put her arms up in front of herself and pushed through more people.

She bounced off of a man dressed in a white robe. The kind of garb you'd see in the markets in Cairo and came to a stop. His lean face looked to be a younger leaner version of Bakari's. He scowled at her and said one word, "Mitchell."

The frantic crowd pressed in on them from all sides. Her mouth fell open and she stared at him. She pressed her lips together. Tears came to her eyes. Time stood still. She couldn't risk her friend's life. Not for a silly old relic... not for anything. Could she trust Bakari to keep his word? Betting Mitch's life on the word of an arms dealer sucked. But it seemed her only option. She wanted Mitch to live. The rest didn't matter.

Sadie nodded. Seb's strong arms encircle her waist. She closed her eyes for a second in response and when she opened them Bakari's look-alike had vanished into the crowd. She looked for Eboni, but the masses and confusion had swallowed her as well. She'd lost them and the treasure.

"I'm ready to go now," she said to Seb.

"A friend of mine has an apartment in central Manhattan. We'll go there. And then you can explain what just happened."

They walked towards the subway, but everywhere they turned hordes of people had gathered to stare at the museum making it hard to make progress anywhere. The anger of the people was palpable. It was as if their own homes had been violated and in a way they had been. The museum, the people's sanctuary for heritage had been attacked. Their cries turned into a stunned silence surrounded by the cacophony of more sirens approaching.

Police cars and barricades blocked off the street. Two fire engines, four ambulances and at least ten police cars lined the area below the museum. At least a hundred policemen were now taking over the steps and the entranceway. The SWAT team headed up the stairs.

It was hard to believe anyone could escape through this dragnet, but they had and she'd helped them.

Breathe. She needed to keep breathing. What had Bakari said, "Things are not always what they seem."

Twenty minutes later Sebastian and Sadie waved down a cab. As they headed back to central Manhattan Sadie told Sebastian about meeting Bakari's brother. She was pretty sure that was who it was. His younger brother Chasisi.

Sebastian held her hand and listened. As they arrived at their destination he got a message from Xander: "Mitchell secure. Found in front of Central Station." He was safe.

CHAPTER 39

Their destination turned out to be a studio apartment in a seven story brown stone only a few blocks away from the hotel Sadie'd been trapped in. Once inside the dizzying noise and bustle of Manhattan stopped.

For that matter everything stopped. Finally, they were alone. Together, alone and safe.

Sebastian closed the apartment door and slipped five dead-locks into place. He turned to her. The warmth of his smile took her first, then his strong arms, then his rock solid chest. She breathed in his familiar scent. A groan came from deep inside her shuddering through her senses.

"Bed." His voice sounded raspy as he scooped her up and into the air like a pirate and walked ten feet to the double bed.

The way he placed her gently on the mattress made her feel cherished. Her heart thundered. She grabbed his shirt and pulled him towards her.

He laughed and sat on the edge of the bed leaning over her. Their eyes caught and held. The intensity of the moment was like no other.

He leaned in and kissed her. Gently at first and then with deepening passion. Their tongues exploring one another. Small shivers of delight ran through her body as his large hands slid under her shirt to her bare breasts.

Her breath hitched as he fondled her, stroking her nipples sending ripples of pleasure through her body. Desire pooled between her legs.

He pulled away for a moment and their eyes caught once again. "Are you sure about this?"

She dug her nails into his back and pulled him down to her. Never had she been so sure of anything.

"I want our first time to be perfect," he whispered into her ear as he let her pull him down.

"Then why are you talking?"

He laughed and pulled enough away from her to take off his shirt revealing a chest that belonged on the cover of a body-building magazine. Then his pants. Then his underwear. Yum.

Broad shoulders, rock hard chest, six-pack abs and a lean waist. And then below all of that an erect penis that would make the Greek gods weep. She reached for it and stroked its length longing to take it into her mouth.

He groaned at her touch. She massaged his balls and reached for the tender spot at the base of his scrotum. His hand stopped hers. "Let's not rush."

His baby blue eyes were on fire with need. A need that could only be matched by hers.

Sadie managed to remove her sweatshirt while he was undressing, but being so distracted by the sight of him she hadn't gotten any farther. Sebastian moaned as he cupped one then the other breast, rubbing her hard nipples until she thought she'd explode. "You're so beautiful."

He leaned down and took a nipple in his mouth. Arching her back she moaned with pleasure. His soft lips and scratchy chin trailed kisses below her breasts then lower and then lower until he came to her jeans. He ripped them off and then her thong flew in the air like an elastic band. She laughed and he responded with his killer, bad boy smile.

Going up on his knees he nudged her legs further apart with his large hands. Tenderly his fingers explored her folds, stroking her clitoris sending shudders of exquisite delight through her body, creating an ache deep inside her pelvis. She gasped.

His tongue found her clitoris and stroked it with precision, while his finger massaged her tender entrance. She moaned as he stroked and suckled her. Exquisite erotic torture. His finger and mouth teased and teased. "Sebastian." Her voice sounded raspy and desperate. Sweat covered her body.

His finger slid inside her and her muscles convulsed on it flooding her. He pulled his finger out, massaged her entrance gently and then went in again. Deeper and deeper he thrust into her, caressing the walls of her vagina as his tongue licked her clit. Her muscles convulsed. When his finger found her G-spot, she gasped. Rhythmically he touched as he suckled her clit.

"I want you," she murmured, but he didn't stop. Panting, she groaned. Stubborn Dutch man. That was her last thought before her body burst into a million pieces of ecstasy in what she would later call the longest orgasm in history.

As spasms of pleasure rippled through her, he held her and kissed her neck gently. She grabbed his rock hard ass and pulled him closer. "Now. Please, now."

"Condom." Lifting his body away from hers, he reached for the drawer beside the bed and grabbed a package. With lightning speed he opened it. She leaned back and moaned at his impressive body of rippling muscles glistening in sweat.

He entered her slowly. She gasped. His hardness pushed into her softness, filling her with his presence, completing her in a way no other man ever had.

Rhythmically he moved his hips, thrusting into her again and again. Her hips lifted to meet him. She dug her nails into his back and wrapped her legs around him to bring him into her as deeply as she could. The sensation wickedly wonderful. And then she came again, pure pleasure bursting and rippling through her body like a cascading waterfall of joy and this time he climaxed with her making a low guttural sound. He shuddered in her arms.

***

Afterward, they lay entwined, sated and complete.

"We didn't do it right," said Sadie.

He chuckled. "Felt right to me."

"No, I think we need practice."

"I plan on lots and lots of practice." His hand stroked the long curves of her body.

"I'm serious we did something wrong."

"Okay. Why do you think we did something wrong?" His emotive blue eyes looked at her with uncertainty.

"Because the first time isn't supposed to be so good."

He pulled her to him. "I like to set high standards."

CHAPTER 40

Sadie couldn't remember the last time she checked her messages. She'd been far too busy having the best sex of her life and falling deeper in love with Sebastian. For the most part, the outside world faded away. But her niggling worry about Mitchell reared its head the following morning. Exactly how secure was he?

At eight in the morning Sebastian's phone jingled. Mitchell had sent a message: "I'm okay." Sebastian handed his cell over so she could have a close look at the screen. Her stomach dropped the length of a runway or two.

Like most men, Mitchell's text messages tended to be cryptic, often including only graphic images and silly emoticons. But two words, okay three if you count the contraction, seemed mighty thin even for him. How serious were his injuries?

The swelling in his eye had looked pretty bad. She sent him a reply, "Sadie here - How okay?"

To her amazement he shot back, "Stoned in an Amsterdam coffeehouse drinking some truly fine Heineken."

"Have you got all your fingers?"

"Last I looked. U ok?"

"Never better." She bit her lip. Indeed, never better.

"C U in Italy?"

She thought about that for a moment. She did love the Italian medieval town of Lucca surrounded by an ancient brick wall. It held a special out-of-place, out-of-time charm, but not one strong enough to pull her away from her present uh moment. "Thinking of staying here in NY," she typed.

"U have a contract."

She laughed out loud at that one. Controlled by words on a piece of paper? Not likely. She considered what to say. How could she put her feelings into a few flashing letters on a screen. I've fallen madly in love with a giant and cannot leave his side. And oh what a wonderful side it is. Oh that sounds so... so... so uselessly feminine. But it was the honest truth.

"Sadie?" Mitchell nudged her over the phone.

"What happens if I don't turn up?"

It took him a while to answer. Maybe his brain had relaxed a wee too much, but then his words came. "1-u lose contract with Hot Lingerie, 2-u weaken your ..." He didn't want to type it into cyberspace, but she knew what he meant. If she lost this contract that would be two of her main employers down and that would weaken her cover as a model. Even though she wanted to throw Jeremiah off the top of a New York office building at the moment, she suspected she'd eventually calm down and want back into the fold. She loved being a spook. And her model cover worked so well. She typed: "C u there." She'd keep her options open.

Handing back the phone to Sebastian, scattered memories of the last few days along with a twinge of guilt flowed through her mind. The op had not gone as well as she'd hoped. Letting Bakari go had been the price of Mitchell's life, but she wished it could have ended another way.

Then she went back to Sebastian's open arms.

***

Twenty four hours later, still entwined in sheets and the long muscular limbs of the best lover she'd ever imagined, some idiot knocked on the door. Sebastian groaned. She laughed. Light filtered through the slats of the venetian blinds. She'd never thought of New York as romantic until now.

Sebastian sat up and put his feet on the floor. Running his hand through his sun-streaked blonde hair he looked like a sexy, sleepy warrior. She stretched her legs and wiggled her toes to increase circulation. Who could be at the door? Who knew where they were?

The tingling anticipation of preparing for the unexpected coursed through her. Damn, she hated not having a gun. Her eyes swept the studio apartment for weapons. A good sized lamp sat on the table beside the door. It would do. Wrapped in a sheet, she gingerly followed Sebastian to the door, noting that he had a gun in his hand, and went to stand by the wall with the lamp. As she leaped to her lover's side she recognized how difficult walking had become and smiled. Having a sore vagina beat high heel blisters any day.

"It's me. Mitchell. Let me in."

Her shoulders dropped and her heart rose. Sebastian laughed as she pushed him aside and whipped open the five locks. He put his massive hand on the door stopping her from opening it fully. He looked through the narrow space before letting Mitchell in.

Mitchell grabbed her into a huge hug. "I'm so sorry Mitchell."

"Me too," he said into her hair. "I had to see you."

She sighed. "I'm glad you came."

"That makes one of us," said Sebastian behind her. "I'll make coffee."

"American," they both said in unison.

"Yah, yah," he said lacing his words with a thick Dutch accent. As he wandered to the kitchen area she caught Mitchell checking out his naked ass and punched him in the stomach.

"He's mine. All mine."

Mitchell smiled and wiped the tears flowing down her cheeks.

"I shouldn't have sold you out to Jonathon. I didn't realize what an ass the guy is. I'll never do that again. I swear." Mitchell's puppy eyes pulled on her. "Please forgive me."

"And I'm sorry you were kidnapped and held hostage, because of me."

He shrugged. "They roughed me up a bit. My chest is bruised, but I'll have no scars. Mostly my ego took the hit. No man likes to be made helpless. Of course unless he wants to be." His lopsided smile returned. That and his sexual innuendo told her better than anything else, that Mitchell was back to normal.

It seemed like everything could be all right. Could she dare believe that?

Sebastian reappeared wearing tight faded jeans he'd picked up off the floor and poured them coffee. She sat beside him on the sofa. Mitchell faced them sitting in a lounge chair. The caffeine hit her system like ambrosia. How long had it been since she'd had a coffee? She took a deep breath and let it out slowly. "So glad it all worked out." Seemed like stupid words to say, but she had to say something.

Mischief played in Mitchell's brown eyes. "You're not getting off that easy."

Her pulse spiked. What now?

"Tell me about your son. If I'm to take charge of him if anything happens to you, I want to know about him. Hell, I'd like to meet him."

Sebastian's brows rose into a question mark and he grabbed her hand. "A son? Good Lord woman you have a lot of secrets."

Oh hell. Here we go. "A year ago I was in Nigeria doing some work for the CIA between photo shoots in South Africa. There was this..." She gulped. She'd never had to describe what happened to anyone. Never had to put it into words outside her head. " A Shaman was burying a newborn baby boy alive."

The silence in the room was deafening.

"He'd strapped the infant to the body of his mother who'd died giving birth to him. It was a remote part of Africa, cut off by deep rivers, a place where old beliefs lived on. The villagers thought the child caused his mother's death. They believed him to be evil.

"His newborn cries grabbed me. Without thinking, I acted. I couldn't let them bury him alive.

"I ripped him from his mother's breast and escaped. Trust me, getting out of an isolated area of the jungle isn't easy, but I did it. I've seen to his care ever since." Tears welled up in her eyes. "His name is JaJa. It means respected. My life has never been the same since he entered it."

"You adopted him?" Sebastian's voice flowed with understanding.

"No. I considered it, but it would be too complicated. I'm single and well busy. I wouldn't know what to do with a baby. I also didn't want to take him out of his culture, albeit a brutal one. So I placed him with other babies rescued from infanticide, in a home run by Christian missionaries in Abuja, Nigeria's capitol. They are raising a group of fifteen children with love and understanding. I send money regularly. When the children are older they will be told their stories. The hope of the missionaries is that when they are grown and fully understand forgiveness, they will be reunited with their kin, someday when the old beliefs have faded. The government is trying to educate its people."

Sebastian squeezed Sadie's hand. "Did you kill the shaman?"

"I wanted to," Sadie said, a bitter taste flowed into her mouth. "But it's a backwater place where the old ways still survive, cruel ways. He was only doing what he believed to be right. He believed the baby was evil, and getting rid of him would protect the village. He knew no better."

"So you just grabbed the baby?" Mitchell asked his eyes wider than she'd ever seen them.

Sadie smiled remembering the satisfaction she felt at that moment. "I attacked the grave digger, a tall lean man, first, grabbed his shovel and hit him on the top of the head with it. He went out cold. Then I pushed the Shaman away from the open grave and screamed Latin words at him to sound scary. He ran away. I grabbed Ja Ja in my arms and ran in the opposite direction. No one followed me. They probably thought I was an evil demon. I can only imagine the story the shaman told the village."

"So I'm an uncle." Mitchell's smile spread across his sculpted face.

"Yes." Sadie said, "an honorary uncle."

"And what does that make me?" asked Sebastian.

CHAPTER 41

The next day in Washington DC

After flying around the world chasing truly wicked people, returning to the offices at the CIA always rankled Sadie. She'd never been an office person and the petty politics, paper-pushing and dust of the place put her into a heightened state of agitation. She likened it to an allergy attack. Part of her wished Sebastian was by her side, but she knew she had to deal with this business on her own.

Right on cue, her stomach became nauseated on the elevator ride up to the seventh floor and a dull throbbing sensation began in her temples the moment she stepped out of it. Normally, she'd shrug off these feelings as part of the price she had to pay for a job she loved. But not today. She felt anything but gracious.

Sadie's chest tightened every time she thought about Bakari. She was a devout patriot. Whatever else she might have questioned in her life, she never questioned her allegiance to her country. She believed in America, like others believed in religion. It was the best place on the earth to live. Its constitution ensured basic freedom to everyone. She was proud of her country's history and accomplishments. Working for the CIA had been an honor and a privilege. She'd been proud to put her high cheekbones and ability to lie to good use.

But after her encounter with Bakari, fifty shades of doubt clouded her mind. He'd sold arms to people who would put them in the hands of child soldiers. His business was an eye sore to humanity. And yet the CIA had funded him. Her CIA, the only family she'd ever had. Sure, they wouldn't have been behind everything he did, but he'd made it clear that they'd been good customers.

Sweet Jesus, she didn't like hearing that. Sure, she understood that the company had to manipulate the world stage. She knew better than most the delicate situations in some areas of the world required a certain amount of smoke and mirrors. But to use Bakari? Evil Bakari? A shudder ran up her spine as she thought of the severed head of his dead wife. She had more than a few words to say to Jeremiah.

Dressed in an Italian black business suit, she walked through the cubicles to Jeremiah's office, her stilettos making a rhythmic clicking sound on the vinyl flooring. She flicked her hair back behind her shoulders and kept a cool all-business expression on her face. People, *her people*, looked up from their desks, but she gave them head nods and kept walking. She needed to set things right.

Jeremiah cocked his left eyebrow when she stalked into his office with as much an air of authority as she could gather in this hollowed place. He wore a suit and tie that made him look like the other million men who went to work in the city that day, but his amber eyes studied her like a tiger. "Welcome home Sadie."

She frowned and took the seat opposite him.

"I'm glad you're safe."

She nodded while she ordered the words and emotions jumbled in her mind. How best could she bust his balls?

"You could have kept in touch." He steepled his fingers, not letting his eyes flinch.

"Jeremiah, I trusted you."

He looked down at his fingers as if an answer lay there. "As you should. I am your handler."

"Then why? Why on God's green earth did you not tell me everything about Bakari?"

"Would it have made a difference?" Not a muscle on his clean shaven face had moved to suggest emotion. The man had to be made of stone to not feel the anger wafting off her.

She looked at his chess board. The pieces had been realigned for a new game. He thought in terms of moves and counter-moves. Maybe, he'd been right. If she'd known, she might not have had the stomach to take the assignment. Bull shit.

"I had the right to know. You sent me in without a full picture of the man. He wasn't at all what I expected."

"What did you expect?" Jeremiah sat back, his face tense.

"Evil. Pure evil."

He shook his head and pursed his lips for a moment. "I suppose pure evil exists somewhere, but for the most part people are a mixture of good and bad. Bakari has more evil than most. We needed your help to take him down."

"You know he wanted the power to heal his daughter."

Jeremiah broke their eye-lock, leaned back in his chair and looked out the window. "Yes."

What the hell? What else was he hiding? Was this all another charade to keep her in the fold? *Every King needs his pawns.* "She's dying of cancer."

"Yes." He looked back at her. His eyes actually softened to a molten orange. "And I can't blame him for wanting to break a few laws to do something he believes will save her. But we couldn't let him steal from the museum."

"Do we have a right to hold artifacts from ancient Egypt?"

He tilted his head the way he did before he offered a gambit, a sacrificial offering in a chess game. "That's debatable. Personally I hope that someday, in a better world, we will make replicas of them and send the originals back to their homeland. For now, we keep them safe and people from all around the world are able to share their beauty."

"They don't belong to us." She'd always known this, but having met Bakari made it even more clear in her mind.

"How safe are they in Egypt? The looting of artifacts has gone on for centuries and continues today. In fact it's increased since the 2011 Arab Spring. New archeological sites are being ravaged and old museums ransacked. There's big money in artifacts. Every day treasures are lost. So is it so wrong to want to protect some?"

"You make all the good points, but I don't blame people for hating the west for interfering with their history and heritage. For taking it from them." She blew out a breath she'd been holding. "Still..." She hesitated.

"Still what Sadie?"

She grimaced. "It's more wrong for Bakari to want to keep the treasures for himself." Jeremiah's chess set grabbed her attention for a moment. Everything about this man came down to strategy. Had he anticipated this visit?

"Right, wrong, the world is more complex than that."

"It bothers me that we've stolen fragments of their past. We have no right to own Egyptian treasures. I understand our intent is to protect them and share them with the world, but I also understand Bakari's anger."

Jeremiah leaned forward again and steepled his fingers on top of his desk. "Do you think he would take better care of them?"

The corner of her mouth twitched. "No. Bakari doesn't share. He wants the amulets for personal power."

"Did you have sex with him?"

"No."

"It sounds to me like the man got under your skin. I warned you about going too deep into this op."

"Nothing I couldn't handle." Her chest tightened. "Have you found Bakari?"

Jeremiah looked at the chess pieces and said nothing. His mouth flat lined.

As silence fell in the room it hit her. *Oh-shit.* All the lost Lego blocks in her head snapped into place one by one in an instant. She closed her eyes. "I'm such a fool."

"You did your job and you did it well. You got the information you were sent in to get and no one was hurt. I'll recommend you for a commendation."

She gritted her teeth. Her people had played her. They sent her to track Bakari and find out the details of his plans. What a fool she'd been to think they wanted to stop him. They had no intention of interfering with him unless he threatened lives. Even then... she wondered. Ancient relics and museums weren't part of the CIA's big picture. Keeping their international operations in play was their sole intent, and they needed Bakari for that. Her mission from the start had been more of a cover story than anything else; a pretense of stopping the man. And she'd almost slept with the man. Well, they could stuff their shiny medals up their yahoos.

Sadie's mouth tasted bitter. "Rashida?"

"She's looking better. But she is a very sick young woman. I don't know that amulets can do what medicine cannot, but faith has a powerful influence on healing."

Okay, maybe she did need to grow up and see the world's not all black or white, but textured in shades of gray. Maybe she needed to let go of her rigid view of good and evil. She grunted. Damn it all—this ending just didn't feel right. It fit wrong, wrong, wrong.

Jeremiah's jaw hardened.

They could have read her in, could have respected her, and could have not treated her like a pretty cover girl. Her mind cast back to all the times Jeremiah had told her how much he liked working with her, what a good spy she was... how much the company valued her. Bull shit—all bull shit. Glaring at Jeremiah she rose to her feet. She'd spit, and that might feel good, but that wouldn't be lady like.

He cocked both of his eyebrows.

She leaned over and slowly slid his chessboard into the trash can. Turning and walking to the door she said over her shoulder, "Don't call me."

CHAPTER 42

Cairo

At midnight, a sealed envelope was delivered to Bakari. The spring air filled Bakari's room with the smell of lotus flowers. He dismissed the two women he'd had mediocre sex with and sat up in his bed. It seemed nothing could satisfy him. A note? Maybe putting his head into business matters would straighten him out.

He reached for the glass of scotch sitting on his bedside table and took a sip. Beside it lay the last quarter report of the family business; a compilation of numbers, columns and bottom lines. After the excitement of the last month, none of it held much meaning for him, but he'd been forcing his eyes over the pages to keep himself from thinking about other things.

And there were a lot of other things to think about.

But getting mail in the middle of the night grabbed his attention. The first thing he noticed was that the envelope was from someone's personal stationary, made of expensive paper in an off-white color. On the front there was only his name. He turned it over. The back flap had been secured with a personalized seal of blood red wax. Did people still do that in this century?

The Eye of Horus sat in the centre of the wax stamp, the ancient Egyptian symbol for protection. The all-seeing eye. As he traced the image with his finger, a tingling sensation flowed into his body. Who would create such an emblem?

Not wanting to break the seal, he grabbed his switch-blade from his bedside table, opened the side of the envelope and turned it upside down. A folded note smelling faintly of kypher fell out. Carefully, he opened it.

"Come to me," it said in Arabic. Just one sentence. Signed Djeserit.

The high sorceress had never sent for him before. He'd always sent for her.

The tingling sensation slid into his body and clutched at the base of his skull like the strong claws of a raptor with sharp talons. Something was wrong. Very wrong. He bellowed for his butler.

***

Five hours later he knocked on the cabin door of Djeserit's houseboat in Amsterdam. Not hearing any response he let himself in. The room smelled of incense and death. He rushed in.

Djeserit lay on a bunk at the side of the hull wrapped in a gold embossed blanket. Her black hair wet with sweat lay tangled across the white pillow. Her face had little color left in it. But her eyes were still lively.

"You came." Her weak voice resonated through him.

He knelt beside her bed and picked up her hand. "Of course."

"I have much to tell you."

Bakari pushed strands of hair away from her face. "Let me summon help."

"No."

"You are suffering."

She nodded. "For once Bakari, really listen to me."

"You need help."

"I have been poisoned and there is no antidote. I should already be dead, but I've used all my powers to stay alive to talk to you."

"I'm so sorry," he said, but the words could only express a fraction of the depth of his feelings. His chest tightened. He hadn't realized to this moment how much this wise woman meant to him. "I don't want you to die." His eyes hardened.

She gave him a weak smile.

"Who did this to you? I will have them killed at once."

"Our son."

"What?" His breath caught in his throat. It was like all the air in his lungs...in the room... had been sucked out. A hurricane of emotions hit him all at once. How the hell could they have a child? He'd never slept with Djeserit. How could this be?

And yet, she sounded so certain. "A fever is touching your mind," he said as gently as he could, but even as he said the words, he knew them not to be true.

"My mind is clear. You must listen. Seventeen years ago I came to you, dressed as a prostitute. I wanted to have your seed, your strength and I got it."

He'd slept with many prostitutes over the years. His mind scanned back, and the vivid memory came to him in an instant. "The red head in the black mini-skirt in Amsterdam."

"Yes," she said.

It had been the most unusual sexual experience in his life, but later he had decided it was just because she was a pro and knew things regular women didn't. Besides they were in Amsterdam a city where sexuality has no limits. He remembered waking in the morning, deeply satisfied, with a raging headache. He told no one, because the details he remembered were... so otherworldly. Shit. That was Djeserit.

And she'd left him and bore him a son. He'd always wanted a son. "How could you keep this from me?" he said. Shock and anger mixed in his blood.

Her thin hand covered in blue veins came from beneath the blankets and held his arm. "Calm down Bakari. We have no time left for emotions. There is too much at stake."

"A son."

"I had hoped he would have your strength and my heart, but children come into this world with their own souls and I fear his is as black as the night."

"Are you sure he poisoned you?" Bakari's body trembled with an anger stronger than any he'd ever experienced. Sweat burst from his pours, his breathing became erratic, his thoughts frantic. He wanted to kill someone. But he could never kill his own flesh and blood. He buried his head in the blanket that covered her.

"Yes. He told me so." She stroked his head. "He wants my power, and by killing me he will gain some of it. But not all. I have made sure of that."

Bakari lifted his head. "I have so many questions."

She held up her hand. "His name is Khalid."

"That means immortal."

"If I have enough strength I will tell you all about his life as a child growing up here in Amsterdam, but my time is running out. There are other things I must tell you."

"More important than my son?"

"More important than us." She took a moment to swallow. "I," she hesitated as a wave of pain crossed her face. "I must tell you."

He grabbed her hand willing his own body's strength into it. He was not a sorcerer, but if there was a god anywhere he wanted them to hear his silent prayer. Let this woman speak.

"I broke my sacred oath to Amun-Ra and did things for you I shouldn't have. I did it..." She gasped for breath. In a weaker voice she continued. "I did it because I love you."

He nodded. "You never said anything."

"Telling you about the amulets did not break my vows, though it weakened them. But in the end, I travelled in a dream to Sadie Stewart and bent her mind. I did that for you. So that you could have The Emerald Ankh and save Rashida. But it broke the sacred bonds of Karma that hold us all in place. And so now I lay dying."

"Bullshit. You were poisoned. You said so yourself."

"Khalid was just the instrument, the manifestation of justice on this plane."

"He's our son."

"Our teenage son, who needs guidance."

I'll give him guidance. The guidance of the back of my hand, just like my father gave me. "Where is he?"

"I don't know, and I don't have the strength to..." She wheezed out the raspy cough of death as her muscles convulsed.

"Is there nothing I can do?" Bakari said these words more to the room than to the dying mother of his child.

Her breathing stuttered.

His throat tightened.

With one last breath she said, "The amulet grows stronger. Now that it has been used for personal gain, it will draw dark forces. You must protect yourself... protect the world. Get my wand to..."

He leaned in to hear her voice which had had turned into a whisper, but she was no longer there.

The wand wrapped in a parchment paper fell from her hand onto the wood planking making a distinct thud that he would remember for the rest of his life.

CHAPTER 43

Venice, Italy
Two weeks later

T*he warm* August sunshine reflected off the water of the Grand Canal making it sparkle like faeries dancing a magic tango on top of it. The mid-day heat rippled the air. Vaporetti and gondolas carrying smiling tourists with cameras slide along the ancient waterway. Ornate palaces that looked like they came out of a fairy tale book lined the sides of the canal. Laughter and cheers of joy spilled into the air. Sebastian held his course in his yacht.

He pressed his lips together. Sadie had said she needed time to close down the case and tie up loose ends, time to do her modelling gig and take care of Mitchell, and... basically time for everything but him. She had promised to meet him in Venice in two weeks. She'd said they'd have their own time then.

Counting the hours until the two weeks were done had been difficult. And now, like a love-sick fool he waited. Two days had gone by and still no Sadie. She could be in trouble, but he didn't think so. She'd probably decided to not get involved with him. Too much work... too much trouble. He had no illusions about her need for independence. It was one of the things he loved most about her. Had she decided he was a complication in her life she didn't need?

He felt hollow like his insides had been scooped out. He'd never met a woman like her. Her beauty—her balls, her sweetness—her toughness. She was a woman of contrasts, a woman of heart. And a woman with a hell of a lot of secrets. His eyes filled. Godverdomme he couldn't imagine living without her.

Scanning the horizon he wondered how many days he should wait. Why hadn't she called? A horn blew behind him and he looked around.

A small motor boat made way on his Port side, Sadie was at the wheel wearing a delicate black lace Venetian carnival mask that accentuated her moss green eyes. With her full lips she smiled up at him and he stopped breathing. His heart jack hammered in his chest. Pure joy rose within him in a flash. "Sadie?"

"Hey sailor looks like you're going my way." With a wide smile, she threw him a rope and he pulled her boat alongside his and secured it with a strong knot.

He offered her his hand and her lithe body slipped up the side of his hull and boarded his boat in short order. She stood before him looking as radiant as ever. The love of his life.

Five horn blasts came from behind him. The warning of disaster. "Dio...Dio..."

Seb turned to see his boat was heading for another and he grabbed the tiller just in time to avert disaster. Sadie put her hand on his arm and laughed. And then he laughed. And then they were in each other's arms.

He broke their first kiss with a low groan. "I know you like danger, but..."

***

Sadie nuzzled her head into his massive chest. Never had she been kissed with such fervor. He smelled of the sea and so damn masculine it made her fingernails curl into his flesh. "I'm sorry I'm late."

Sebastian smoothed her windblown hair away from her eyes. "Don't apologize. I know you were busy."

She took a step back. Busy, that's an understatement. "Wait till I tell you the whole story."

His roguish grin appeared. "Really? You came here to tell me stories?" His sun streaked shoulder length hair looked ruffled, his day old beard rugged and his blue eyes tired but happy.

How did he always know what to say to her? Her stories could wait. The time for two of them to be together and make their own stories had come. "Do you know how to dock this boat?" she asked.

"Just tell me where princess." He traced her cheek. His touch sent quivers through her system.

"I left my luggage in the lobby of the Bella Giornata."

He turned the boat around.

"I've never taken a lover there."

His look so hot it sizzled touched all her senses at once, telling her more than a thousand words ever could. That was his way.

***

Three wonderful days and three even more wonderful nights later, they lay entwined in each other's arms, sated with passion, filled with love and content. Sadie sighed. "You're one hell of a sailor."

Tracing her hip with his hand he chuckled. "And you're one hell of a spook."

She put her hand on his rock hard chest and rose above him. Looking into his rugged face made her heart stop. She'd wanted to say something, but she'd lost the words. She blinked.

Laughing, he grabbed her hips and flipped her under him. "I want you to come back with me to Amsterdam." He said, his tone urgent. "At least for a couple of weeks. We need time to give our relationship a proper start."

Smoothing his back with her hands she replied, "Only if you promise to never stop getting in my way."

The End

Dear Readers,

Welcome to the world of Mata Hari. If you enjoyed reading Sadie and Sebastian's story, you can help me spread the word. Consider telling your friends about the book and writing a review (e.g., Amazon, Goodreads). Word of mouth and written reviews are pure gold for new writers, like me.

Learn about my latest publications from my newsletter. I am on Facebook, Twitter and Pinterest. Links can be found on my website: www.jo-anncarson.com.

To send me a personal note, email me at connect@jo-anncarson.com. I'd love to hear your thoughts on my stories.

On the next page you'll find information about the other books in the Mata Hari Series.

I know your time is valuable. Thank you for sharing it with me and my books.

Best Wishes,
Jo-Ann Carson

Aknowledgments

Covert Danger took over a year to write and publish. I couldn't have done it without the support of a wonderful group of people. In particular I'd like to acknowledge:

My husband, Piet, who patiently listened to every wild idea I came up with and encouraged me to "go for it."

J.C. McKenzie, my awesome critique partner, whose wit and sharp eye kept me going through my first draft. Someday I'll share on my blog what she said about my sex scenes. <blush>

Hannah Myles, one of my two beta readers, who's solid feedback helped me strengthen the plot.

Marisa Radcliffe, my other beta reader, who taught me how to swear in Italian and understand men better <grin>.

Dr. Philip Newey, my copy-editor, who

straightened out my grammar.

Nina French, my cover designer.

Eric Baetscher who granted me permission to use his photo of the NYC Metropolitan Museum of Art on my cover.

And last, but never least, my writing buddies who support and inspire me.
All errors are my own.

The Mata Hari Series

#1 - Covert Danger

#2 - Born of Magic

#3 - Ancient Danger

Let me tell you about the other stories:

****

Born of Magic

The Egyptian Sorceress wants a child of her own. The arms-dealer wants power at any cost. Their desires conceive a son destined to change the world.

****

Ancient Danger

A single woman – a complicated life

International, super-model Sadie Stewart meets her Dutch lover Sebastian Wilde in Venice to celebrate their six month anniversary in style. But having lived a double life as a CIA operative for ten years, her life is never simple.

During a charity costume ball in an ancient Venetian palace, an assassin tries to take her out. Sebastian gets over-protective, which drives her crazy. Her old boss offers her information, but wants something in return.

Arms-dealer, Bakari al-Sharif is planning to steal more ancient Egyptian treasure. This time he's after a scarab from the tomb of Tutankhamen about to be revealed at Highclere castle near London. Sadie is the only person who has ever gotten close to al-Sharif and lived. The CIA wants her to stop him.

Or at least that's what they say. When

it comes to the world of espionage, the true motivation of the players is never clear.

Can Sadie return to the life of a spook and maintain a relationship with Sebastian? Can she nail the arms-dealer? Can she figure out why the masked man tried to kill her?

Life is complicated for Sadie Stewart.

a cross between Covert Danger and Indiana Jones

smart, sexy suspense

all my books available on: <u>Amazon</u>

www.ingramcontent.com/pod-product-compliance
Lightning Source LLC
Chambersburg PA
CBHW030414180626
46812CB00005B/2001